Broken Petals

Tasha Hutchison

ISBN (pbk) 978-1-955062-03-9
ISBN (ebook)978-1-947041-97-4

To my family and friends who've always believed in me.
I dedicate this novel to each of you.

Chapter 1

Saturday mornings in the summer were for sleeping in, not trips to the airport at six o'clock in the morning. They especially weren't for Uber rides with a driver who refused to take a break from scarfing on his artery clogging breakfast sandwich to lend a helping hand.

What happened to chivalry?

Sure, the lines of grease dripping down the side of his double chin should've given me an indication that he didn't care one way or another, but it's about the principle.

After I managed to extract my last oversized piece of luggage from the trunk, I slammed it hard enough to rock the tiny car, and if lady luck was on my side, even knocked a bit of his sandwich out of his hand and onto his lap. It'd serve him right.

Outside of the airport, near the corner of the building, an older man ogled a teenage girl. All I could think about were the constant news headlines of girls being taken. I'd never forgive myself if this girl ended up as a headline in the *Highsea Daily Newspaper*. I could see it now: *June 20, 2021, Teenage Jane Doe Found Dead in the Forest.*

Highsea was never short on crime with the beach attracting tourists from around the world. Not to mention, the forest stretched for miles. It was the perfect place to make someone disappear.

Not this girl. Not today.

I raced to her before the man made his move. "Are you okay?"

She drew her dingy green bag to her chest with questioning eyes darting side to side at the both of us.

"You're obviously scaring her. Please back away." I knelt down. She smelled of spoiled milk and dirty clothes. "My name is Brooklyn Monti. I want to help you. What's your name?"

"Bianca," she whispered. "Bianca Hamilton."

"That's a pretty name. It's nice to meet you, Bianca." She pulled her legs closer to her chest along with her bag. I took the hint and backed away a few steps. "Are you here by yourself?"

She gave me a look while never uttering a word.

"Well, I'm by myself. Actually, I'm by myself often. My parents travel a lot, and I'm an only child. Are you an only child?"

She looked away.

"Can I tell you a secret?" I squatted down and sat Indian style across from Bianca. "I have Huntington's Disease. It's an inherited disease that will cause my brain to stop working. I was adopted when I was a baby, but I got it from my birth mom. She passed away. I never had the chance to meet her. I often imagine what she looked like, the sound of her laugh—all those little things. The only thing I know about my dad is his name is Britt Thornburg."

"That sucks."

"Tell me about it."

"What will happen to you if your brain stops working?"

"I could die."

"Are you scared?"

"Out of my mind," I said.

"Life sucks."

"Yeah it does for me, but surely not for you. Why do you say that?"

"I ran away from home."

"Why'd you do a thing like that?"

"My mom and dad are always gone too. I figured they wouldn't miss me."

"I'll bet they're worried out of their minds. Where are you from?"

"Goldgham." She released her bag a bit and pulled on the strap of her backpack.

"That's over four hundred miles away. I should call security and the police so we can get you back to your family."

"Good, I want to go home. I thought I was making the right decision, but I was wrong. I haven't eaten all week. I've been sleeping outside. Strange men keep coming up to me like that other guy. I'm scared."

"How old are you?" I asked while I dialed security.

"I'm sixteen."

I spoke to a woman at the security desk inside the airport.

"They're sending two security guards out here with us. No more weird guys, okay?"

"Thank you."

"Hey, I have a couple of granola bars I grabbed on the way out this morning. Would you like them?"

Bianca grabbed the bars and tore into them within seconds. Clearly she wasn't exaggerating about not eating.

The security guards appeared outside within moments as promised. I waved them over and explained the situation while speaking with the Goldgham Police Department. Turns out, they'd been searching for Bianca for weeks. I gave the detective our location and made sure she was in safe hands with the security guards before carrying on with my day.

"Bianca, I have a plane to catch, but I want to make sure you feel safe with the security guards before I go." Luckily, one was a woman.

She reached out and grabbed my arm. "Thank you, Brooklyn. I hope your brain doesn't stop working."

"That's the nicest thing anyone has said to me this week. Make the best out of your life, Bianca. It goes by so fast."

Helping Bianca filled my heart. God knows I wish I could've helped my friend, Veronica. She ran away during our sophomore year of high school. She met the guy online. Her Prince Charming turned out to be a married man with three children. He took her life. The news rocked all of us, and it stuck with me over the years. I should have told her parents where she was going instead of keeping secrets. We were so naïve, just like Bianca. I will never again turn my back on helping a young girl or a woman.

Save one, love one.

I entered the air conditioned terminal, which mimicked leaving the sweltering Southern heat for an Alaskan winter, and was startled by a sharp chime from my cell. I'd set up a special ringtone to alert me whenever our event company, Three Angels, had new account inquiries. This particular job was for a multi-million dollar firm in Santa Bay that would pay a hundred thousand dollars to plan an event for the announcement of their company's expansion. My partners, Tammy and Lorraine, were going to hit the roof.

I hurried to the counter ahead of a huge group traveling together in matching t-shirts and passed my bags and documents to the TSA agent. "They're your problem now."

"Oh, it's no problem," he laughed. "This is what I do."

I gave my chest a little pat where my heart beat for his kindness and followed the signs to undergo the scan and search. I took my shoes off and placed them inside a small bin. The TSA agent waved his wand around me but he got a little too familiar while patting me down.

"Hey." I smacked his hand.

"You know I could have you hauled off for assault of a public servant."

"I've got two bee stings up here. It doesn't take all that."

"Get out of here, and word of advice." He waved his wand. "Don't try that with anyone else. You're lucky I'm nice."

"Practice what you preach." I stuck my AirPods in and cranked up the volume to listen to my daily affirmations about allowing love to flow freely through me and how I deserved the utmost happiness.

The glorious smell of coffee beans and fresh pastries pulled me toward the food court.

Just what the doctor ordered.

A young twentyish man with spiked hair pushed out coffee orders like a machine. He mixed the cups before customers could finish spouting their orders. It's almost as if he had the menu emblazoned in his mind. He made my spicy pumpkin coffee within seconds and topped it off with a thoughtful design from the frothed milk.

"That'll be ten dollars."

"One second." I searched through my bulky bag for my wallet. The line had already grown by four people. The nerves jumped in my shoulder hard enough to knock the bag off my arm onto the floor. I hated being vulnerable in public. All those eyes staring at me—judging me, wondering what the hell was wrong with me. I scrambled to gather my runaway tampons. Before I knew it, tears stung the rims of my eyes. I didn't have the guts to look up. I felt foolish crawling around the dingy airport floor.

The young man slammed my cup down and screamed. "Do you see the line behind you? I don't have all day, lady."

"Hey, buddy, show the lady some respect. Be patient." A baritone voice boomed with a sexy Persian accent that sent chills throughout my body. "I see I'm not the only one having a hell of a morning."

A pair of mint green Nike shoes stood before me. My gaze crawled up his legs. He was a bronze hottie with a tapered haircut. He resembled the kind of man who appeared on the cover of romance novels with thick eyebrows and green eyes. He shoved a twenty dollar bill at the barista to pay for both our orders.

Mr. Hottie had huge muscles in places I'd never seen before. His five o'clock shadow looked more like six o'clock. A long scar ran down the right side of his cheek. Strangely, it complimented him. He even smelled like he'd cleaned his house before coming to the airport. The scent roused my OCD, which made a smile spread over my face from ear to ear.

"I appreciate your kindness. I'm going to pay you when I find my wallet in all this mess."

He dangled a pair of my red silk panties from his finger. "Sexy."

"Wow, how immature. You don't even know me." I snatched my unmentionables away from him and stuffed them inside my bag along with my other runaway items. "Thanks for your help." I held out a crisp ten dollar bill. But he refused it.

He followed close behind as I walked away from the kiosk with the little dignity I had left.

"Consider your coffee a gift and an apology for my immaturity."

"Apology accepted."

Our hands touched when he passed me the coffee. I nearly dropped it. People often talk about sparks, but this was the first time I'd experienced it. I thanked him again before taking a seat in the area marked D12.

"Are you following me?"

"No, I'm in the right place. I have a layover in Pinemoor. Are you in the right place?"

"Yeah, I guess we're on the same flight."

Mr. Chatty Hottie sat across from me while I nervously guzzled my coffee. Every few seconds, I glanced up to see him still watching me with curious eyes. I wondered if he was trying to figure out why my arm spazzed out. But deep down inside, I hoped he didn't see it. I tucked my hair behind my ears. I'd straightened it the night before and brushed it down with a middle part.

My mother had drilled into me over the years, *"A woman should never leave home without putting effort into her appearance."* However, I'd gone against everything she'd taught me when I'd dressed in a baggy sweat suit for my flight. Fortunately, I'd put myself together in a manner that complimented my five-foot-five frame even though I had on very little makeup. Men often gave me a second look, but this guy's persistence was new to me. I hugged my waist with my free hand to avoid eye contact altogether.

"I'd like to start over. My name's Kai Rahimi." He stuck out his hand.

"I don't know if I should talk to a man who'd show my underwear to a group of complete strangers."

"Oh, come on. I apologized and I bought you a cup of coffee. I was stupid. Please forgive me." He held his hands up in prayer style. "You're the most beautiful woman I've ever seen. It'd be a shame if I never got your name."

"Whatever." I gave in and shook his hand. "My name's Brooklyn Monti."

"Brooklyn? I like that." He gulped his coffee without breaking his gaze.

"Why do you keep staring at me? Are you thinking about my underwear again?"

"No. But now that you mentioned it, I am imagining you modeling them for me." He sucked his teeth. "Oh boy, it's a sight to see. Your butt in that string and lace would drive any man insane."

I covered my eyes and peeked through my fingers.

"I see you checking me out. I don't blame you. I look good."

"You're so conceited."

"I sure am. You should be too. Look at you—beautiful hair, gorgeous brown eyes, and full lips with a nice figure."

"Please stop."

7

"Loosen up a bit." He set his cup on a table next to his chair and moved beside me to place a hand on my shoulder. "There you go— slouch, relax."

"I don't know how to slouch. My mom spent years knocking me straight whenever I slouched." I bent forward and laughed as if I'd told the joke of the decade.

He clumsily put his arm around my shoulders. Perhaps the scent of bleach piqued my interest, or maybe it was his sexy muscles, but whatever the case, I didn't smack him.

"I'm on my way to train a bunch of stockbrokers in Bay Valley. What about you?"

"I'm going to my college homecoming. I haven't seen my friends in over a decade since we graduated, except for my best friend, Iris. I consider her to be more like a sister. She flew ahead last night." I drummed the side of my coffee cup causing the spicy pumpkin scent to infiltrate my senses. "I'm not ready to see them, but Iris twisted my arm. Now, here I am."

"A weekend catching up with old friends is a good thing—or at least it is in my world."

The nerves in my hand started to dance. I clasped them together. Kai gently pulled them apart.

"Want to hear a funny story?"

It fascinated me how he calmed my nerves faster than any anxiety medicine ever had.

"I embarrassed myself like hell this morning." He propped his elbow on the back of the chair. "Earlier, one of the wheels on my luggage got stuck on a piece of paper. Before I knew it, I face-planted on top of my bags. Two immature teens recorded the entire ordeal. I tried to snatch one of their phones, but I guess he was a pretty good basketball player because he faked me out so bad I almost twisted my knee. Now, I have a bad feeling that the video will go viral any moment."

My laughter shot out like a machine gun.

"You know what? I think you've got a wild side buried deep down inside."

"Is that your thing—wild women? Typical."

"Actually, my thing is a woman with intelligence, but my heart beats for a woman with a personality."

"Good for you."

Kai never stopped talking. Usually, I'd avoid people like him. But his personality slowly coaxed out the sexy and playful side of myself I usually kept under lock and key.

"I can't help but wonder what your thoughts consist of when you have that blank stare."

The gate attendant invited the first-class passengers aboard, and I gathered my bags and walked away to avoid his loaded question. I moved quickly, almost taking out a sobbing woman when our shoulders collided at the gate.

"2B, 2B," I whispered as I searched for my window seat. "Bingo."

Passengers were lightly scattered throughout the cabin, which gave me hope that I'd sit alone in silence for the entirety of the flight. I pulled out my phone and thumbed through the texts. No more than a few minutes passed when a shadow hovered over me. It was him again with a goofy smile. From the lower angle, I could see age lines around the corners of his eyes.

He fanned his ticket. "My seat is behind you. I don't like that." He signaled for the flight attendant.

"Wait. What are you doing?"

"You're in luck." He shoved his bag in the overhead storage. "Since this isn't a full flight, the nice attendant said I could sit next to you." He plopped down. "I don't know how often you fly, but you're supposed to put your phone on airplane mode or you could have us lost in space—not that I'd mind being lost with you."

"Oh, I see. You're one of those people who can't tell when they're being ignored."

"Stop pretending you don't like me."

"I don't know you."

"Well, I told you my name is Kai Rahimi. I'm a stockbroker, and I have a son. His name is Dylan." He showed me a picture. "He's my pride and joy."

I squeezed my arm and wished I could stop my nerves from jumping.

"Maybe you don't like me. I should leave you alone."

"No, I'm sorry. My mind is all over the place. You have an adorable son." I pulled my arm close to my waist. "It's not you. I told you I was nervous about going back to Pinemoor."

"I don't know what happened, and it's none of my business." He held his hands up. "But I'm a firm believer that it's best to face uncomfortable situations head on, especially if it bothers you this much."

I squeezed my eyes and clawed the armrest as the airplane rolled down the runway.

Kai put his hand over mine and belted out an off-key tune. He caught the attention of the other passengers, but he didn't care. He sang until I pulled my claws out of the armrest.

"For the love of God, stop singing."

He took that as a cue to sing even louder.

I couldn't wipe my tears away fast enough. By the time I opened my eyes, we were sailing through the electric blue sky, hand in hand. I quickly pulled away.

"I hate flying."

"I figured as much," he chuckled. "That's good for me because I got to hold your hand, even if it was only for a few seconds."

"Oh, Kai," I rubbed the side of my neck where his warm breath grazed my skin. An inch closer and his lips would've touched my shoulder. I moved away with a deep sigh and sank deeper into my seat. I often wished the pieces that made me were more like my best friend, Iris. She lived without fear. She went after what she wanted and even if it didn't work out, she knew how to move on without setbacks bringing her down.

"Ah, see you remembered my name. My plan is working." Kai kissed my hand and placed it back on the armrest.

"What plan?"

"I can't tell you," he laughed. "My goodness, you're beautiful. I'll bet you hear that all the time."

"Not as often as you imagine." I turned my attention to the window.

The clouds resembled the ones I studied from my glass condo on the top floor of our high-rise. The blue and amber were a sight to see from fifteen stories up.

I bought my condo a year after we started our Three Angels business, which took off like a rocket. We were operating in the black in no time. I tore down the walls and started from a blank canvas. My condo was the one place in my life where I had control, and I took full advantage of it.

"Meeting new people is a good thing." Kai showed all of his pearly white teeth when he smiled. It was yet another thing that attracted me to the handsome stranger.

"So you aren't flirting with me?"

"Oh, I'm flirting. Make no mistake about it. I'm flirting big time."

I began to relax next to Kai after an hour of gliding across the golden sky. The flight attendant offered us a miniscule amount of food that didn't match the prices we'd paid for first-class seats, but I didn't dare decline it. I pulled the shade down and turned back to the small screen I shared with Kai to finish watching *Along Came Polly*.

"You're probably the only person on earth who hasn't seen this movie," Kai teased.

"I don't watch much T.V., and I can't remember the last time I went to a theatre." I pointed to the screen, holding back my laughter in fear of disturbing the other passengers. "Is that how you tripped over your luggage this morning?"

"Hey, I told you that in confidence."

The attendant touched his arm. "Buckle up for landing."

"Damn, it feels like we just took off."

I squeezed my eyes and clawed the armrest while the small plane bounced up and down as it made its descent.

Kai sang again—as off-key as he had the first time. He rivaled a box of wounded cats.

"Please, stop. I can't take it anymore."

He kept singing until the plane stopped, but this time he got a round of applause from the passengers.

"Make sure you've got everything. I'd hate for you to leave those sexy red panties behind."

"You're way too focused on my underwear."

"I better stop before I scare you away." He followed me through the tunnel.

"How do you plan to spend a whole hour in dear old Pinemoor?"

"Actually, I'd like to spend it with you," Kai said.

"Oh no, you can't meet Iris. You'll learn how interrogations work."

"Who said anything about meeting Iris? We could stay here at the airport and talk—just the two of us." He stroked my arm with his rough fingers, raising goose bumps over my skin. "So what do you say? Are you staying or leaving me here all alone?"

I couldn't bring myself to say no. There was something between us, and I wanted to explore it a bit more.

Kai stuck out his arm to escort me. "Come on, I'll buy you a mimosa."

"Now you're freaking me out. Mimosas are my favorite. If a bearded man with crazy eyes opened the backdoor of an unmarked white van and told me he had free mimosas inside, I'd be as good as kidnapped."

"See, I knew you had a wild side in there," Kai laughed. "Thanks to you, this has been a great morning."

"You've pleasantly surprised me." I covered my smile with my hair.

"Please don't hide." He put his fingers under my chin to lift my face to his. "You have a gorgeous smile."

We wandered upon a snazzy restaurant dipped in gold and leather with a long bar. He guided me to a stool and interrupted the young bartender who zealously typed on her phone.

"Hello, please tell me you guys make a mean mimosa?"

"The meanest in Pinemoor." She placed a hand on her hip to emphasize it.

"Ah, see, you've already earned yourself a healthy tip, young lady."

"Gee, thanks." She snatched the twenty dollar bill from Kai. "I'll add this to my, get the hell out of Pinemoor and never look back my savings account."

I gave her a high-five. At least Iris and I weren't the only ones who felt that way about Pinemoor.

"Ah, see. Now we're talking." Kai rubbed his hands together. "Let's see how you act after you get a few mimosas in you."

I pulled out my phone to ask Iris to hold off for an hour before coming to the airport.

"Are you texting your boyfriend?"

"I don't have a boyfriend."

"You're pulling my leg."

"No, but I'm sure you have a harem of women falling for your long hair and muscles."

"You've got me all wrong. I'm the monogamous type. The world can have the rest. I believe we were created to live in pairs."

"I see."

"What? You don't agree?"

"I agree with you. But most of the men I've met don't think this way."

"How is that possible? If you were my lady, I wouldn't glance at another woman." He paid the bartender and tipped her another twenty.

"That's what you say now. You don't know anything about me." We strolled to his gate.

"Here's my phone number. I hope you'll call."

"How long will you be in Bay Valley?"

"Seven long dreadful weeks," he huffed. "I busted my ass to get into this training program because I needed a change. But lately, I've been regretting it. They keep me on the go." He gently brushed the hair away from my face.

I knew exchanging phone numbers meant I should tell him I have Huntington's disease, but I couldn't say the words. Meeting someone new always scared the hell out of me because Huntington's has ruined every milestone in my life.

First, I lost my mother, and my father gave me up for adoption. Then my diagnosis interfered with my college years, and my college boyfriend changed after he learned the truth. Then every man I've met since has run away from me.

Without warning, Kai wrapped an arm around my waist and pulled me into him. He placed a gentle kiss on my forehead then his lips wandered down to mine. He held me close, and we stood there looking into each other's eyes until the attendant tapped him on the shoulder.

"Sir, this is the final call for Bay Valley. Are you still going?"

"Yes, coming now." He kissed my hand. "Are you going to call me?"

I gave him a nod because he'd left me speechless. I watched him until he disappeared, touching my lips, thinking about our kiss.

Life finally gave me lemonade instead of lemons.

Chapter 2

Iris showed up at the airport exactly an hour later as requested. Thankfully, Kai was already long gone before she could interrogate him. I wasn't ready to let her loose on him. If Huntington's didn't run him away, her overprotectiveness would.

She looked beautiful in her strapless red and white striped dress. She'd pulled her hair back and covered her head with a scarf as protection from the high winds that came from riding around with the top down on her rented convertible. How she was able to drive around in six-inch high heels was beyond me.

We woke up early to have breakfast before heading to the college for the festivities. Iris and I were asked to speak to a women's group that consisted of current students about our career and life after Pinemoor. Then later that evening, we attended the football game.

We took a walk around campus before the game. Every place brought back a memory, some good and some bad.

"Did you see Professor Williamson? He's still handsome. Right? Hello? Brooklyn."

Iris hit my thigh. It's a wonder I wasn't covered in bruises. She's a physical talker. The more she made a point or tried to get your attention, the more she'd hit you. So I was in trouble with Iris and prone to her hitting because Kai dominated my thoughts.

"I'm sorry. What did you say?"

"Welcome back to the real world."

I gazed beyond the cliffs to the forest, clutching the door handle as Iris sped around the mountain's sharp curves. I love her, but she's the worst driver known to man. It's bad enough to give me heart palpitations. One wrong move and we'd be flying over the cliff like Thelma and Louise.

I touched my lips and once again thought about the kiss I shared with Kai. It'd been so long since I kissed someone that I'd forgotten how it felt.

My phone alarm pulled me out of my daydream to remind me to take my daily dose of medication.

Once again, Huntington's had ruined a good thing.

I swallowed the handful of pills with a gulp of water and reached down inside my gray leather bag for the fancy camera my dad bought for my birthday last year.

"I never wanted to come back here, but boy did I miss this view." Iris threw her head back to suck in the fresh air, leaning her body with the car as she navigated the winding roads. "I used to drive out here every evening to recenter after my parents died."

I grabbed the steering wheel. Sure, it was risky, but I had to do something.

"Touch it again, and we'll be flying through the air."

"Do you ever stop talking?"

"You know the answer to that," she said with a chuckle. "Do you remember the summers we spent at the beach? All we cared about were hot guys, sun, and cheap wine." She pointed to where the water beat against the golden shoreline and a colony of seagulls played near the tide. "Sunsets in Pinemoor remind me of a Leighton Annenberg painting. It's breathtaking."

I rolled my eyes in a huff. Iris took one art class and from then on thought of herself as a curator.

"You never admit when I'm right."

"Pinemoor sunsets are underrated compared to Leighton Annenberg." I wouldn't call myself a know-it-all. But I did know a lot, and Pinemoor wasn't all that spectacular. "Annenberg's use of color is remarkable. Think about the painting, *Dance Under the Rain*. It tells a story of old romance. He painted a couple kissing in the rain, but the man is so into the woman that he doesn't realize he's dropped the umbrella. Though, neither of them seems to mind. The trees burst with color, and old post lamps line the sidewalks. It doesn't look anything like Pinemoor. It's all green here. It's a beautiful green. But, green is green, and green isn't Leighton Annenberg. Oh, and what about his painting, *A Beautiful Night* with the stone bridge and grand architecture. In Pinemoor, they slap a coat of paint on the crumbling walls, hang a few paintings, and call it a renovation."

"Pinemoor has plenty of modern buildings downtown. And there's color when the cherry blossom trees are in full bloom," Iris insisted with raised eyebrows.

"I'll give you that. But everything else is green." I looked down at my emerald green nails. I hated the color after I got them painted, but now they reminded me of Kai's beautiful green eyes.

Iris snapped her fingers at me again. "Hello?"

"Too close." I slapped her hand away.

"Do you remember the last time we were at the beach? You screamed *carpe diem* and ran into the ocean. You almost drowned under a huge tide. What in the hell were you thinking? You don't even know how to swim."

"I wasn't thinking." My smile flipped upside down. "I used to have fun. You know, before…"

"Huntington's, I know." She patted my leg this time instead of hitting it.

"I was only nineteen. My life was just beginning when I was diagnosed.

17

Talk about a life coming apart. I wish I'd never let my curiosity get the best of me when the school held an event for genetic testing. I mean, I'd still have Huntington's, but I wouldn't live in constant fear."

"Well, I'm glad it didn't work out that way because you're able to treat it and keep it under control." Iris pointed to the top of Ans Hollow peaks. It was the tallest mountain in Pinemoor. "I used to sneak out to the peak after midnight to meet my boyfriend. We didn't care about animals, murderers, or the dead backpacker."

I slid down in the seat and covered my face. "Please don't start with the dead backpacker stories. I don't want to hear it."

"Ah, baby Brooklyn can't handle a scary story. That's fine. I'll save them for Halloween. You've got five months."

"Pinemoor has been bearable since I haven't run into Adam. I can actually breathe."

"You'll never change. Relax and enjoy yourself. It's only two days. I told you Adam's a washed up Arena Football player. Even when he suits up, he's riding the bench. You know he can't handle not being the center of attention."

"I don't know what I ever saw in Adam."

"You smiled!" The tail ends of Iris's scarf flapped in the high winds. "When you said his name, you smiled. I saw you. Do you miss him or something?"

I turned the music up to drown out her jibber-jabber. The sun hovered over the city like a giant orange and turned the horizon the same color.

Iris turned the music back down. "I'm not crazy or blind. I know what I saw. You smiled when I said his sad, sad name. After everything that idiot did. You must be some kind of masochist."

"Pay attention to the road you delusional freak." I yanked the steering wheel again. This time she hit me. "Cut it out. You're going to leave bruises on my leg."

"Don't put your hands on the steering wheel while I'm driving. Me sentare felizmente en el lado del pasajero." Her fiery Spanish side surfaced. "Now back to what I was saying before you momentarily lost your mind. I never liked Adam, and I'll bet he hasn't changed one bit." She sped off the highway north of Ans Hollow Peek, leaving the smell of burnt rubber behind.

"I'm not proud of my decisions, but he was a top athlete. My reputation meant everything to me back in those days, so I put up with his crap to enjoy the perks. But it taught me some painful life lessons—and when I say painful, I mean painful."

"I wish you could see yourself the way everyone else sees you."

"Back in college, I used to love getting dolled up in a sexy dress for a hot date—before Adam, of course. I felt like I had endless possibilities. I'd have intellectual conversations and a few laughs over wine with a hot guy. My hands would be sweating by the time my date walked me to the door. I'd make sure to inhale his cologne because that's the best part of a man—his scent. I'd let my date know he could kiss me by resting my hand on his shoulder and drawing my body closer to his. Huntington's stole my confidence. I want to enjoy my life again."

"You can and you will once you let go of your fears. You're no different from any of us. We're born then we die. Hopefully, you get to do some amazing shit in between." Iris put the car into overdrive on the last stretch of highway.

"You usually cruise like Morgan Freeman in *Driving Miss Daisy*. Now you're racing as if you've got gasoline coursing through your veins."

"See, that's your problem. You want to control everything and everyone around you, but you can't control me." She sped off the ramp into a sea of cars proudly displaying Pinemoor State's school colors.

"The sun must've baked your brain because you're not thinking straight."

"Be quiet." Iris gestured toward the building that loomed ahead. "I've got a surprise for you."

There it stood, tall and proud—the familiar sign hovered over the parking lot. "The Paragon Mill Hotel," I read with a smile. "This place holds a special place in my heart. This definitely makes up for that horrible hotel we stayed in last night."

The grand water fountain sat proudly at the entrance of the hotel. I remembered the night the manager caught us having an impromptu foam party in the fountain. We all piled in after Iris filled it with soap. It was amazing. We splashed and jumped around until the manager spotted us. I ran until my legs turned into jelly. I couldn't afford to go to jail or pay a fine, and there was no way I'd call my parents. I'd have to listen to a long speech about responsibility and why they sent me to college.

"Look at this place." I stepped out of the car. "One night here would force us to eat noodles for the rest of the week, and we didn't care. We always had a good time."

"You almost got us banned after your catfight with Stacy."

I stuck my fingers inside my ears and began humming.

"Oh, no. You're going to hear this. You weren't embarrassed when you went bat shit crazy on that poor girl." Iris recalled the big fight of 2009.

Mostly every student at the college had the same bright idea to blow off steam before finals. We all ended up at the hotel. After I started dating Adam, I'd sit beside him while he played the piano. A group would stand around the piano and sing along. He soon caught Stacy's eye. I wasn't having it.

"I didn't do anything wrong. I stood up for myself."

"I can't believe you're still playing the victim card."

"Oh, please, you were there. You saw what happened."

Iris untied her black scarf to smooth her hair back into a neat bun.

"Yeah, and I don't know why you'd fight over a piece of…"

"Watch your language." Iris had the mouth of a sailor. If I didn't stop her, she'd drop bombs all night. "Stacy disrespected me."

"We all knew how she operated. Every man within a hundred mile radius was fair game, but you took it too far. I'll never forget the size of Stacy's eyes when you pushed her over the bar and she crashed into the liquor shelves. You cost the hotel hundreds in damages. You're lucky the manager didn't send you to jail because if it were me, you'd be wearing an orange jumpsuit, fighting off Big Bertha after lights out. And I still would've made your parents pay for the damages." She tossed her keyring inside her silver clutch and refreshed her plump red lips.

"If I'd known then what I know now, I would've taken my chances to fight Big Bertha. That old man had me cleaning hotel rooms for months. That's why I never make my bed. It gives me flashbacks."

"All I'm saying is keep your cool. You're a grown woman with your own business. You have a brain. Use it instead of your hands."

"You need not worry yourself. I'm not in that space anymore." I pulled my bags from the backseat and followed Iris.

Smiling familiar faces of old classmates huddled throughout the posh hotel. Lydia, the campus comedian, stood amid a crowd of chuckling friends. Stan, a devout Christian, comforted a sobbing woman. Ralph signed autographs for his old buddies who'd become fans of his tattoo reality show. We were all superstars in our own right.

The hotel had finally replaced the old disgusting brown loop carpet with a beautiful marble floor. Back then, it didn't matter how often they vacuumed. It always looked filthy. Business has been good for them.

I stopped at the black Steinway piano and leaned over the silver railing where it sat on a high platform near three arched windows underneath a crystal chandelier. I could see us as young kids dancing and having a good time. We were oblivious of the real world.

Then a ghost raced to the piano. It was the one person I was afraid to see—Adam. My entire body went numb.

"Forget him." Iris tugged my arm.

"He's playing the song he wrote for me. He's unbelievable."

"Pull yourself together."

"I'm doing my best." My heart raced. Adam was the only person who could make me come unglued. My feet wouldn't stop moving. I was practically tap dancing. Thankfully, it wasn't from Huntington's. Just old fashion nervousness.

Iris caught Adam's glance and flipped him the bird. A woman standing next to him with two little girls quickly covered their faces. He stood from the piano and gave her a kiss. The girls stuck to his legs so much he could hardly walk. He bent over to whisper to them. They quickly let go and ran to the woman. She was tall and thin with a sassy short haircut. Adam gripped the back of her arm tightly and kissed her again. She gathered the girls and hurried away without saying a word. Then he started our way.

"Why is he coming over here? I have nothing to say to him."

"I'll kill him if he tries anything stupid."

Adam made my skin crawl, but he still looked damn good. He'd managed to hold onto his athletic build over the years. The only difference was he'd let his hair grow longer. He'd pulled it up into a man bun.

"Are my eyes deceiving me, or is it Brooklyn Denise Monti in the flesh?" He stuck his hand out even though all I could focus on were his evil eyes. "You're even more beautiful than I remember."

He moved in to give me a hug, but I hastily pushed him away.

"You're a sight for sore eyes." He stuck his hands inside his pockets. "It's good to see you."

"You think this is a good thing?"

"Yeah, I do. Aren't you happy to see me?"

"Maybe you've taken too many hits to the head on the field if you think us being in the same place is a good idea."

"I was too quick on my feet to take that many hits. Come on now, you know me. No matter how much you try to forget about me."

"Iris?"

"Yes?" She stood next to me with her arms crossed over her chest as if she were my bodyguard.

"Take my credit card, and go get my room squared away, please." I passed her my wallet.

She tapped her foot on the marble floor and drummed her fingers against her folded arms, totally ignoring me.

"Iris, I know you hear me. Please take care of that for me?"

"Fine, I'll go. But you just proved my point, masochist." She snatched the wallet and marched away.

"It's good to see you too, Iris." Adam teased.

He looked as proud and handsome as he did years ago, and he smelled of cologne, leather, and expensive scotch.

"Could I get a hug?"

"Do not touch me. I hoped and prayed I wouldn't see you. I thought, maybe, just maybe, if we crossed paths, you'd keep your distance. What a disappointment."

"You don't know anything about disappointment."

"Seriously, Adam. I don't have any desire to go blow for blow with you about disappointment when you obviously have none. I see you have a beautiful woman in your life and kids. They look just like you."

"She is my wife. And yes, they're my twins, but that doesn't mean I haven't faced disappointments. Actually, I've been looking forward to seeing you because I'd like to discuss business with you." He reached for my shoulder.

"Do not touch me with the hands that almost killed me. There is not enough money in the world to make me want to do business with a man who is violent toward women, especially when it started with me."

"What makes you think I have a history of it? I made one mistake."

"No man who did what you did to me stops after one time."

Adam circled me with his hands still shoved inside his pockets. "You're holding on to the past. You need to move on from that shit. Let's go to the bar and drink until we remember why we ever liked each other. What do you say?"

"No."

"Damn, after all these years you still hate me," he laughed. "I've been told love and hate go hand in hand. This is no coincidence. The two of us being here at the same time has to mean something. It may never happen again. So stop acting crazy and have a drink with me." He stood there trying to look innocent as if he never tried to take my life.

"There's nothing coincidental about us being here at the same time. It's a familiar place."

"I've moved on from that night. How many years has it been since we've seen each other?" He rubbed his beard.

"It's been seven years, nine months, two days, seven hours, two minutes, and thirty seconds. Selfishly, I'd like to keep the time rolling."

His eyebrows raised and his eyes widened. "You've never said no to me before."

"Actually, I said no the night you tried to kill me and I ended up in the ICU." I waved him away. "I can't do this. I can't be close to you. I don't want to talk to you." Tears burned the rim of my eyelids, but I held it together. Adam didn't deserve my tears.

Adam was my emotional kryptonite. He knew how to get under my skin. When we first met, he was charismatic and thoughtful. We'd laugh, listen to music, and dance. I wanted to spend all my time with him. And he was right. In the beginning, I hardly ever told him no. He was my boyfriend—the first man I'd loved and made love to. But after my diagnosis, his love for me turned into hate, and I was too stuck to him to walk away. He was my first love, or so I thought it was love.

"Seriously, I need to talk to you about a business opportunity. Forget about the past."

"You have got to be kidding me."

"I'm serious. A production company wants to do a biography about my life and football career, but they won't move forward unless you're on board. I have the paperwork upstairs in my room. I'll go grab it."

"Adam, you weren't even in the NFL. You play in the Arena Football League. You're not as important as you think. The only reason they want me on board is to sensationalize your little bio to get people to watch it. I'm not doing it. Get out of my face."

"Maybe I'm not important to you because you're clouded with hate."

"Why in the hell do they need me to move forward? Say whatever you want to say. I don't care anymore."

"I've tried to get them to give up the idea of you being onboard, but they won't do it since you're the reason why I never went to the NFL. There is no way around it."

"YOU are the reason you never went to the NFL, you piece of shit."

"I can tell you're still hiding your disease from everyone, except for Iris. Don't worry, I won't say anything." He walked away, shaking his head as if I was the certifiable one instead of him.

"What did he say?" Iris crept up behind me. "Do you need me to take care of him?"

"Not today. Do you have the key card to my room? I need some peace and quiet after my encounter with the devil."

"Okay, this is the deal." She scratched the back of her head. "We will have to share a room. They're all booked up. I told you to reserve your room weeks ago, but you spent that time fighting me about coming here. My room has double beds, so we'll be roommates just like the good old days."

"This weekend is officially busted. I love you as a friend and sister, but I hated you as a roommate."

"Whatever, Brooklyn, it's only for one night. It won't kill you."

"You can't sleep without your annoying sleep machine. I'll bet it's in your bag. I mean, who in the hell finds the sound of crickets relaxing? No way, I can't deal tonight."

"It's too bad. You don't have a choice, and for the record, it's not crickets anymore—it's rain."

I forced myself to hold my head high instead of balling up in a corner like I wanted. After years of counseling, Adam still had the power to steal my joy with a simple hello.

Money well spent.

Chapter 3

Later that evening, I spotted Adam riding up the glass elevator adjacent to ours. I bit my lip. My ability to be around him had become null and void. So in order to keep my emotions in check, I clasped my hands together and whispered a prayer.

"Please, God, I'll give up my castle in the sky as long as he doesn't stop on the same floor as us."

Unfortunately, my prayer went out a little too late.

"So, we meet once again." Adam emerged from his elevator and stuck his hand out to Iris. "You took off before I could say hello."

She turned away with her arms folded over her chest.

"You haven't changed. You're still a mean bitch. All you've gotten is older. Soon you'll be a gray-haired old bitch."

"Cuidado con la boca antes de sacarte la lengua." She drove her nimble finger into the side of his head. When Iris was excited or upset, her native tongue dominated. "You're lucky I don't slap the shit out of you for what you did to Brooklyn. Do you know one in four women experience domestic violence in their lifetime? Thanks to you, Brooklyn became one of those statistics."

"He's not worth it, Iris. Let's go."

"I'm not surprised neither of you have a ring on your fingers. No man in his right mind would marry unstable lunatics like you." He slammed the door to his hotel room.

"I could strangle him," Iris said.

"He's a disrespectful jerk."

Iris walked inside our room, which was on the other side of Adam's, swinging her arms wildly and speaking in Spanish.

"Calm down before you give yourself a heart attack."

She took more than a few deep breaths.

"Adam brings out the worst in everyone. I never should've let you talk me into coming back here. Pinemoor is a bad, bad place." I threw myself across the queen sized bed near the window and sank into the gel mattress with my eyes closed. It smelled of fresh strawberries and vanilla.

"This is ridiculous." Iris paced the room. "We've got to pull ourselves together."

"When I saw him, the only thing I could think about was the night he almost killed me. He hit me so hard everything went black, and he wouldn't stop. All because I refused to have sex. At one point, I accepted my fate because I knew I was going to die right then and there."

"I don't even want to think about that." Iris froze mid-stride. "I don't know what I would've done without you."

"I will never forgive Adam, never."

"Oh, hey." Iris snapped her fingers and danced in a circle. "I know where we should go to get your mind off things." Her crazed smile resembled a court jester.

I stood and leaned against the window. The heat from the blazing sun warmed my back in contrast to the hotel room's frigid AC. The window framed the downtown skyline and showcased the landscape of cherry blossom trees, larkspurs, and peonies.

Maybe I couldn't appreciate the color back then because we were poor college students who could only afford a cramped room with a tiny window overlooking the hedges and the hotel gardener's shed. Now, we could afford a hotel room with a city view, and our upgraded room was a true testament of how far we'd come since those days.

"No way. I don't feel like it."

"Oh, come on," she coaxed. "You love Pizzaandu as much as I do."

"I could go for a couple slices right now," I sighed, "and maybe even a glass of Merlot."

"That's the spirit. Now, let's get out of here before you do something stupid. You can't pull off an orange jumpsuit these days. You'd look like a thirteen-year-old boy with your flat chest."

I elbowed Iris for her harsh comparison as we latched arms and made our way back downstairs. I admired the hand-painted murals of the mountains on the ceiling and noted our collection of classmates had dwindled down to a few newcomers scattered here and there.

"Why did I ever waste my time with him? I know he hasn't changed because I saw how he grabbed the back of his wife's arm to shoo her away."

"I saw that too," Iris replied.

"I shouldn't be this close to him. Who knows what he'll do when he doesn't get his way again."

"I feel the need to rescue that poor woman." Iris shook her head.

"Adam is still a narcissistic abuser. He can play kissy-kissy with his wife all he wants. I know the real him, and I'm not falling for it. I feel sad for his daughters having to be raised by him."

"Well, well, well, if it isn't the terrible two."

A masculine voice boomed from across the room. I'd faced my kryptonite, now it was Iris's turn.

"Danny? I can't believe it's you." Iris ran full speed into his arms. "You're wearing a suit—and it's Ralph Lauren. How cute is your bow tie? I love your beard. You look like a rough James Bond. I've missed you."

"Oh, honey, hands off." A woman with smooth skin and dreamy eyes stepped in between them. They made an unlikely couple. She stood at least six-three, and Danny was a mere five-nine.

"This is my beautiful wife, Besa. She's hot, huh?"

Hot, indeed. There wasn't an ounce of fat on her body. Her face had the perfect bone structure. She'd surely make any woman feel intimidated in her presence.

"Honey, I told you about my closest friends in college," Danny explained. "This is Iris. We call her Firecracker. You never know what'll come out of her mouth."

Iris scrunched her brows. "You're kidding, right? Is Besa her real name?"

"Yes, that's her real name. She's Albanian."

"Albanian's the closest you could get to a Latina, huh? You miss me, admit it?" Iris salsa danced with one hand on her stomach and the other in the air.

"Please excuse my friend." I put my hand around Iris's waist to make her stop. "I've asked her a thousand times to ease new people into her wackiness."

Besa rolled her eyes and pulled Danny closer. She did everything but pee around his feet to stake her claim.

"This is Brooklyn." Danny placed his hand on my shoulder. "We call her Fu-Fu. She kept us all in line."

"It's nice to finally meet you, Fu-Fu." She stuck her hand out with a smile.

I accepted her handshake and knew full well it'd come back to bite me in the butt with Iris.

"Sooo, tell us how you two met," I asked.

"I was Besa's accountant for a year. She was so kind, intelligent, and beautiful. One day, I gathered the courage to ask her out for coffee. We've been together ever since."

"That coffee date was magical." Besa raked her red nails through his thick curly hair. "I love you, honey."

"I love you more." He pecked her cheek. "What are you doing these days, Firecracker?"

"I'm the Chief Forensic Medical Examiner of Fallbush County. It's been six years now."

Danny freed himself from Besa's grip long enough to lift Iris off the floor in a tight hug. "Check you out, Firecracker. I'll bet you look great in your white coat."

"Wouldn't you like to know?" She strutted in a circle and held her collar as if it were the lapels of her white coat.

Besa cleared her throat to more than likely put an end to their shameless flirting.

"What about you, Fu-Fu?"

"I partnered with two amazing women five years ago, and we started a business: Three Angels Event Planning." I passed Danny and his wife a business card. I never missed an opportunity to network. "I've also been toying with the idea of leaving my business to start a career totally dedicated to marketing." I covered my left cheek to hide the twitches. This time it wasn't nerves. It was Huntington's trying to make its grand appearance at the most inopportune time.

"You'd be a fool to walk away from your own business to work for someone. You have it good because my boss is a major thorn in the ass."

I slapped his arm. "Watch it, Danny."

"I forgot you were the profanity police. I promise it won't happen again, dear Brooklyn." He flashed her the Boy Scout Salute.

"Don't pay Brooklyn any mind. Her business is top-notch. You should see the events they've planned." Iris whipped out her phone. "These aren't sweet sixteen parties. They're extravagant events for Fortune 500 companies. The women wear sequin dresses, long gloves, and old money."

"You weren't kidding." Danny gushed over the pictures. "Are you still living here in Pinemoor, Firecracker?"

"Fallbush County is Woodcrest." Iris giggled. "I couldn't stay here after my parents died." She hung her head and fiddled with her hair. "Thankfully, Brooklyn's parents welcomed me into their home. When I left Pinemoor, I never looked back."

"It's really good to know you have each other."

"What about you, Danny Boy?" I asked. "Tell us more."

"I'm a boring accountant these days. I'm your man if you're worth a million or more. It pays extremely well, which comes in handy because my wife has caviar taste. So I need more than a malt liquor budget to stay in her good graces."

"I'm not the only one with expensive taste, my love." Besa kissed Danny on the cheek and wiped away her fuchsia lipstick with the tip of her thumb. "And just so you know, I'd love you no matter what."

Danny pulled out a handful of business cards trimmed in gold.

Iris crossed her arms over her chest and refused to take one. "I don't have a million dollars lying around. I'm not your ideal client."

"I'm no millionaire either." I held up my hands and followed Iris's lead.

"Ah, but you hang with millionaires on a daily basis. Share your rolodex. Help me out."

He passed me a few more business cards.

"You may as well forget it. Brooklyn won't discuss anything with her clients outside of their need for her business. That's probably why she hasn't landed herself a millionaire man."

Danny chuckled, "Maybe she's holding out for—"

"It's been great catching up," I snapped, "but we were on our way out before we ran into you."

Iris held Danny's hand longer than she should have. She only let go after Besa cleared her throat three times.

"Do you need some water?" Iris stared at the Albanian beauty. "You keep clearing your throat. You must be parched."

"Um, hey, what do you say we meet at the bar around eight o'clock?" Danny interjected.

"Sounds like a plan. We'll see you then, Meathead."

"Meathead's a thing of the past."

"If I'm still Firecracker and Brooklyn's Fu-Fu, you'll always be Meathead." She blew him a kiss.

"Pinemoor State grads are in the house." A voice wailed from the other side of the hotel lobby.

I wandered inside the gold and blue lounge and sat on a sofa by the window overlooking the large pool. People swam around a floating bar surrounded by artificial palm trees. I could hear them screaming and laughing over the loud music, sounding as if they didn't have a care in the world. I wanted the same for myself—if only I could escape my thoughts and emotions.

"I'll bet you half of those women are lonely housewives who can't pay for a compliment at home, and the men are escaping from their out-of-shape, micro-managing wives to flirt with old college flames." Iris teased with a shoulder bump. "Ah, I got a smile."

"I don't feel like laughing. I just want to deal with my feelings."

"Fine, I tried," she huffed. "What brought this on?"

"I knew dating with Huntington's disease would be challenging, but I wasn't prepared for this life. I'm lonely, and this weekend has me comparing my life to everyone else. I need time to think, and I don't want to fight with you about it."

Iris touched the side of my face. Her eyes held concern and pity.

"You want to know the truth?"

"What?"

"You are your own worst enemy. It's not Adam, me, or anyone else. What do you want out of life? Say it and be honest for once."

"I want romance. I want love. I want a family of my own. Are you happy now?" I chased the tears streaming down my face. "I'm envious of the possibilities you all have because I'm afraid I won't have time to experience them for myself."

"Okay. Stop crying about it, and do something to change it. Go mingle. Have a one night stand. Just do something."

"Maybe I would if you'd get out of here and give me a second to think."

"Fine. I'll go, but don't get us kicked out here."

I waved her away and kicked off my heels to stretch out on the sofa. Her constant blabbering wouldn't help me find my center. A group of musicians had set up their instruments around the piano across the hall and had started to play an old jazz song about luck being a lady. The song gave me a sense of courage, and it was high time I used that courage. So, I pulled out my phone and sent Kai a message.

Hello, this is Brooklyn. I hope you haven't forgotten about me? lol

While I waited for a response, I called my parents via video chat. They were in Saint Falls. My mom answered with a soft smile. She had a white flower stuck in her hair, and her lips were painted a tropical red.

"Honey, how's Pinemoor going? Have you seen all your friends?"

"Yeah, and the one person I didn't want to see."

"Adam?"

I nodded.

"Oh honey, don't let him ruin your time with your friends. You need to enjoy your time away to relax and reset your mind. You're always so worried about the end when you really don't know when or if that will happen. You're young and beautiful."

"My birth mom was young and beautiful. Look what happened to her."

"Brooklyn, I went back and forth with myself for years about whether to tell you the truth about your birth mother's death. But in the end, I knew you had to know. Sadly, the truth comes with many fears and never-ending questions. Yes, your mother died young, but that doesn't mean your story will end the same way. I need you to hold your head up and enjoy life. You'd have a great one if you would only step out of the darkness to see it for yourself."

"I love you, Mom."

"I love you too. Tell Iris I said hello, and I love her."

"I will. Tell Dad the same." I hung up and sang along with the music as the band played.

"You still have the voice of an angel."

I leapt from the chaise. "Roxie Kavangla, is that you?"

"It's Roxie Hill these days." She wiggled her finger to show off her diamond wedding ring.

"Hill?" I screamed like a schoolgirl. "Did you and Jace get married?"

"What can I say? He's my soulmate."

"Wow, that's great. Congratulations. I'm still waiting to find mine."

"You'll find each other when the time is right. Be patient." She kissed my cheek. "Tell me everything that's been going on with you since we left Pinemoor. I've been thinking about you nonstop over the years."

"Hold on, where's Jace?"

"He couldn't make it. He started a business with Eleni's husband. Their grand opening is tomorrow. So while you guys are asleep, I'll be on a red-eye back to my baby's side. I can't miss his big day."

"Wait a second. Back up. Did I hear you say El's married?"

Roxie muffled her laugh with her hands.

"What do you mean she's married?" I added a chuckle of my own. "El changed boyfriends more than I changed my underwear. She used to say marriage was a nice dream, but that's all it was, a dream."

"All that changed after she met Nolan, and it's a good thing too because I was worried about my girl." Her stomach jiggled whenever she laughed. She tried to hide it with her jacket, but it didn't work.

"I can't wait to make her eat her words. Where is she?"

"She's too pregnant to fly—doctor's orders—but she specifically told me to tell you that people can change."

"You're blowing my mind. El's married and pregnant." Jealousy coursed through my veins. "Did she start her design company?"

"Actually, we're business partners. We focus more on hotels, resorts, and airports. That's where the bulk of our money comes from whenever we can agree on the details without missing a deadline. That girl still doesn't know how to make up her mind in a timely manner."

"Okay, you and El need to stop hogging the key you've found to perfect bliss and pass it to me. I'm in desperate need."

"My life's not perfect." Roxie sat down on the edge of the sofa with her elbows propped on her knees.

"Maybe your life isn't perfect, but it doesn't sound too shabby."

"I'm serious. I'd give everything up for the one thing I can't seem to get."

"Oh, really? I find that hard to believe. You have a great husband, and you both have thriving businesses. I don't have a husband or a boyfriend for that matter. I have no idea if I will ever have a family of my own. I'd trade with you any day."

"Brooklyn, I'm going to share something with you because you've never broken my trust before." Roxie fiddled with the chain on her Chanel purse. "I can't have a baby. We've been trying for three years with no luck. So when I say my life isn't perfect, I mean that and I need you as my friend to understand that."

I held her hand. I hardly knew how to keep my emotions under control. I wasn't equipped with the right words to comfort her.

She wiped the tears from her eyes and blew out a belly full of air. "Okay, enough of my problems. I really have to ask you something that's been bugging me since college."

"What's that?"

"Junior year…"

"No, don't go there."

"You don't even know what I want to say."

"Fine, say it."

"You were gone for six or seven months during junior year. But when you came back, you were different. You walked slower. You weren't as carefree anymore. Plus, you and Adam started to fight a lot just before he left Pinemoor. What happened?"

"If I didn't talk about it then, I certainly don't want to talk about it now."

"Sounds like I struck a nerve."

I twisted my hand around my wrist to calm my twitching muscles. A silver vase filled with lilies sat in the center of a round table. I walked over and touched the petals. "Do you see these flowers?"

"Yes."

"Junior year, I was in the hospital for seven months—ICU. My mother kept fresh lilies by my bedside. The colors didn't matter much as long as they were lilies. One of her neighbors grew them special for me, and he'd give them to my mother. He believed flowers had healing power because they were also living organisms. So now, when I see these beautiful flowers, they make me think of that time and of Adam because he was the reason I was there. That's all I'll say." I plucked one of the beautiful petals and flicked it to the floor.

"I knew you were taken away in an ambulance, but that's all. Did he hurt you?"

"I told you. I don't want to talk about it. But thanks to Iris, I'm stuck in a room next to Adam for the night."

"That girl marches to the beat of her own drum. Where is she?"

"We're in Pinemoor. Where do you think?"

"Pizzaandu." We said simultaneously with a chuckle. Thankfully, it was enough to pull us from the heavy stuff.

Roxie scrunched her face. "You'd think she'd be burnt out on that place by now."

"It's an addiction. Every time she comes to Pinemoor, it rears its ugly head."

"What's crazy is how much she'd eat without ever gaining weight. I've never been pregnant, but look at me." She grabbed her love handles and jiggled them. They moved like a bowl of jelly.

"I'd say she's gained about thirty pounds since college."

"Seven years, a baby, and that's all? She's an alien."

"I only said that to make you feel better. Her pregnancy weight melted off like cotton candy after she gave birth. She's looked the same since college."

"I remember when we'd go on insane diets and eat nothing but rice cakes and air. Then Iris would come around, stuffing her face with pizza and hamburgers. I hated her abnormal metabolism. I would gain five pounds just from the smell of her fast food." Roxie reclaimed her spot on the chaise. "What is she doing these days? How old is her baby?"

"She's doing exactly what she said she'd be doing, and my godson is four years old."

"Wow, good for her. Just add one more thing on the list of reasons why I'm jealous of that girl."

"We ran into Danny and his wife, Besa, about an hour ago. You should see her. The woman looks like a supermodel."

Roxie's eyes widened. "Are you talking about our friend Danny who wore thick glasses and cuffed jeans with his graphic T-shirts tucked at the waist?"

"Yes, his wife is slim with long hair and blue eyes. She has uneven peach lips that are arguably her only imperfection. Her hotness must've rubbed off on Danny because he looks amazing. Wait until you see him. You wouldn't believe it if I told you."

"Yeah, right. No way geeky Danny looks that good. You're exaggerating."

"I'm serious. He looks good. We're meeting up with them soon. You should come."

"He must be rolling in dough to land a woman like that."

"Nope, try again. Besa is worth more than Danny. We talked to them for less than twenty minutes, and a blind man could see how much she loves him."

We'd sat in the same spot for over an hour, catching up and laughing about old times when Iris came running full speed with her arms out. "Roxie-Loxie, it's really you."

"You haven't changed a bit. I heard all about you, Ms. Forensic Medical Examiner."

"Yup, that's me. That's most definitely me." Iris did her strut.

"It's been a long damn time." Danny walked up and joined our exuberant circle. "It feels good to be together again, minus a couple of us."

"Danny, Danny, Danny, I heard all about you," Roxie giggled.

"What did you hear? These two love to exaggerate."

"Don't go there." Iris said. "I don't want Brooklyn to have one of her meltdowns."

"You've got to love that Brooklyn." Adam pranced toward us, clutching a small glass of scotch.

"What are you doing here?" Iris asked.

"Danny invited me to hang out with the gang. So here I am— hanging." He did a little dance.

"I didn't think it was a problem. Is it a problem?" Danny asked.

"Adam, why don't you explain to the group why it's not a good idea for you to hang out with us?" Iris cocked her hip and braced a hand on her waist.

"Don't bother, I'll leave." I backed away and held up the palms of my hands to the group. "Roxie, Danny, take care. I'm so happy I had the chance to see you guys again. Danny, please give my best to your wife if I don't see you guys in the morning. I wish you all the best. We should make plans to meet under different circumstances—a more controlled get together. Iris, please get everyone's phone number. Goodnight, guys. Enjoy."

Iris was hot on my heels. I punched the button about a thousand times to summon the elevator.

"No, Iris, don't say anything. Don't try to save me. Don't try to fix me. I'm tired of people telling me how I should feel and what to do. Adam is over there making people think I'm crazy. I can't pretend I'm okay with him being around. I won't do it for you or any of them. So don't ask me."

"Who knows if we will ever get together again? You go on and on about finding your happiness, but you're running away from what could be the start of it." Iris stuck her hand out. "Come back."

"I doubt I'll find happiness in the company of Adam."

"Forget about him. It's about us—your friends."

"I know it's unhealthy for me to harbor all these unresolved emotions, but I can't be around him."

"I know what you need. How fast do you think you could grow a pair of cojones?"

"Cut it out. I don't feel like laughing."

"I'm serious. You need them quickly. Guys with huge cajones have macho personalities. Big cajones make you feel like you can take over the world. That's all you need right now."

"Iris, I'll be thirty-one this year. You know how significant that age is for me."

"Please don't."

"People with Huntington's disease die fifteen to twenty years after their symptoms start. I'm fidgeting, restless, and having crazy mood swings. I'd say I'm at the first stage of my curtain call. Time is precious, and I don't want to waste it being in the company of Adam. I wish you would try to understand my position."

"You're breaking my heart."

I pressed my hand against Iris's chest and fought to speak through the ball in my throat. "The pain you're feeling right now is the pain I feel every single day. Please, let me go."

Iris moved away from the elevator doors with tears in her eyes just as a notification came on my phone.

How could I forget you, beautiful Brooklyn? I just made it to my hotel room. Give me a call.

Kai had impeccable timing. His text pulled me out of my suffocating world. I smiled at the possibilities of my new friendship.

Perhaps Kai could be my key to happiness after all.

Chapter 4

I'd been home from Pinemoor for three days when a dozen cotton candy fragranced bath bombs in the shape of colorful cupcakes arrived for me at the concierge desk. They were from our new clients, thanking us for a successful launch. Tammy and Lorraine made sure it was waiting for me upon my return from Pinemoor since I was so stressed out about going in the first place. Surely, they'd help wash away the stench of Adam.

"Well hello there, Ms. Brooklyn." Mr. William had been a security guard for the building long before I came. Many of us tenants looked at him as a father figure. He was protective of us. I always felt safe knowing he was in the building.

"Hi there, Mr. William, how are things going today?"

"Ah, busy as ever." He stepped out from behind the security desk. "Your friend came around looking for you today, but I told her I haven't seen you. Just like you asked."

"You're the best." I gave him a high-five and hurried to the elevator.

Before the doors closed, my neighbor ran inside. His cologne smelled like two of my mortgage payments. He wore a blue suit with dark sunglasses. His tie was undone and hung around his neck.

"Hi, it's Brooklyn, right?"

"Yes, that's right. I don't think I've gotten your name."

"Excuse my manners. I'm Nicholas. I own the other condo on our floor. I never see you this time of day."

"Yeah, I've seen you, but we've never talked." I fiddled with my package. "I took the day off for a mental break."

"I hear that. Mental breaks are so underrated but often needed." He held the elevator door to let me off first. "Meraki."

"What does that mean?"

"It's Greek. It means, whatever you do, do it with soul and creativity. Do it with love and passion, and always put a piece of yourself into it. Live your life loud and free." He gave me a nod and disappeared into his condo.

His words gave me the courage to muster up the sexiest pose in my repertoire to send Kai a picture. I straightened my back and smiled big and bright for the camera.

Last night I had the wildest dream, and you were in it. Call me if you want to hear the details.

I took a deep breath before I sent the message, and switched on my daily affirmations. "I am worthy of being happy. I choose to create a happy life."

Kai called within seconds. "Wow, you look amazing. I was wondering when you'd call me. I didn't want to bug you too much."

"Oh, now you don't want to bug me after you practically held me hostage in Pinemoor."

He chuckled a bit before clearing his throat. "I've been busier than I thought I'd be with training. Please don't hold it against me. Once this is over, we should make plans to get together, but right now I have to run. People are returning from lunch and giving me that look. I'll call you later."

I couldn't get a word in, but as a woman in business, I understood.

Chapter 5

It'd been three glorious weeks since Kai and I met, which meant three weeks of regaining my sanity from the combustible reunion with Adam. So I took the girls up on their invitation to meet at a new bar downtown, Baroof.

It was a rooftop bar smack dab in the center of downtown. The place was crawling with the city's socialites, which was a great way to drum up more business. Lorraine took full advantage of it since she handled all the sales. When she wasn't dancing, she was schmoozing. The girl was great at it.

Lorraine and Tammy had been a driving force in my life. We were more than business partners, but I never told them about Huntington's so that when I'm with them, they don't treat me like a dying patient. I've done great keeping them away from Iris, so there won't be any slip ups. Hopefully, they'll be too busy dancing and drinking, they won't have time to make my illness the topic of conversation if Iris slipped up. She often became a blabber mouth when she drank. I hoped she wouldn't make me regret inviting her.

I met Tammy first at a coffee shop while I perused the classifieds. I'd moved home six months earlier after graduating from Pinemoor State. Dad lectured me day and night about wasting my education since I hadn't put my degree to work. But one day after dinner, he laid down the law and told me the only way I could live under their roof was to get a job or go back to school. So the next morning, I packed up my laptop and headed to Coffee Joe to come up with a plan.

It was six o'clock in the morning and Tammy was on a date. She sat a couple of tables away from me with her beau. They shamelessly flirted with each other as if they were the only two people in the coffee shop. Every so often, he'd lean in to kiss her cherry cheeks. Then she'd return his affection the same way. For a moment, I envied her, until he left.

Tammy chugged the last of her coffee and threw the empty cup into the trash. She refreshed her lipstick, and at precisely seven o'clock, her second date walked into the coffee shop. He wore a muscle shirt with nonexistent muscles and gray sweatpants with a fresh layer of gym sweat. They shared kisses for an hour, hardly able to keep their hands off each other.

After he left the coffee shop, I gave Tammy a standing ovation. She curtsied with a wide smile and joined me for her third cup of coffee. We talked like old friends, and from that day on, we remained in contact. Eventually, we came up with the idea for Three Angels Event Planning. The Angels were my birth mom, my adopted mom, and Tammy's mom.

Neither Tammy nor I had a chance to meet Lorraine. She met us. A month into the business, she came into the office and explained why we needed her and how she could increase our bottom line by landing large accounts using her virtual presentations and gift for gab. She also brought in a third of the finances to officially become a partner. Three Angels then became something totally different. We were the three angels.

I smiled at the memory and inadvertently caught the eye of a guy who leaned over the bar and winked at me. I turned away. I'd already seen him talking to several women in a span of thirty minutes. He was a player, and I wasn't interested in being played.

"Come dance with us." Tammy's limbs moved out of control. "Are you going to sit there all night pointing your camera?" She kicked her legs and flung her arms in a circle. "Get out here."

"You call that dancing?"

"At least I'm having fun, unlike you."

After refusing to embarrass myself on the dance floor, the girls joined me at the bar.

"Why are you so down? You abandoned us to go live it up in Pinemoor with Iris. You should be on top of the world." Lorraine passed out more business cards.

"Actually, there's something I'd like to talk to you guys about while we're all together."

"Ooh, this sounds juicy." Tammy sat on the leather bar stool next to me and held up her glass. "Bartender, I need another. Sorry about that Brooklyn. I'm all ears."

Iris chuckled and patted my hand as if urging me to speak.

"I met someone at the airport the morning I was flying to Pinemoor."

"Hold on," Iris interrupted. "Why is this the first I'm hearing about it? You could've told me this when I picked you up at the airport."

"Do you want me to tell you now or not?"

"I'm just saying. You sure have been keeping secrets lately."

Lorraine and Tammy elbowed Iris. "Go on, Brooklyn."

"His name is Kai. He's a stockbroker. But the thing is, I haven't dated anyone seriously since college. I've spent so much time guarding myself that I don't know if I'm able to open up and get to know him."

Iris touched my shoulder. "Tell me this, do you think he's worth it?"

"Yes, he's a wonderful guy. Totally different from any man I've ever dated."

"Okay then, what could it hurt for you to give him a chance. All those things that happened in your past are over," Iris explained. "It's time to move forward. If this guy can help you do that, I'm all for it."

"I want that."

"Good, all you need to do is be present with him. It will be what it will be."

"She's right." Lorraine swung her bar chair around. "You haven't seriously dated anyone since we've been in business together. Sure, you go out on dates, but nothing serious has come of them. You're an amazing person. You deserve an equally amazing man."

"Don't obsess over it. Put yourself out there, and give him a chance." Iris thrust her hips to the music. "None of us know what the future holds. Heck, even Betty Bates, the tarot card reader, couldn't tell you about your future."

"She sure had you fooled. You called more than a dozen times."

"I only called three times. I wanted to know why people thought she was so damn special."

"She said you'd be wearing red the day you meet the love of your life. You walked around campus dressed in red for so long someone started a rumor you'd joined a gang."

"I went through a red phase. It had nothing to do with that fraud."

"Tell your lies to someone who wasn't there to witness it. I still think you were the one who had the poor woman investigated."

"Poor woman my ass." Iris folded her arms over her chest. "I want my two hundred dollars and ninety-eight cents back."

"Face it. You fell for her scam."

"Whatever. This isn't about me. Give the man a chance." A tall guy in a gray suit pulled her back out on the dance floor. "I'll be back." The other girls followed her.

I looked down at my phone at an email from Adam. I walked over the end of the bar to be alone.

Hello Brooklyn,

After the way we left things in Pinemoor, I know I'm the last person you want to hear from, but I figured this was the best way for us to talk since you can't stand the sight of me. I need your help. I have an opportunity to tell my story in a documentary. The film will cover the rise and fall of my football career. I need this for my family, but there's a catch. They won't do the documentary unless you tell your side of the story of what happened in college. It'll be a win-win for both of us if you think about it. I'll be in Woodcrest soon with the paperwork for you to sign. Oh, and by the way, you looked fucking amazing at the hotel. Not that I'm surprised. You were always a looker. I'll see you soon.

Your first love,

Adam Williamson

Nicholas's advice came to mind—*meraki*. So instead of allowing Adam to ruin my entire night, I called Kai.

"Hello, beautiful Brooklyn."

His voice conjured a smile. "How are you?"

"I'm better now that you called. I'm surprised you're not on a hot date."

"My friends have dragged me to a bar for a girls' night. That's the music you hear in the background." I found myself twirling my hair like a teenage girl with a crush.

"I feel special. You're at a bar with friends, but you called me."

"I actually didn't think you would answer. It's Saturday night. I figured you'd be out on the town meeting people with that sparkling personality of yours."

"No need. I've already met the woman of my dreams."

I pulled a handful of wild hair over my face to cover my wide smile.

"Take a selfie so I can see how sexy you look at the bar. I want to see your beautiful smile."

I smiled into the camera and snapped. "Don't be too hard on me. I'm not very good at taking selfies."

"My goodness you are breathtaking."

"You're too kind. When will you be back in town?"

"I'll be there in a couple of weeks."

"I can't wait to see you."

"I can't wait to see you either, beautiful Brooklyn. Thank you for the picture. I'll be looking at it for the rest of the night."

"You sure know how to put a smile on my face. I'll call you tomorrow."

The girls surrounded me. "Were you talking to that guy?"

"Yes."

"Ooh, I hope he gives you good sex," Lorraine drunkenly said.

"Yeah, I hope he turns your brain into goo. You need a good time in the sack." Tammy danced provocatively.

I ignored the girls and admired the picture Kai sent me of him lying on his back with a bare chest. His muscles were on full display, and I was mesmerized. I needed a drink. He had me, hook, line, and sinker.

Chapter 6

I hated Huntington's appointments. You never knew what news the doctor would bring you. I glanced at my shoes and grimaced, regretting our night of dancing and drinking at the bar last week. My feet still ached, so there was no telling what was going on with my insides.

I studied the old-fashioned wallpaper in the exam room while I waited for my doctor to return. The place hadn't changed in the nine years since I'd become a patient. But as long as they upgraded their medical tools in a timely manner, I wouldn't complain too much.

"Brooklyn Monti, we meet again. How are you?" Dr. Hall entered my exam room staring at his tablet. "I've got good news."

"Good news?"

"I've reviewed your neuropsychological testing results, psychiatric evaluations, CT scans, and your blood work to make sure your medications haven't harmed your organs. You're not even in Stage 1. The muscle spasms come with the territory of Huntington's. You're good to go, young lady."

"Are you sure? The spasms are occurring a lot more now."

"I'm one hundred percent sure. Get out there and enjoy life."

"Look at you being the bearer of good news a day before the weekend. Thank you, doctor."

His report couldn't have come at a better time. It was my green light to test the waters with Kai, even with Huntington's hanging over my head like a gray cloud.

Chapter 7

The next day after getting a clean bill of health, I sat amongst the ten people who made up our support group for Huntington's. With a new lease on life, my spirits were riding high, not even recounting my encounter with Adam could change it.

Everyone sat on the edge of their seats and listened to the story of me going back to Pinemoor for the first time in seven years. That's also how long I'd been in the group. My mom had urged me to join after we met the leader, Gina, at one of my doctor's appointments upon my return home from college. So, they'd heard all the Adam stories except for this most recent one.

"I enjoyed everything up until we got to the hotel. I prayed Adam and I wouldn't run into each other, but that hope was all gone."

Rosemary pushed her salt and pepper hair behind her ears. Her gangly, frail body showed the weight of her world. "You remind me of my daughter. She died two days before her twenty-ninth birthday. By then, she could hardly swallow. She choked in her sleep." She leaned forward with her elbows on her knees. "My daughter couldn't enjoy life anymore. Poor thing was scared of everything. That's why I come here every week. I want to encourage you all to live your lives. She gave up many years before her death."

"I don't get it. Where's your growth? You've been in the group long enough to have gained the strength to not give a damn about him."

Angeline bit off a piece of her beef jerky.

"Yeah, yeah, you should've ripped him a new hole." Ernestine ripped her bagel in half.

"I get where Brooklyn's coming from. This shit is not easy. My biggest fear is choking to death," Erica said. "I don't want my eyes all bugged when I die. That's not popping."

Ernestine rolled her eyes. "Why can't you ever be serious? You consistently bring the group down to a garbage level."

"Yeah, you missed the point," Rosemary chimed in. "I wish you'd stay on topic."

"So what, I made a joke, big damn deal." Erica picked at her fingernails and slouched in her seat.

"Erica, look at me. I can make you forget about Huntington's for at least two hours." Marc drew his finger up her arm.

"She's a married woman. Show some respect." Rosemary shook her finger at him. "Just because you choose to sleep your way through life doesn't give you the right to bring your destructive energy here."

"Okay, we're going off the rails. Let's bring it back in." Gina paced the circle.

"Kick Marc out of the group, and we could stay on track."

Ernestine demanded the same thing every time the group met.

"No, I've told you a million times we're not doing that. Everyone deals with this illness in their own way. We should be supporting one another," Gina explained. "Brooklyn, please continue with what you were saying."

"My friends have created amazing lives for themselves. It made me sick to see how much of my life I've wasted feeling sorry for myself." My words moved everyone to tears—even Marc, but they all shied away from making eye contact with me.

"Brooklyn, you have made an amazing life for yourself. You have a thriving business, loving parents, great friends, and a beautiful home life. What have I told you a million times?"

"You've said that I'm intelligent and beautiful. Stop allowing Huntington's to stand in the forefront. Live life."

"But you've made yourself seem small in comparison to your friends. I want you to get to the point where you won't compare your life to anyone else's and you believe you are just as great."

"I want to get to that point too."

Gina walked over to the snack table and dumped a stack of paper plates in the trash. "Okay, you guys, the next group will be here any moment. I understand how hard it is for some of you to live with Huntington's, but you owe it to yourselves to keep pushing. Make every second count. Seek God's help to accept the things you cannot change, courage to change the things you can, and the wisdom to know the difference." She lifted her chin toward me as the group disbanded. "Brooklyn, do you have a moment to talk?"

"Sure."

"I'm worried about you. What will become of your life if you can't figure out how to let go of your fears?"

"Your guess is as good as mine."

"I want you to soar. Do you want that for yourself?"

"Sure I do."

Gina reached out to touch my shoulder. "You're an amazing person. You deserve an amazing life as much as the next person. Fight for it."

I walked outside into the golden sunset and dialed my best friend's number. The air smelled delicious thanks to the quaint bakery next door. It mixed well with the spring flowers. I sucked in a deep breath to take it all in while making my first attempt to take my control of my life.

"Hello," Iris answered.

"I have something to tell you, but promise me you won't go crazy."

"No way. I don't make promises I can't keep. Now spill it."

"Adam's been in contact with me—"

"Why in the hell have you been in contact with that piece of shit?" Iris snapped.

"I haven't been in contact with him. He's been in contact with me. He's trying to get me to sign a contract to appear in a documentary about his football career."

"He's got some nerve after all the damage he's caused. I'm guessing you failed to tell him off because you said he's been in contact."

"Oh, I told him off, but Adam is like a rash. He just keeps coming back."

"This is harassment. You wait right there, and I'll get the police on the line."

"No, Iris. I can handle this on my own."

"You better put an end to it quickly." Iris huffed and puffed. "I don't like the idea of you speaking with him. He almost took your life— almost took you away from us."

"It's complicated."

"Adam won't stop bothering you because you're a damn pushover. You need to stand up for yourself. If you can't do that, block him."

"I'm only telling you this because you're my sounding board. I'll keep you updated."

I threw my head back to allow the cool wind to blow through my hair. The change of seasons helped confirm my continued existence, but mere confirmation was no longer enough. I needed to know more. I needed to know my purpose.

Chapter 8

I spent the weekend relaxing at home and talking to Kai on the computer. Friday night after my support group, we cooked together on Skype, drank wine, and talked until six in the morning. We both slept until noon on Saturday just to get back on Skype and talk for the rest of the day. Sunday night, we gave each other time off to prepare for the start of the week. And oh, what a Monday it was.

First, Lorraine came into the office late on the day of her sales pitch for a huge account. Then a fire was reported at one of the venues we needed in a month, so we had to get all hands on deck to move that mountain. And, as if we hadn't scrambled enough for the day, our system went offline for an hour. The story of my life. I have a great weekend then I pay for it.

I arrived at my condo just as the stars began to blanket the sky. A couple snuggled on a bench next to the water fountain statue of a woman surrounded by small lights. The stone woman gazed up to the sky with one arm stretched toward the clouds. For me, it served as a daily reminder to reach for my highest goals—love, family, career, and peace.

As I rolled into the parking garage, I noticed my neighbor sitting on the trunk of his car. He pushed a tuft of hair from his face. His thick black mane was shaggy on top and tapered on the sides like Elvis's infamous pompadour.

"How are you doing, Brooklyn?"

"It's Nicholas, right?"

"Yes, you remembered. Cool." He jumped down from his car and tugged on his gray button down shirt. Then he gave me a hand with my bags. "I've been waiting for you. Mind if I walk with you?"

"How long have you been sitting here?"

There were only two condos on the penthouse floor, and we owned them. However, our conversations only consisted of a quick hello in passing, which didn't happen often.

"About twenty minutes." He glanced at his watch. "You're usually home by now. I guess you're not a creature of habit after all."

I gave him a nod even though I was wary of him knowing my schedule. I didn't know he thought about me, much less paid attention to my comings and goings.

"You do know personal shoppers come with the building, right?" He followed me to the elevators.

"I've used the same butcher for five years. I'm way too picky to have someone else shopping for my food. I use their other services, though, especially the car detailing."

"When you drive a black on black Mercedes C-Class convertible, it should shine." Nicholas spread his hands out like the host on *Wheel of Fortune*. "I need your butcher's name. Last week the shoppers brought me steaks so thin I had to eat them like lunch meat."

"Sure, but he won't give you the same deals as me. You're not exactly his type." I shook my two bee stings. They might have been small, but they got the job done, especially with my butcher. He'd missed the memo that he wasn't supposed to flirt with young women, seeing how he was pushing fifty with a wife and grown kids.

"The power women embody is amazing."

"You better believe it." I pointed toward the gym where a group of sweaty men raced around the basketball court. "Don't you usually play ball with those guys?"

"Not today. I told you. I've been waiting for you."

"Why?"

"First, I need to double back and remember my manners. How was your day?"

"Dreadful. I'd rather hear about your day." We hustled off the elevator after reaching the top floor.

I held my door open for Nicholas so he could bring my bags inside. The scent of every cleaning product I'd used before leaving for work attacked us, mainly the bleach.

"So here's the deal. I recently landed a huge account that'll put my company on the Forbes list."

"Good for you. Congratulations."

"So the reason why I was waiting—"

"Oh, first, would you like a drink? I really need wine after the day I've had."

"No, thank you. But you go ahead."

"Cool, you talk. I'll pour." I threw my head back with my eyes closed to savor its sweet taste.

"My company is throwing a black and white ball in my honor, and I wanted to know if you'd be my date."

"Repeat that." I pushed my hair behind her ear. "You want to take me as your date?"

"Yes."

I stood in silence for a moment. First Kai, and now Nicholas. Lemons kept falling from the sky for my lemonade.

"Don't answer now." He interrupted my silence. "Take some time to think about it. I'll get out of your hair now."

"Actually, Nicholas, I have two beautiful steaks. One has your name on it if you're interested."

"You...want me to stay for dinner?"

"Yes. Unless you already have plans."

"You're serious?"

"Yes. Would you like to stay or not?"

"Hell, yeah, I'd like to stay. I was going to order a greasy pizza and suffer from heartburn in the morning."

"You don't look like you eat anything unhealthy."

"What do I look like?" He put his hands on his hips as if he were Superman without the cape.

"I mean, you have a nice body with hardly any fat. If I didn't know, I'd say you only ate kale and drank green smoothies." I kicked off my heels and ran around the kitchen like a seasoned chef, taking two silver pans from the iron rack hanging above the island.

Growing up, my mom would only cook dinner two days out of the week. So on her days off, I'd pull out her cookbooks and follow intricate recipes. Soon, I didn't need the recipes. If I wanted, I could have easily gone to culinary school and ran a successful restaurant.

"Some nights I have had to stop myself from knocking on your door when I smell your cooking. It literally makes my mouth water."

"If you keep paying me compliments, you're going to have a hard time getting rid of me."

"Ah, you shouldn't have said that. Now, I'm going to bombard you with compliments." He chuckled when I almost dropped the steaks on the floor. Honestly, he was laying it on so thick, it had me frazzled. "You look amazing in that dress."

"Thank you." I wiggled a bit. "Do you eat pizza and things like that often?"

"Hey, it's the price I pay for my bachelor lifestyle."

"That body of yours must be from good genes. If you don't watch out, it's going to catch up with you. One day you'll wake up with a double chin."

"I can burn in the kitchen, but I save those skills for special occasions."

"What qualifies as a special occasion?"

"An evening with you would be considered a special occasion."

"If that's the truth, why is this our first time having a conversation?"

"I don't want to offend you."

"Usually, when people say they don't want to offend you, they end up offending you."

"We've been neighbors for what, two years now?"

"Yes."

"From my point of view, you aren't that approachable. You never smile—at least when I see you—so I steer clear." He tapped his foot against the tiled floor. "Do you ever date?"

"To be totally honest with you, I'm kind of seeing someone now. That's why I'm hesitant to accept your invitation."

"If you say you're 'kind of seeing' him, it's not that serious."

"Never mind. It's brand new. We're getting to know each other." I flipped the sizzling steaks and gulped more wine. "Forget I said anything."

Nicholas ran his hands up and down the side of his black slacks.

"Are you one of the microwave people?"

He lifted an eyebrow. "What does that mean?"

"It means you want things to happen instantly. You'd rather snap your fingers, and boom, you're good to go—microwave."

"Oh, no. You've got me all wrong. I don't need things to happen instantly." He admired my kitchen and ran his fingertips along the marble countertops. "Do you need help with anything?"

"Now you're talking." I gave him a pat on the shoulder. "How good are you at cooking asparagus without making a mushy mess of it?"

"Asparagus is easy. All I need is salt, pepper, a garlic clove, Parmesan, and mozzarella cheese."

I sat all his requested ingredients on the counter. "Show me what you've got, Chef Nicholas."

"Come to my place for dinner tomorrow. I can show you more."

"Could I take a rain check?"

"Consider it an open invitation." He sliced the garlic. "You're pretty cool, Brooklyn."

"Thanks. You're pretty cool yourself." I slid each steak on a plate and lightly poured my special sizzling mushroom sauce over them.

The meat was cooked perfectly, and the smell took me back to when I was sixteen. My dad wouldn't allow me to cook my first steak without his guidance. He'd claimed that no cookbook in the world could teach his daughter how to cook a steak better than him, not even Julia Child herself.

"Were you going to cook all this for yourself?" Nicholas sautéed the garlic and carefully placed the asparagus inside the hot pan.

"Hey, I'm worth a steak dinner."

"I won't disagree with you there."

Ten minutes later, Nicholas proudly paired his asparagus with my steaks.

"Good job, they look pretty tasty."

I led him to the dining room. Our condos had the same floor plans, but I tore down the walls to create a blank canvas. Each room was painted with a neutral color. I also changed the oceanside walls in the living area, master bedroom, and dining room so that the windows stretched from floor to ceiling.

"You put way more thought into your condo than I did. I took the safe route with leather sectionals and flat screens."

Our fifty-five story building was built on the edge of Crystal Reel Ocean. We awakened to the rumbling blue waters and slept as the city lights danced upon it. I consider our view a privilege.

"Oh, no. You've got to do better. Your home should be your prized possession." I took a bottle of wine from the side-by-side wine coolers I had installed in the dining room. "I have a confession."

"What's that?"

"I'm the third owner of Three Angels Events, and I oversee the marketing and finance."

"Wow, congratulations to you. Three Angels is a booming business."

"Thank you, but it's not enough. My goal while in my pursuit of my master's degree was to have a career fully dedicated to marketing."

"I didn't know that."

"How would you?" I giggled and covered my mouth with a linen napkin. "My mother gives me grief about it all the time, but she's right. I use my business as an excuse not to follow my dreams."

"Marketing is the way to go. No business can operate without it."

"I love the creativity that goes into it."

"What's stopping you?"

"Life." I gulped my wine.

"Damn, that sucks."

"I should stop you there. I'm a firm believer that profanity cheapens the conversation."

"You're the boss."

He propped his elbows on the table. I let it slide.

"What in your life keeps you from chasing your goals?"

"Obstacles turned my dreams into distractions." I winced and stared out the window. "Then they eventually faded away. Some people are lucky enough to get back on track. Others, like me, find it almost impossible. Thankfully, I have a pretty successful business."

"If you don't mind me asking, how old are you?"

"I'm thirty-one." Pride extinguished my growing frown. In my world, thirty-two was a big deal. It meant another year I've held Huntington's at bay and outlived the one person whose early death scares the hell out of me—my birth mother.

"You don't look a day over twenty-five."

"Oh, please, now you're being nice."

"I'm serious." He smashed a fork-full of steak into the mushroom sauce before devouring it. "If you're interested, I could get you an interview with my marketing company. You'd skip the crawling process of the early stages."

"Don't sell me lies, Nicholas."

"I'm serious." He set his fork down. "Our company is growing fast. We need more educated people who can deliver impeccable work under impossible time constraints. If that doesn't scare you, then you're perfect for the job."

"I'm a businesswoman, and I know there's a screening process before you bring people on board. How could you be so sure about me if you don't know my work ethic or my knowledge in marketing?"

Nicholas uncrossed his legs and straightened his back. "You have a successful business. I know about Three Angels Events. You mentioned your education—master's degree in marketing—and you have the passion for it. I don't know what you see when you look at me, but I'm a damn good judge of character. You'd be an excellent fit."

"The offer alone means the world to me. I've been feeling so unsatisfied, and no one seems to understand. All they see is the success of our business, and they go deaf to everything else. I could kiss you."

"Don't fight the feeling. Lay it on me." He stretched his arms out.

A chime from the doorbell saved me.

I opened the door to find a twentyish woman with purple highlighted hair wearing a tight red dress and smacking on bubble gum.

"I'm sorry. You've got the wrong door."

"No, I'm at the right place. I'm here for him." She popped her gum and pointed at Nicholas, who stood in the dining room.

Nicholas rubbed the back of his neck. "Damn, I forgot. How did you find me here?"

"You said you were waiting for your neighbor while we were on the phone. Since this is the only door, I figured this was the neighbor you were talking about. Who is she?"

"Who are you?" I asked.

"I'm someone with youth on my side." She twirled the gum around her finger. "That's who I am. Any more questions, oldie?"

"Wait a second, ladies. This is my fault." Nicholas stepped in front of me. "Brooklyn, please accept my apology. Faith, here are my keys. Go to my place. I'll be there in a second." He shut the door. "I apologize for that. When you invited me to stay for dinner I obviously lost my mind."

"Go home, Nicholas. It's rude to keep your company waiting."

"Will you forgive me?"

"You asked me on a date, but you're already involved. Why?"

"I'm dating the same as you," he shrugged. "Didn't you say you were seeing someone?"

"You're right, but she acted territorial as if you two are doing more than dating." I held the door open. "Oh, and I think I'll pass on the date. You should take Faith."

"For what it's worth, I really enjoyed your company this evening. Maybe we could do this again sometime?"

"I enjoyed your company too until Faith reacted like a wounded girlfriend." I closed the door with a great sigh. "So much for that."

A ring from my cell brought me back to reality. I strolled outside on the balcony with a glass of wine and sank into the cushioned lounge chair. Thank God. It was Kai. His timing was impeccable.

"Hello handsome."

"Hello beautiful, I was just thinking about you for the millionth time today."

"What were you thinking about?"

"I want to know more about you—your hopes and dreams, all of it."

"I have simple dreams, you know, a loving marriage, a kid or two if I'm lucky."

"You're an amazing woman. I have no doubt you will have all those things and much more."

"Okay, tell me about your hopes and dreams."

"I was married before. It wasn't perfect, but it was everything I ever wanted until it went downhill." His voice hitched. "I don't blame anyone but myself. I put my career before my family, but I didn't do it out of selfishness. It was quite the opposite. I took them for granted, thinking they'd always be there when I had time. But my time ran out, and I accepted that. I'm saying all this because I know my ex-wife wasn't the person I was supposed to grow old with. If she were, she wouldn't be my ex-wife. She didn't sit me down to tell me how she was feeling. She didn't want marriage counseling. She took our son and left. My dream is to find the woman who was created for me. A woman who will be committed to our union and love me enough to fight for me. I desire to have a woman in my life who doesn't forget about her happiness. In all honesty, I'm hoping that woman is you. I'm not ashamed to say, I'm hopeful this could turn into something more."

"How could you say that without knowing enough about me to come to that conclusion?" I cleared my throat. "You see, I'm different from other women, which helps me see things for what they are. I don't live in the clouds of hopes and dreams. I like you, Kai. You're easy on the eyes. You're funny, and you must have some intelligence to have successfully thrived in your career. But today, I've learned about one of your faults—you have a history of taking people for granted. You say you've learned from it, and I have no doubt that you have. But I need to see the other layers of your personality before I can say, you're the one I want to pursue as the last man I'll ever love."

"Touché," Kai whispered. "Since you're an open book today, tell me something else about yourself that I wouldn't know."

The moment he said it, I instantly regretted my transparency. "I'm adopted. My mother died when I was a baby. My father knew my adopted parents and decided I would be better raised by them. I've never met him. I have no idea if he's alive or dead."

"Thank you for trusting me enough to share that with me. I'm sure it wasn't easy sharing that part of your life."

"No, it wasn't." I sighed and gazed out at the dark sky. The stars had finally made their appearance, but one stood out more than the others. Its shade was more yellow than white. I thought of myself. I may be different, but I stand out for the better. My life serves a purpose. But would Kai see it that way? This wasn't the time to lay more heaviness on him.

"I've enjoyed talking to you."

"I've enjoyed you too. Same time tomorrow?" he asked.

"Yes, same time tomorrow. Goodnight."

Kai had wedged his way into my life, and I was surprised to discover my heart actually welcomed it.

Chapter 9

The bakery perfectly executed my idea for Dad's birthday cake. The bottom two layers resembled a suitcase with the world sitting on top while a candy-coated airplane hovered alongside. Mini toothpick flags stuck out of the globe marking every place my parents had traveled. White circles made of fondue marked the name of each country.

I carefully walked out of the kitchen, holding the elaborate cake with two sparklers on top. Dad warned me not to overload his cake with fifty-two candles so that we wouldn't burn the house down.

"On this day, August 1, 1969, the best man I've ever known was born. Some men leave it up to the mother to bond with a girl while they provide and protect, but you were present with guidance, wisdom, understanding, patience, and an endless pool of love. I haven't had the opportunity to meet my birth dad, but as far as I'm concerned, you are that shining light for me. I love you with my whole heart. Happy birthday, Dad. Now make a wish before the sparklers burn out."

He bowed his head with his eyes closed, but his voice boomed. "My only wish is for my beautiful daughter to live beyond my years."

"Ah, Dad, you're going to make me cry."

"Look at me." He took the cake from me and placed it on the table. "You are a very special person. You were such an unexpected blessing to our lives."

Mom rested her head on my shoulder and stroked my arm.

"Your birth father made a difficult decision. It wasn't easy for him to leave you. Never doubt that for one second. He loved you very much," dad explained.

"I know. You guys tell me that all the time. I don't have any issues with him, but I would like to meet him one day."

"I wish I could tell you he will reach out to you one day, but I can't promise that. How will you handle it emotionally if that never happens," Dad asked?

"I'm thirty-one now. Whatever deep-rooted issues have come from his absence already exist, and I'm surviving just fine. I can't miss what I've never had." I rolled my shoulders. "Now, let's cut into your cake so I can go for a walk because you know I don't like to eat sweets."

"When did you start walking?" Mom asked with questioning eyes.

"Today." I chuckled as I watched my parents devour the red velvet cake. Such a small token for the people who'd diligently anchored me through the ups and downs of my illness. When they retired and made the decision to become world travelers, I initially felt abandoned. But I quickly realized they deserved to live out their dreams. Besides, I wasn't alone. I had Iris, so I gave them my complete support.

"I'll be back." I kissed them both before taking a stroll through the upscale neighborhood. A burst of purple and red painted the setting sky. The silhouettes of the robust palm trees did a tribal dance along the pavement, and the warm wind carried a floral scent that overpowered the salty smell of the ocean.

I waved at old man Coleman, who watered his garden. He had the biggest one in the neighborhood. He was the reason I always had fresh flowers in my hospital room.

"Well, look-a-there. I ain't seen you around here in a while. How ya' doing, young lady?"

"I'm well, but it looks like you could use a little help." I chuckled at the sight of him becoming tangled in the long water hose.

"Ah, don't worry ya' pretty lil' head about it. This happens all the time. I'll get it together eventually. I ain't got nuttin' else to do."

"I don't mind helping."

"I'm sure, young lady. You go on and enjoy ya walk."

In the corner of my eye, I saw a shadow running down the sidewalk in my direction. I pressed against the fence to get out of the way when I heard a familiar voice saying my name.

"Brooklyn, Brooklyn, it's you. I can't believe it."

"Kai?" I smiled in great relief because it wasn't a crazed maniac. "What are you doing here?"

He straightened his shirt. "My mom lives down the street. I was outside when you walked by. Do you live in this neighborhood? I've never seen you here before."

"My parents live about four blocks over. I usually go to their house, hang out for a while then hit the road."

"I almost forgot how beautiful you are in person." He slowly ran his finger along the side of my face.

I shyly turned away, unable to control my jaw muscles as my mouth fell open.

He put his finger under my chin and pulled my face toward his. "May I kiss you again? I can't stop thinking about our first kiss."

"Could we hug for now and work our way up to a kiss?"

He obliged with a long embrace and joined me on my walk. Most of the residents hung out by the ocean in the evening, so peace resonated over the neighborhood. It was calming after a long day in the office.

We stopped at the corner, and Kai stared into my eyes for a moment as if they were a rare pair of emerald jewels. "Would you like to check out the new coffee shop?" He pointed across the road.

"I'd like that. I was surprised to see they allowed them to build it inside these gates. The residents aren't exactly open to retail zoning or construction for that matter."

"Tell me about it. They gave my dad the blues when he built a greenroom for my mom."

A car full rowdy teenagers and loud music zoomed down the street, cut the curb, and almost ran into me. I leapt head first into a row of hedges to avoid the killing machine.

Kai yelled at the kids and helped me to my feet, but his gaze lingered on my curves. "Are you okay?"

"I was almost run over, and you take it as an opportunity to check me out."

"Look at you. I couldn't help myself."

"Stop it." I avoided his stare.

Kai tipped my chin to face him. "Why do you always look away when you smile? You're far too beautiful for that."

"I'll bet this is what you say to all the women."

"I'm not a playboy. I go after what I want with tunnel vision. Right now, you're it." He rested his hand on my lower back to help me across the street. "Level with me, Brooklyn. You're intelligent, funny, and easy on the eyes. Why are you single?"

"Put it like this, it's going to take a special man to see beyond my flaws."

"I've been called special all my life. Just ask my mom. She'll tell you."

Again, he turned my head so that my eyes met his own, but he was so focused on me that he almost tripped on the cracked sidewalk.

I couldn't contain my laughter. It spilled out of me and echoed through the block.

"I lost cool points on that one."

"You fell at the airport. Now, you're all over the place here. Do you fall often?"

"I'm kind of a klutz. I'm not ashamed to admit it."

The coffee shop had a unique design. The entire front wall was made of glass doors that completely opened to create an indoor-outdoor environment. They'd placed vases of bright orange flowers throughout the small space. It had a country feel to it. No wonder my mom loved it.

"Order whatever you like," Kai urged.

"Ah, you're a big spender."

"Hello, what could I get for you?" A young girl sat a pink piece of broken chalk on the counter. She'd written the first part of a daily inspiration on a small glittered chalkboard that sat behind the counter.

Know what sparks the light in you...

"I'll have a small cappuccino, thank you."

"Is that all? I can afford a muffin or two."

"No thank you. I don't require much."

"Are you sure?" His right eyebrow shot up. "I don't want you walking around hungry. You're tiny as it is."

The young barista hummed along to the classic jazz of Dizzy Gillespie while she mixed the coffee.

"What could I get you, Sir?"

"I'll have a black coffee with a raisin bagel." He passed her a hundred dollar bill. "Keep the change."

"Oh, no. I couldn't possibly accept this. It's way too much."

"Sure you can. Consider this a small investment toward your educational journey. I'm familiar with your Biomedical Engineering book." He pointed to the text on the counter behind her. "But you're a baby. No way you're in college. Are you one of those kid geniuses?"

"You could say that. I'm in the dual college program at my high school. So by the time I graduate, I'll have my bachelor's degree. Engineering is my goal. My dad says I need to stay ahead of the pack. He's never steered me wrong." She slid our steaming cups of coffee across the counter.

"Your dad is a wise man. Always listen to him."

"I know. Look at this place." She stretched out her arms. "People went nuts when he started building the shop. Now they're all loyal customers. Some even come in twice a day." She finished writing the quote on the chalkboard.

...then use that light to illuminate the world.

Kai and I pointed at each other with a chuckle. She'd unknowingly confirmed our skepticism.

He helped me to my seat and quickly kissed my cheek.

"Pine-Sol?" he asked.

"Original lemon scent," I snorted. "I cleaned my parent's house while I was waiting for them to return home earlier."

"No worries. I probably smell like glass cleaner. My mom's got me cleaning windows today."

"Cool." I drummed the rim of my coffee cup. "I like how you encouraged the young lady back there. It says a lot about your character."

"That girl's going places. Mark my words." He pointed. "I want to know more about you."

"Well, let's see. You already know I'm thirty-one with no kids." I tapped my chin. "Oh, have you heard of Three Angels Event Planning?"

"Who hasn't?"

"I'm one of the three owners."

"Oh, wow. I feel like I'm sitting with a celebrity. Why haven't you told me that?"

"I don't know. It makes me feel like I'm bragging when I tell people."

"Who handles what areas?"

"I have a master's degree in business marketing, so I take care of that department as well as accounting. Lorraine brings the customer's visions to life with a visual 3D presentation that usually lands our accounts. The girl is a computer genius. She also handles sales. Then there's Tammy," I sighed. "She's a social butterfly. She secures all of our vendors. We get the best deals no matter where the event is held. We've made a lot of money from her connections."

"I'm impressed."

"Thanks." I brightened, but kept my eyes on my coffee cup. "That girl reminds me of my younger self. I had my life planned at her age then everything took a major turn. I hardly recognized myself."

"I've been trying to figure you out for weeks now."

"How's that going?"

"You're not an easy person to read."

"Bingo." I winked.

"What do you do for fun, Beautiful Brooklyn?"

"What is fun? My personal life is stale. Sitting here having coffee with you is so out of the norm, it's frightening."

"It won't be stale anymore." Kai smiled with a lopsided grin.

"Why is that?"

"I'm here now." He winked. "Tell me about the rest of your friends. Why were you so nervous to visit them at Pinemoor again?"

"I don't want to talk about that today." I straightened the ruffles on my shirt. "It's your turn to tell me something about you."

"I attended Winford University. I made some pretty good memories, met a lot of people, one of them being my ex-wife. My birthday is a month away, and I'm not looking forward to turning the big 3-5. It's a slippery slope into adult diapers once you're over the hill."

"Thirty-five isn't so bad." I gave his hand a pat. "How long were you married?"

"Five years too long."

"Divorce scares the hell out of me. If I ever get married, I want it to stick."

"I know what you mean, but divorce was easy compared to the pain of her moving my son back to her hometown. A month after they moved, I'd still find myself waking up, hoping to hear my son say,

'Good Morning, Daddy.' I prayed it was a nightmare. But nope, it was my new reality." He ran his thumb along the corner of his eye to blot away the pool of stubborn tears.

"How are you dealing with the change now?"

"Missing my son causes me physical pain. A boy needs his father, but the toxic environment wasn't good for any of us."

Despair resonated over his face, and I connected with it. "What else should I know about you?"

He leaned back and crossed one leg over the other. "I have a younger brother. He's been sight unseen for some time now. I couldn't tell you the first thing about him except he has a healthy appetite for women, judging by the myriad of ladies who call my mother's phone on the hunt for him. We moved here from Port de Flores when we were babies. Does any of this make you want to run for the hills?"

"Please, this is child's play compared to my life." I knocked back the last of my coffee. "How is your relationship with your son?"

"We're best buds. I fly out there to see him as much as possible. That's the best part of being a stockbroker. I can work from anywhere."

"Why are you single?"

"When did I say I was single?"

I hopped up from the table and rolled my sleeves up. "Why wouldn't you tell me that? I don't spend time or text men who are in relationships."

"Please, sit down. It was a joke that went terribly wrong. I'm single." He pointed with curious eyes. "Do you know you have a huge vein that bulges out the side of your neck when you get upset? That can't be healthy."

"I've known about the vein all my life. Thank you for pointing that out." I covered it with my hand.

"You should loosen up. When was the last time you did something spontaneous?"

"What do you mean?"

"Oh, God. If you need a definition, it's been way too long. Come with me." He led me down the street toward the ocean to a narrow terra-cotta house covered in ivy.

We followed a stone trail that led to a linked fence. Kai climbed through an open part of the fence and reached back for me.

"Where are you taking me?"

"You're going to love it. Trust me."

"I've seen those crime TV shows. You could be the killer."

"I'd be a stupid S.O.B. to hurt you, beautiful Brooklyn with the red panties. Now come on."

"The sign says no trespassing."

"Come on, Ms. Goody Two Shoes. No one's going to call the police on you. I come here all the time."

"I can't believe I'm doing this." I grabbed his hand.

Kai jumped off a steep ledge to a path that led to a rock formation near the shore of the ocean. He reached back to help me climb down, and we walked to a spot where we could sit close enough to hear the ocean water splash against the rocks.

"This is magnificent. How did you find this place?"

"I'm too embarrassed to say."

"Don't tell me you used to bring girls here."

"No, I used to come here with my notepad to write poems."

"You write poetry?"

"Yes." He turned a soft shade of red.

"Recite one so I know you're telling the truth."

"Hell no," he shrieked.

"Please."

"I'm rusty. I haven't written anything in years. You'll laugh at me."

"Oh, come on. Practice what you preach. Be spontaneous."

"How about I make one up right now, special for you?" Kai exhaled. "There are a million stars in the sky, but only one stands out. It is perfect, and it captures my attention without a doubt. There's no such thing as space or time. For I could grow old and gray, but I'll never stop doing what it takes to make that beautiful, perfect star mine."

How did he know about the stars?

Kai was in touch with himself. He was secure. He was all man. He could stand on the rocks and beat his chest, and I'd believe him.

"I told you I'm rusty."

"No, I loved it." This time I touched his chin to pull his face up to mine.

"You're just saying that."

"Seriously, I loved it."

"Thank you, beautiful Brooklyn. The sun is setting. We better get out of here. But first, could we take a selfie?"

I grabbed his arm and put it over my shoulders while he held his phone up.

"See, we look perfect together. Do you have any plans next week? I'd like to take you on a date."

"I'm available as long as you're single."

"I'm not single anymore. I've got you." He licked his lips.

"Like I said, you're a smooth operator."

"I walked right into that one, didn't I?"

"Yeah you did, but I'll let it slide since you're so darn cute." I poked his chest.

"Compliments are rare in my world, so I'll take it."

We latched hands and hiked back out to the street.

"You look like that, and you expect me to believe women don't compliment you."

"They don't." He shrugged.

"I hear you, but I don't believe you." I stood on my tip-toes to softly kiss him.

"That was well worth the wait."

"Call me later."

"Let me walk you to your parent's house. It isn't safe for you to travel alone at night."

I touched my chest where my heart raced.

What a man.

"I can take care of myself." I blew him a kiss and walked backward until the darkness swallowed the both of us.

Chapter 10

It'd only been a few hours since Kai and I parted ways, yet I couldn't stop thinking about him. He was patient and kind with everyone he encountered and that meant the most to me. I was bursting at the seams and wanted to share my good news with Iris.

"Hello?"

"Why are you breathing so heavy?" I balanced the phone between my ear and shoulder as I navigated my vehicle. "Are you and Rodney…"

"Hell, no," Iris spat. "I'm in the middle of a dance workout, and it's killing me."

"That crap doesn't work. It's not exactly a real workout."

"Oh, you think? Well, the next time you come over, we're working out. So come prepared with no excuses because I'm seeing dots."

"You're only seeing dots because you're out of shape."

"If you're my best friend and you think I'm fat, I can only imagine what other people are saying."

"You're being dramatic."

"How do you expect me to feel when my best friend—no scratch that—my sister says I'm fat and out of shape?"

"I never said you were fat and out of shape."

"You implied it, and it hurt my feelings."

"I apologize for hurting your feelings. You're not fat, but you are a bit unhealthy."

"I've been a size four since high school. Now I'm up to a size eight. That doesn't work for me. I hang out in Highsea too much. People stare once you're over a size five."

"Why do you care what those superficial people think? I'm a size twelve and proud of it. Embrace your beautiful body."

"Who the hell am I talking to? There is no way this is Brooklyn."

"Stop playing around."

"I'm serious," she said. "I'm usually the one giving pep talks."

"I'm growing, okay. Now leave me alone."

"Keep it up. I like where this is going. How was your dad's birthday dinner?"

"It was fun. I'm so happy they came home so I could celebrate with them."

"How did he like the cake?"

"He loved it, but that's not why I called you." I exited off the highway to head home. "I went for a walk in my parent's neighborhood this evening, and guess who I ran into."

"Tell me, tell me," Iris urged.

"Kai," I shrieked. "It turns out his mom lives down the street. We went out for coffee and watched the sunset by the ocean."

"Oh, so that's why you've turned into Ms. Positive Patty these days. You like him."

"More than you know," I admitted. "His name is Kai. He has an amazing sense of humor. He's a possibility. Can you believe it? I finally have a possibility."

"Don't say another word until I mute the TV. I don't want to miss anything."

"Are you ready now?"

"Yes." Iris made a heavy sigh as if she was settling into a comfy spot. "When will you see him again?"

"He asked me on a date for Friday." My nerves tingled in a good way. "Where's my little godson?"

"He's giving me the blues. There's no pleasing him today."

"It's not his fault. He's not feeling well."

"You should come by and take him home with you for the night. We need a break from each other."

"No way. I'm going to my peaceful home by myself. I need some sleep."

"Sometimes, I think you try to hurt me on purpose."

"I'd walk in your shoes any day." I hurried out of the car and rode the elevator to the top floor. The blue moon illuminated my path and spilled specks of light into the hallway. "I'm home now. I'll call you tomorrow. Goodnight."

"Hey, Brooklyn, how are you?" Nicholas stood in the doorway of his condo with his hair disheveled and shirt unbuttoned to the waist. "Could we talk for a moment?"

"I'm not sure. Is the coast clear, or should I be worried about Faith?" I looked over my shoulder.

"Why are you so angry with me? We're just building a friendship. It's not like we're exclusive and I cheated on you."

"You come off as a playboy. My intuition is never wrong. I've had experience with men like you. I don't need that in my life."

He pinned me against the wall and let out a menacing laugh that could rival the hiss of a serpent. "Do you make it a habit to tease men to get your way? When I offered you an interview with my company, you were ready to do just about anything."

"Take your hands off me. You smell like a drunken bum."

"Yeah, you're a damn tease." He tightened his grip. "I still have something to offer you. Do you want to come to my place to collect it?"

"Get your hands off me." I wiggled until I was free.

"You're a bitch."

"You're an idiot."

"Go to hell." He slammed the door with so much force the sound pierced my eardrums.

"He's as looney as Adam. Is there something about me that attracts loons?" I mumbled, scrambling inside my condo. I quickly locked the door and rested against it. My cell dinged with a message from Kai.

I met a beautiful woman with the sweetest voice. She drew me in, beyond my control or choice. Her eyes held me captive, or perhaps it was her subtle seduction that captivated me. She doesn't know it, but I will soon make her mine.

Goodnight, beautiful Brooklyn.

I'll call you in the morning.

I pressed the phone to my chest. "I can hardly wait."

Chapter 11

Next Sunday, Iris and I decided to spend some time with Junior on the beach. A wide expanse of ocean lapped the shore. The wind whipped over our faces and pulled on our cover-ups. Salt water invaded our noses, and we washed it away with wine coolers while we relaxed on oversized beach chairs underneath large umbrellas that shielded our golden skin from the blazing sun. We played music through a small Bluetooth speaker and sat close enough to the water for the waves to nip at our toes.

Iris slid in the sand as she chased after her son, Rodney, Junior. The older he got, the faster he moved. Unfortunately, the older Iris got, the slower she moved. When she finally caught him, she held his hand with the other propped on her hip, huffing and puffing.

"So how's it going with your new friend?"

"He's growing on me." I rolled a cool drink across my forehead.

"Do you think he could be *the one*?"

"I can't say just yet, but I adore him."

"He's a good influence on you." She dusted the sand off Junior's butt.

"You think so?"

"Oh, I know so."

"He was so unexpected. I never imagined a man like Kai would be interested in me."

"You don't think you're worthy of a man like Kai?"

I moved to the edge of my beach chair with clenched teeth and stared at my phone.

"What's wrong?"

"Here. Read it."

Brooklyn, this is Adam. We need to talk as soon as possible. My phone number is 540-709-6644. Give me a call to set up a time and place.

"Allow me to respond." She took the phone.

This is Iris. Brooklyn asked you to stop contacting her. She doesn't want anything to do with whatever scheme you've got going. Stop harassing her, or I'll make sure she files charges against you.

She silenced the phone and tossed it inside my green and white beach bag. Didn't matter how she handled it. The damage was done. The mere mention of Adam's name had ruined a perfectly beautiful sunny Sunday afternoon.

Chapter 12

Kai and I decided on an intimate dinner at his home to wind down from the end of the work week. I was excited to spend some time with him in person now that he was home. I was also happy to spend time with someone on a Friday night besides Iris and Junior.

I undressed for the third time after losing another round of strip poker to Kai. Left with nothing on, except my black lace panties and bra, I'd exposed the only place where I had freckles.

Chestnut logs crackled in the fireplace. The subtle nuttiness of the fire's smoke mixed with the lemons and peppers drifting down the hallway from the oven that held Kai's secret masterpiece.

We'd stretched out along the alpaca wool rug, slowly making our way to the bottom of a tall bottle of wine.

I titled my head to the side. "I don't know why my game is off. I never lose in poker."

"Because I'm the new sheriff in town, and I don't take prisoners." Kai slammed a handful of cards down one by one. "This is what we call a full house. Now off with your bra."

"No way, you get the sunglasses. The bra stays on." I threw them on top of my red dress.

He fell backward in a fit of laughter and clutched his stomach.

"You've been reading my cards through my glasses." I threw my cards at him. "You're a freaking cheater."

"I don't know what you're talking about."

"You can't be trusted."

He sucked in a belly of air while wiping tears from his eyes. "You were hell bent on wearing sunglasses, talking about you'd have something else to take off other than your clothes. I guess you forgot about reflections."

"I feel so stupid. I should've known better after the second round. You're unbelievable."

"There can only be one winner. It's not my job to tell my opponent about her weaknesses."

"Is this the only way you could get me naked, Mr. Playboy?" I drug my finger down the side of his arm. "Cheating isn't sexy, Mr. Rahimi."

"Hey, I like to win." Kai tugged on my hips to draw me closer. "You smell sweet."

"Don't try to flatter me. You, Kai Rahimi, are a cheater, and now you owe me."

"I'm a bad boy." He softly kissed my earlobe. "I'm so bad I may need a spanking."

I stroked my neck and unconsciously parted my legs. The warmth of his breath hypnotized me. My body relaxed from the weight of him resting on top of me. I held my breath as he passionately kissed me.

"Whoa, wait a second." I fanned myself. "It's burning up in here."

"That's what happens when you're aroused."

I took control and climbed on top of him. His body became my playground—a living map of fun places to visit one by one. I made a trail of red lipstick kisses down his smooth chest. My small hands could hardly grip his bulging thighs, but that didn't stop me from trying.

Kai relaxed on his back with his arms behind his head, staring up at me, enjoying my reactions as I explored his body. I was just about to claim the ultimate prize when the doorbell interrupted us.

"Who in the hell is that?" He glanced at the clock.

"How am I supposed to know?" I slid my dress over my head and quickly sat on the white leather chair.

Kai hurried to the door, adjusting himself all the while. "Who's there?"

"It's Jeesamyn. Open the door. It's freezing out here."

He cracked the door enough to poke his head out. "What are you doing here?"

"Does it matter? Open the damn door."

"This isn't a good time."

"I thought we were in a better place? You wanted us to work on our friendship so we could be better co-parents."

"It wasn't a standing invitation for you to show up uninvited."

"It's cold out here you big jerk."

She wedged her foot in the door and pushed it open before Kai could lock her out. She made a beeline to me as if she'd sniffed me out the moment she walked inside.

"Who the hell is she? Is she why you didn't want me to come inside?" Jees towered over me. "You need to go. We have important things to discuss."

"You don't call the shots in my house." Kai bellowed. "Brooklyn, please don't go anywhere. Give me ten minutes to get rid of her."

I located my purse and set it beside me. "Ten minutes, and that's it."

Kai took a couple of breaths before marching away. "Get the hell out of here."

"Who is that woman sitting on the sofa I picked out?"

"She's not you. That's all you need to know."

"You're right, she doesn't matter because if she did, I would've met her by now. Isn't that the rule? If relationships get serious, we introduce the person." She didn't give him a chance to speak. She wandered from room to room, circling back to the doorway of the den where I sat. She stared at the fur blanket, half empty bottle of wine, discarded stems from the chocolate covered strawberries, and the well-tended fire before settling her gaze back on me.

"I'll bet you think you're special." She marched toward the kitchen. "Aren't you the gracious host? You're cooking for her too." Jees grabbed the tall pot, sniffed it, and slammed it down. The red sauce splattered over the white counter.

Kai's OCD kicked into overdrive. He hurried to clean it before it stained. "You're acting like a scorned woman. You left me, or did you forget? What I do is none of your damn business."

"An unknown woman is sitting on the sofa where we conceived our child, and I'm not supposed to care? You haven't changed anything since I left. You know you still love me." She drove her fingernail into his chest. The same place where I'd left stains of my kisses. "How long has this been going on? Do you hold her the same way you used to hold me?"

"We can talk about this when you can think rationally. I don't know why you're so emotional when we're over…"

She barreled down the hallway. "Do you remember how this stain got here?"

"I don't give a damn."

"Oh, you give a damn. We were drinking wine to celebrate your career change. We got so carried away you dropped the bottle. You never had it cleaned because you didn't want to forget the passion we shared in that moment. You think you can replace me, but you can't. You never will." She knocked over a Chinese vase then doubled back to the kitchen where a long knife sat on top of a wooden cutting board.

Kai pried the knife from her and cut the side of his hand in the process. Red blood dripped onto the stone floor. The sight of it snapped them both back into reality.

"As of tonight, you are no longer welcomed in my home. I will always be there for my son. I will continue to be the father he needs and deserves, but you cannot come back here—ever." He wrapped a towel around his hand to stop the bleeding. "Now get the hell out of my house."

My breathing had become raspy. I was stuck—frozen, standing in the hallway witnessing pure insanity. Once my throat opened, I addressed them both. "This is too much. I'm leaving. Don't ever call me again."

Kai barricaded the door. "Please don't go. I'm begging you. Give me the opportunity to make this right."

"You asked for ten minutes. I gave you ten minutes. You can't possibly expect me to stay here with the two of you acting like complete idiots."

He touched my chin. "Please, let me make this right. Give me that much. I'm begging you."

"Look at your hand. I need to get out of here before she turns that knife on me."

Jees cackled from the other side of the room.

"I won't let that happen."

Against my better judgement, I stayed.

Kai marched toward Jees with cold eyes. His breathing rivaled a pit bull with asthma. "If you don't get the hell out of my house, I'll have your ass thrown in jail. The decision is yours." He held the phone in the air.

"Don't call me when you're done playing with your little toy." Jees pushed him aside to show herself out.

"Fine. Don't ever come back here."

The force of her departure shook the pictures on the entryway wall.

After a moment of silence, Kai kissed my hand. "I apologize from the bottom of my heart. Please accept my apology."

"What was this all about? She ran around here like an angry wife who'd caught her husband cheating. It doesn't seem like you two are over, and if that's the case, where does it leave me? She's the mother of your child."

Kai led me to a bench in the foyer next to a tall clock. It lightly chirped as the second hand changed.

"You're the first woman I've invited into my home, so she knows this is serious. She doesn't want me. She thinks of this as a game. I'm sorry this happened. I will make sure there are rules going forward. She will never be allowed back into my home."

"Are you sure about that? She's the mother of your child."

"You have my word." He drew a cross over his chest. "How are we supposed to recover our night after this madness?"

"Like this." I leaned forward and rested my head against his so that our lips brushed against each other and our tongues intertwined.

"Oh, okay. That'll do it." He beat his chest. "How did I get so lucky to meet you?"

"You wouldn't leave me alone at the airport."

"I give myself a pat on the back every time I think about it."

"Sometimes we get lucky to meet people who add value to our lives, and there are people who add nothing. I'd been wondering what value you'd add to my life, but after tonight, I'm not sure if I'll ever find out."

"I'm going to show you in due time," he assured me. "Dinner's ready if you still have an appetite."

"Kai," I took his hand in mine, "I like you a lot. There is something about you that calms me, so you have the ability to add something invaluable to my life—peace. But with that said, I'm only willing to continue this journey with you as long as what happened here tonight will never happen again." I grabbed my stomach. "Now feed me. What's your main dish called, again?"

"Chicken piri-piri with a special sauce." He beamed. "For the sides, we'll have wild rice and a garden salad with Italian dressing. My grandma taught me how to cook it when I was seventeen, but I've perfected it over the years. You're going to love it."

"I'll be the judge of that."

"You're the boss." He grabbed two large white platters from the cabinet and garnished the plates with enough fresh herbs to bring Chef Gordon to tears. "What do you think?"

"It smells awesome. It looks appetizing, but I'll need to taste it before I hand you the blue ribbon."

I helped Kai bring the platters and bowls to the dining room. He held my seat out and kissed the side of my cheek.

"How long did it take for you to cook the chicken?"

"I marinated it for four hours. Then I let it grill for an hour and brushed the rest of the dressing mixture over it for the last fifteen minutes. It's complex enough but doesn't require too much time away from me kicking your butt in poker."

"Why did you have to bring that up? I'm never playing poker with you again."

"Even if you weren't wearing shades, you would've lost. I'm that good."

"You should be a comedian with these jokes. There's no way you could ever beat me without cheating because I'm that good."

I appreciated the effort Kai put into planning our special dinner down to the romantically decorated table with a centerpiece of white roses, four white taper candles, one round white candle, and five tea candles.

"Honestly, I did more harm to myself for cheating. It's been a battle trying to compose myself with your sexy body on full display."

"You're such a hound dog."

A wide grin spread over his face. "Thank you for staying."

"Honestly, I have so many regrets in my life I've lost count of them. I don't know what we have between us, but it's worth exploring. I've had such a difficult dating life. I don't want to get into the specifics tonight. We've had enough drama."

"I appreciate you." He set his fork down. "But something's bugging me."

"What?"

"I keep wondering, where the hell was my son?"

"I didn't want to say anything, but wouldn't it make sense to bring your son if she's working on co-parenting?"

"Let's move on from her for the rest of the night. I want to focus on us. I'll deal with that tomorrow." He fed me a bite of his chicken. "You won't ever have to worry about anything like that happening again. Enjoy your dinner, my love."

I accepted his peace offering, and it tasted so good I did a little dance in my seat.

"See, I knew you would like it."

"You're growing on me."

"Please say that again."

"You're growing on me."

He closed his eyes and held his hand to his heart.

"I know you see it. I grin like a deranged psychopath every time I'm in your company."

"I'm so happy you're here with me."

I held my glass with my eyes fixed on Kai. There was a shift in my heart, and I was excited for where this was going—flirting, dating, kissing, love, doubts—all of it.

"What's on your mind over there?"

"My thoughts aren't innocent right now." He chuckled and brought his glass to his mouth.

"Please tell me. I want to know."

"Have you ever heard the saying, curiosity kills the cat?"

I leaned into him. "Meow."

"I'm thinking about asking you to come upstairs for dessert."

"What's for dessert?"

"You." His stare was firm, and he moved closer until our lips touched.

"It looks like I backed myself into a corner here. I'm not sure we're ready to go there tonight."

"Come upstairs with me. I'll turn on some soft music and kiss you in places that will make you have out of body experiences. I'll start at your neck and make my way down to your navel…and further if you want."

I wiped a layer of sweat from my forehead and reminded myself to breath. "No, no, I couldn't. It's way too soon."

Kai unbuttoned his shirt and traced the faint lipstick kisses I'd placed on his muscular chest.

"That won't work."

"Okay, fine." He kissed my hand. "You can't blame a guy for trying. Take all the time you want. I'll wait for as long as you need."

"Thank you."

"Now, let's talk about how fast you ate your food. You liked it, huh?"

I covered my face with a napkin. "I scarfed it down because you starved me with your strip poker and drama."

"I want to make it up to you. I'll do whatever you say."

"No questions asked?"

"No questions." He held his hands up. "I can't have you thinking poorly of me."

"I want to dance."

"That's it? That'll square us away?"

"Clean slate."

"You're making a big mistake."

"How?" I asked.

"Do you know Kizomba?"

"Wait? You know it?"

"Sweetheart, I invented it."

"Well, put those words into action, Mr. Kai Rahimi."

"If we're going to do it, we need to do it right. Go put your sexy red heels on and meet me in the den."

I raced down the hall in a split second. I saw a couple dance Kizomba at a dance club and it intrigued me so much I took classes on it. The dance is so sensual and sexy. It makes me feel all my desires. Not to mention it brings out my sexy side.

The night from hell was beginning to shape up. I hadn't danced with a man since the mysterious man I met at a fundraiser in Bellborough. We danced all night without ever exchanging names. That night, I got exactly what I needed—companionship.

Kai led me to the middle of the floor. He rested his hand on the small of my back and lodged his leg between mine. I came alive when the music began to play. We started off at a steady pace, careful not to boil over.

"You make me feel alive," Kai whispered. His lips brushed my earlobe. "My feelings are getting involved here. I would never do anything to intentionally hurt you. Do you understand?"

"Yes."

"I'm falling for you, Lyn." He cupped my face and softly kissed my lips, sending me into a tailspin.

"Are you sure what you're feeling is love or could it be lust?"

He held me closer and gracefully swept me across the floor. "I want to explore you, not sexually but mentally. I constantly think about you when we're not together. I wonder what you're doing. How are you feeling.? What can I do to put a smile on your face? It's only been you since we met."

I exhaled as the song faded. "I'm not going upstairs. Does that change your feelings?"

"Not at all." He kissed me even deeper this time.

I held my head and stumbled back a few steps.

"Are you okay?"

"Oh, wow. I'm a little dizzy." I clasped my hands to calm the jumping nerves that decided to take life at the worst possible time.

"Hey, hey." Kai guided me to the floor with worried eyes. "What can I do to help? Should I call an ambulance?"

"No, that isn't necessary. It must've been the food."

"I can tell you're trying to make light of what's happening. But just so you know, in my past life, I was a white jacket wearing, world-class chef. It wasn't the food. What can I do to help?"

"I'm sorry. This will pass in a moment." I melted against the wall and gazed down at the mosaic tiles.

"You don't need to apologize. Jees probably made you sick with her antics."

"You may be right." We shared a laugh.

"Do you remember when you told me it would take a special man to see beyond your imperfections?"

"Yes."

"Is this what you were talking about when you said imperfections?"

"Not tonight." I clawed my arm.

Kai kissed the side of my face and made his way down to my neck. Then he connected his hand to mine and kissed our connection.

"What are you up to?"

"I see a gorgeous neck I want to taste." He nuzzled closer.

"It feels great, but I need a little air."

Kai fell into a chuckle with his head on my shoulder. "Was that a nice way of saying I'm suffocating you?"

"I don't want to hurt your feelings, but I've been here before. This scares me."

"What scares you? This is the start of something great."

"That's what scares me. When things get too good in my life, it usually turns into crap."

"I'm sorry things have gone that way in your life, but I'm here now, baby. You could never go wrong with someone who wants the best for you and thinks the world of you."

I raised an eyebrow and looked into his eyes. "For me to believe what you're saying, the carpet stain of love has to go."

"It's gone."

My secret sat on the tip of my tongue. All I had to do was say the words, and he'd know what caused my doubts. He'd know what caused my hesitation. He'd know everything—the good, the bad, and the ugly—but the fear of his reaction held me hostage.

And with that, my secret went back safe and sound in the chambers of my heart. All I could do was relish in the moment of this beautiful man.

Chapter 13

Four beautiful months of dating Kai and my motherly instincts were being put to the test with an extended visit from Kai's son, Dylan. Thankfully, the boy welcomed me with open arms. Things were easy with him. He talked openly. He listened and followed directions. He loved to cook with me. I blended into their lives well.

We met Jees at the airport in Highsea. She wasn't too happy having to fly Sunday morning. She also wasn't happy about me being there with Kai.

She blew her top when Dylan said *Bye, Mom* to me after our first meeting weeks earlier, but I was elated he'd called me mom. Those two words made my heart leap out of my chest. On this most recent visit, we were cooking spaghetti when he looked up at me and said, *Mom, is the water boiling now?* I held back my tears so I wouldn't scare him. I don't know what it is about a five-year-old's voice that turns emotions to mush. They're the cutest.

Unfortunately, it hadn't been easy coordinating a playdate with Dylan and Junior because Junior is usually with his dad on the weekends. Today, all the cards fell into the right place. I'd arranged a playdate at Legoland with the boys. Their personalities mixed well. However, Junior was a bit bossy. He was truly his mother's son.

Junior placed a red block on the top of the blob they were building. "My mom says you and Kai are going to get married. Are you?"

Dylan darted over and wrapped his little arms around my legs. "You and Dad are getting married. So that means you'll be my mom forever, right?"

"No, no, boys listen to me," I said. "Marriage is serious. Two people should always take their time to make sure they are making a good decision to commit to someone. Kai and I are taking our time getting to know each other. Maybe one day we will get married but not right now. Dylan, do you understand?"

"Yes." He nodded with sad eyes. "You and Dad aren't getting married."

"Why the sad face?"

"I want you and Dad to get married. I love you."

"Oh, I love you too sweetheart. But right now, I want us all to get to know each other so we will be together for a long time." I kissed his forehead.

"Okay." He raced back to the blob of blocks.

"But Auntie Brooklyn, that's not what Mom said." Junior stood his ground. "Mom said you and Mr. Kai were going to get married soon. She says you're in love. Are you in love?"

"Well, yes. I guess I do love Kai." It was the first time I actually allowed myself to fully express and admit my feelings for Kai.

"You love my dad?" Dylan abandoned his blocks once again.

Now they both were standing in front of me, looking for answers. Kai and I had yet to sit down and profess our feelings and expectations. Just like I didn't want anyone to spill my Huntington's secret, I didn't want the boys telling Kai my feelings either.

"Okay, little dudes, follow me." I led them over to a table to have a heart to heart. "Do either of you know what love means?"

"It means you kiss and stuff."

"Yeah." Dylan jumped up and down. "You and Dad kiss all the time. I see you."

"That's a part of it, but love is much more than kissing. Love is about two people making a commitment to be there for each other emotionally and physically. When Kai is weak, I am strong. When I am weak, Kai is strong. We will be a team. Do you understand so far?"

"I guess so. Can we finish building our treehouse?" Junior hurried to end the conversation.

"Is that what you're building?" I giggled.

"Yes, see. This is the tree, and this is the swing." Dylan pointed and his little eyes connected with mine. "I hope one day you and my dad will get married because I love you so much."

I kissed his forehead and gave his butt a little pat. I never expected to fall in love with him so quickly. I wasn't sure if it was me wanting to be a mother or having some semblance of a family with a husband and child, but he gave me a feeling I would otherwise never get from anyone...it scared the hell out of me.

Chapter 14

It'd been a month since Dylan went home with his mother, and I wasn't taking it well. My spirit was off. I enjoyed stepping into some kind of role in his life on a daily basis. It wasn't easy having him here for so long then moving on without him after he'd gone home.

To cheer me up, Kai invited me on a date to a five-star restaurant, Ourir Touit. He stood tall over the crowd of people and waved me over.

"What took you so long? I was beginning to think you stood me up." He gave me a bouquet of red roses and a kiss on the cheek.

I wore a short black, backless cocktail dress to show off my long legs and torso. The fabric draped down around the dip in my back just above a scar that wrapped around my hip and stomach—compliments of Adam.

"Oh, you bought me flowers. They're beautiful. Thank you." I cradled the bouquet in my arms as if they were a newborn baby. "I apologize for being late. I've had a crazy day." I looked around the modernly decorated restaurant. Large canvases of abstract art hung side by side on the tall walls, leading up to a tempered glass ceiling. It framed the electric gold sunset streaked with red flames. "If it ever snows in Woodcrest, I want to see it from this view."

"I'll make a mental note of that, but you know it hasn't snowed since the early eighties," Kai said. "Excuse me for a moment. I need to let the maître d know you're here. He's a hard ass—wouldn't seat me without you."

I swayed to the soft music and watched the women pointing and smiling at Kai. They couldn't keep their eyes off him in his perfectly tailored black suit. He'd left half the buttons open on his shirt to show off his burly chest.

Kai returned and stuck his arm out to escort me to our table. "Are you ready?"

The tables and chairs were covered in white linen. Gold flakes circled the edge of the china coupled with gold flatware on either side of the place setting. Origami folded tan linen napkins, resembling flickering flames, sat inside the brown tinted wine glasses. A tall crystal vase of long-stemmed yellow stargazer lilies acted as centerpieces.

I bent over the table to inhale their sweet scent. "Oh my God, I love lilies."

"How did I not know that lilies were your favorite? You've been accepting roses all this time and never told me."

"Consider this your lucky night." The maître d nodded at a mature couple cuddled in the lounge area. The old man kissed the nape of her neck while she massaged his thigh. "Two more seconds, and I would've given your table to that lovely couple."

"See, I told you he's a hard ass," Kai chuckled.

"I wonder how long they've been together, how many ups and downs they've experienced and managed to stay true. Love is a beautiful and rare thing to experience with someone."

"It looks like they've been together since pockets were invented."

"Stop it. That isn't a nice thing to say."

"I know, I know. I'm sorry. Truth be told. They have what I want. I want to grow old with the love of my life. I don't ever want to start over again."

"How many women have you wooed here?"

"Let's just say, it's a good thing walls can't talk," Kai laughed.

"Wow. Here I am thinking I was special."

"You are special." He touched my chin to lift my face. "You've outshined them all. I only come here because this is my favorite restaurant. But if it makes you uncomfortable, we don't ever have to come here again. Your happiness means more to me."

"I'm not insecure. I don't care about the other women. I only asked to see how honest you'd be with me."

"Damn, I could take you right here on this table. What do you say?" Kai pulled my chair close to him and gently kissed my neck.

My head rolled back. My eyes soon followed.

"You knew what you were doing when you wore that sexy dress. You're not innocent." He powered off his phone and slid it inside the inner pocket of his black suede blazer. "Did you make it in time to see your parents off for the next adventure?"

"Yes, that's part of the reason why I was late. They were going on and on about Dylan. They already love him so much."

"He loves them too." Kai put his hand over his chest where his heart rested. "The love you all have for my son and he has for you guys make me love you even more."

A tall waitress with long brunette hair towered over us at the worst moment. I'd been waiting for Kai to profess his love because I was drowning in mine. She had the eyes of a lioness on the prowl and ample bosoms like Dolly Parton, which she proudly showcased.

"My name is Sarah. I'll be your waitress this evening. Would you like to start with a bottle of wine?" She passed a brown leather menu to Kai.

"Blue Label Pinot Noir for the table."

"Excellent choice. I'll bring it right out. Oh, and by the way, that suit looks amazing on you."

Sarah's hips swayed side to side when she walked—a true seductress.

"Where did your parents go this time?"

"Fiji." I folded my arms over my chest and leaned back with my eyes glued on Kai.

"Ah, hell. I know that look. It's universal amongst women. What have I done to piss you off?"

"The waitress complimented you."

"Perhaps, does that upset you?"

"I remember you telling me women never complimented you. But whenever we're out, women practically throw themselves at you. Why didn't you think I could handle the truth? You're a handsome man. I expect it."

"I didn't lie."

"What do you call it?"

"Women don't compliment me. They flirt excessively," Kai explained. "I'm an old-fashion man. I prefer to be a hunter. I don't understand this new breed. One day, I actually witnessed a woman propose to a man. Can you believe that? She got down on one knee, and he stood there and let her put a ring on his finger. I mean, can you believe it?"

Sarah returned with our bottle of wine. "Here you go." She filled Kai's glass and set the bottle on the table.

"Excuse me, what about my glass?"

"Silly me. I forgot you were there." She slopped the wine in my glass and quickly turned her attention back to Kai. "Would you like an appetizer?"

"Yes, my beautiful date and I will have the Maple Leaf Duck Breast."

"Are you ready to order your main courses?"

"Yes, my lovely date will have the Lobster Bouillabaisse. I placed my order a couple of days ago for the porterhouse steak."

"Ah, you know the rules around here. Most people end up disappointed when they order a porterhouse."

"This isn't my first rodeo, but I don't remember seeing you around here before."

"Yeah, this is my second week." She placed a hand on her hip and bit her bottom lip. She held her gaze on Kai a little longer than necessary before slowly walking away.

"I want to take you somewhere," Kai said.

"That came out of nowhere."

"I've been thinking about it for a couple of weeks. Ask me where I want to take you."

"Okay, I'll play along. Where do you want to take me?"

"I own a lake house in Meuburn. It's on five acres of land with lots of trees and has access to the lake. We could take my boat out to watch the sunset, drink wine, and have a great conversation. If you don't want to talk, we could sit in silence while I bask in your beauty. What do you say?"

"It'd be nice to get out of the city for a little R&R." I rested my pinky finger in the corner of my mouth while the wheels turned in my head.

"Is that a yes? I figured I'd have to spend most of the night trying to convince you to go."

"No way, you had me as I *own a lake house in Meuburn*. Sometimes I curse myself for not buying a lake house because the tourists in the summer are the worst."

"Don't sweat it. Now, you own a house in the city, a lake house, and a condo. What's mine is yours."

"Oh, really, it's that simple." I snapped my fingers. "You open your life to me that easily?"

"Listen." Kai straightened his back the same as I do when I mean business. "You're smart, funny, beautiful, and so damn classy. I love the way you carry yourself. You're everything I've ever wanted in a woman wrapped up into one. I'm not going to beat around the bush and play games with you. Neither of us has that kind of time. My goal is to connect to your soul. I'm making you aware of my intentions upfront so there won't be any questions later."

"Here are your appetizers." Sarah bent over so her breasts would be eye level to Kai. "Could I get you anything else?"

"That'll be all." He touched my thigh as she walked away. "I'm not blind. I see what the waitress is doing. If you want to go, just say the word."

"I've got what she wants. I'm not going anywhere." I rested my hand on top of his. "You're a good man, and I appreciate how you make sure I know I'm a priority in your life." I swallowed hard. Huntington's did a taunting dance in the back of my throat.

Kai held his wine in his mouth for a moment to savor its taste. "Something happened to you in the past—something profound. I can tell from the way you get uncomfortable. Please don't insult my intelligence by saying I'm wrong. Tell me about it."

I looked up to the dark, starry sky through the glass ceiling and twirled my hair between my fingers without uttering a word.

"Talk to me. I won't judge you. This is how we connect with each other's soul."

"You're right. Something changed me, and now I'm terrified of relationships." I blinked back tears.

"Hey, hey, I'm sorry. I shouldn't have brought it up here. Let's talk about it in Meuburn. We'll take the boat out and make a day of it." He pulled me into his arms.

"I was right about you."

"What?"

"You're one of a kind."

"I owe it all to my dad."

I smiled while Kai rocked me in his arms. His touch had a way of taking my pain away. It gave me a source of power.

"I just realized something," I said. "You've never told me your dad's name."

"Emmitt," he replied. "I wish you could've met him. I married Jees because of him. He'd say, 'Son, it's not right for you to carry on with a woman, live under the same roof with her, and not offer her anything more than a meaningless relationship on a fast track to nowhere.'"

"Your dad sounds like my kind of man."

The waitress returned to the table with a few more buttons opened on her blouse. In such an establishment, I wondered how she got away with her behavior. "I can take your appetizers away if you're done."

"I'm done. What about you, Lyn?"

"If I eat anymore, I won't have room for dinner."

"Yes, please, take it away." Kai held the plate in the air. "You're not getting out of dinner that easily."

"Are you always so animated?" Sarah laughed.

"Laughter is good for the soul."

"I'm a freaking waitress. My life is a joke."

"Why are you in this line of work if you hate it so much?"

"If I had a man like you, maybe I'd be off somewhere living my dreams."

"Your happiness shouldn't reside on the shoulders of a man or a woman. It resides within you. That way, no one has the power to ever take it away."

"I disagree." The waitress flipped her brunette hair. "It's better when you have someone special in your life. Enjoy your dinner."

"If there's one thing I could say about our waitress, she's efficient in unprofessionalism."

"Oh look, there goes the vein."

"It's okay. I'm calm," I inhaled. "Please go on. I want to know more about your dad."

"My dear old Dad," Kai sighed. "He loved to give advice, and I took in every word, unlike my brother. He only listened to the devil on his shoulder. Honestly, if it wasn't for my dad's wise words, I would've tried to jump your bones the first day we had coffee."

I wiped my mouth, careful not to smudge my ruby red lipstick. I'd spent too much time getting the color just right. "You had me right up until the end." I clasped my hands, looking up through the glass ceiling again. "Thank you, Mr. Rahimi, for teaching your son values."

"I'm not joking. You may not realize your sex appeal. But woman, it's strong and it has had a hold on me since I met you."

"You're serious, aren't you?"

"Hell yes. It gets hard for me to keep myself in check." He pounded his chest after swallowing a large bite of his steak. "Damn, I always find a way to embarrass myself when I'm with you. It must be your beauty. It throws me for a loop."

"You're way too stuck on my looks. I have more issues than a magazine. Quite frankly, I'm a mess."

"I'm up for the challenge."

"Most successful men are a-holes, but you're down to earth. What else makes you so different from them?"

"I'm a man who was too selfish to see his faults, so now my son lives in Winford with his mother. I can't be an asshole to anyone. We all have issues."

"You're preaching to the choir."

Kai filled our glasses with the last of the wine.

"You ate like a hungry hostage. Didn't leave anything behind," I teased.

"I didn't eat that fast. You were picking at your food like a cute little bird, but I don't know why. The first time I cooked for you, you ate so fast I don't think you chewed your food. I didn't run away then. I won't judge how you eat."

"This is the thanks I get for having manners."

"Enlighten me," Kai said. "You have your good and bad days. Some days you're not in control. What's up with that?"

"What do you mean by ' control?"

"Your body jerks. You try to hide it, but I see it. You have mood swings. Most of the time you're upbeat but not all the time. I'm not blind. This isn't all about what happened in college. There's more to it. Tell me."

I twisted my hair around my finger and hung my head, afraid to look him in the eyes. Afraid I'd start spilling my guts and he'd leave me sitting there alone. "I'm not comfortable going into details of my life here. I won't do that for you or anyone."

"I wouldn't have asked if I didn't love you."

"What did you say?"

"I said, I love you."

I wove the napkin between my fingers. Those three words made me hyper aware of everything going on inside my body. The butterflies danced. My heart raced. An electrical jolt coursed through my body. "I've been waiting to have this talk with you."

"I wasn't sure if you were ready."

I took deep breaths and savored the moment. "Tell me why you love me. I need to know it isn't lust."

Kai reached out to hold my hands. "I've never had a hard time telling someone I loved them, but I always did it with a Plan B. With you, I don't need anyone else waiting in the wings. I'm willing to give you my heart without fear of what could happen. In a world of uncertainty, you are my antidote. You have breathed new life into me. I know you are my destiny. Because I've lost before, I know how to be the man you need if you will give me the chance." He caressed my hand with his thumbs. "Do you love me? Am I alone in this? I don't mind you taking your time to get where I am if you need it."

"I love you Kai," I exhaled. "When I was in college, my ex-boyfriend almost killed me. His name was Adam. He was the star football player at Pinemoor State."

He moved his chair closer to me.

"He love bombed me when we met. I'd wake up each morning in my dorm to find sticky notes pressed to the door filled with his confessions of love. Then it turned into flowers and love letters every night. He said all the things he thought I wanted to hear. He bought me a diamond bracelet, earrings, and designer purses. He'd compliment me so much I felt obligated to compliment him back so he wouldn't think of me as a selfish witch."

I dabbed the corner of my eyes with my fingertips.

"He walked me to my classes and made sure everyone saw him kissing me and holding my hand. All the girls were jealous, and I felt superior to them. I had the guy all of them would give a limb for, but things changed over time. He turned into an abusive jerk. The compliments became criticism. There were no more love notes. No more flowers. I hate myself for sticking with him. I was young and naïve. I wanted to hold onto my status and the perks that came with dating the big man on campus. Then one night, I was studying for an exam, and he wanted to fool around. When I told him no, I ended up on life support with a broken collarbone, nerve damage down my left side, and broken pelvic bones. That's where my scars came from. I stared death in the face, and I haven't been in a relationship since. I love you because you make sure I know I have a place in your life. You build me up without tearing me down. You make sure I'm safe and happy. I feel special with you."

I rested my head on Kai's shoulder. He wiped my tears away. "Your ex is a coward and a fool. You shouldn't waste another tear on him."

"You made a joke about how slowly I eat. I do that so my jaws won't pop. The sound is a trigger for me."

"I understand." He kissed my hand. "Did that bastard go to jail?"

"The school made sure their star player never missed a game. There was a core group of us in college, but Iris is the only one who knows what happened. That's why I was nervous about going back there. I bottled it all up and tried my best to forget about it. Now, I realize I made a huge mistake because I have no idea how to let it go."

"I'll help you. I want you to live life, not just get through it. I could kill that son of a bitch."

"I told you I had issues." I bowed my head, flushed with the guilt of having spoiled the mood. "This evening wasn't supposed to get heavy. Tell me about your day."

"Whew." He sipped his wine. "I have new clients—a married couple. They took turns driving me up the wall. At one point, I turned everything off and sat in the dark to reflect on my career decision." Kai took another long sip of his wine. "I figured you had a crazy day too because I couldn't get you on the phone."

"When you called, I was at the doctor's office. Then I forgot to call you back."

"Is everything okay?"

"Yeah, it's nothing serious." I avoided his gaze. "I'm so full. I couldn't eat another bite."

"Impossible. You've barely touched your food."

"I'm a tiny thing. It doesn't take much to fill me up."

Kai pulled out his credit card and beckoned for the waitress.

"Leaving so soon?"

"As soon as you take care of the bill," Kai replied.

"I'll be right back."

"What do you say about a walk before we call it a night?"

"Sure, I could stand to burn a few calories. Thank you for dinner."

"I should be thanking you for being here with me." Kai tucked the plastic card back into his wallet. "You lead the way."

I gave the waitress a devious smile as I headed out arm in arm with Kai. "How in the world could any woman let you get away?"

"Some people don't know when they've got a good thing." He stuck his chest out with a slight smirk. "Did I survive another date without making it on *the list*?"

"What list?"

"Don't play coy with me," Kai said. "Everyone has a list of people they'll never date again."

"Tell me about someone on your list, and I'll tell you about one of mine."

"Okay, I've got a good one for you." He stopped walking and bent forward in laughter. "My friend set me up on a blind date a month after my divorce was final. The woman was a kleptomaniac. She stole my wallet when I hugged her goodbye."

"Are you sure that person who set you up with her is your friend?"

"Oh, he's a great friend, but a terrible judge of character."

"One of my *friends* set me up with a thief too."

"What?"

"Yeah, we had an amazing date. When he walked me to my door, he asked if he could come use my bathroom. I went against my better judgment and let him inside. He did his business and took off. Later that night, I realized he stole my LED showerhead and all my face towels."

"Rookie move," Kai chuckled. "You never let a first date inside your home. Don't you know that?"

"I told you I went against my better judgment."

"We have a lot in common, beautiful Brooklyn." He stopped walking. "Do you ever want to become a mother someday?"

"I know you aren't asking me to have a child with you. I mean, we just got to the I love you stage."

"No, I only want to know if you ever want to have a family. A yes or no will suffice."

"Yes."

"I ask because of Dylan. We're a packaged deal. I can't completely fall for you if you don't want that role."

"I completely understand."

Kai leaned in to feed on the sweetness of my lips. His hands wandered my body as if he were trying to memorize every inch of it.

"What was that for?"

He touched the side of my face. "I'm not dating anyone else, but I don't want to keep assuming we're exclusive. You're always on my mind, and I want to date you with marriage as the goal. How do you feel about that?"

"What took you so long?"

"I'm a fool." He glanced around the dimly lit area. The lights of the store fronts went out one by one and darkness fell upon us. "We should go. The last thing I need is some stranger hurting you to prove his manhood for a few bucks."

"How cute. You're protecting me."

"Of course, you're my treasure." He kissed my cheek.

"Will I see you tomorrow?"

"Or we could wake up together. Come home with me."

"Not tonight."

"I've gotten used to having you around. We've been together for months now. I'm going to be lonely without you there. Come home with me."

"I won't get any sleep. We'll end up talking until dawn. Then I'll be cranky and drive my partners insane. I can be a piece of work when I'm running low on sleep."

"I don't buy that. You're always upbeat." He held my car door open.

"Stick around long enough. You'll see."

"In that case, go home and sleep tight."

"Goodnight, *boyfriend*." I blew Kai a kiss and sped away with a goofy smile.

Sappy music filled the cabin of my Mercedes. I was on top of the world until I noticed a car swoop in behind me, blinking its headlights. I pushed the gas, but I couldn't escape the souped-up muscle car. I jerked the steering wheel to the right and rolled into a small parking lot to avoid the car running me off the road.

"Adam." I narrowed my eyes as he approached my window.

"Roll your window down. We need to talk."

"What the hell are you doing in Woodcrest?"

"We need to talk."

I hit him so hard with the car door, it knocked him back a few steps. "You've got some nerve popping up in my life."

"We need to talk."

"We don't have anything to talk about."

"I saw you kissing that guy. Man, he has a sweet ride. You don't have to worry about him seeing us together. I saw him go in the other direction. Is that your boyfriend?"

"That's none of your business. What do you want?"

"You've got two choices. Talk to me tonight, or I'll talk to your friends—and that includes your boyfriend. Does he know everything about you—the Huntington's and all?"

I could feel the vein pulsating in my neck. I wanted to dig into his throat and pull out vocal chords so no one would ever hear his vile voice again.

"Don't you threaten me, you snake."

"What do you want from me? Do you want an apology for the incident?"

I balled my hands into a fist. "You call what you did to me an *incident*? You almost killed me."

"I was a dumb kid, but I've grown up now. I've made a good life for myself. Looks like you have too. Why won't you let it go?"

"You're begging for help from someone who hates you. How good is your life?"

"Damn. Kick a man while he's down," Adam said. "I mean, yeah, some things have happened that's affected me financially, but I have an opportunity that could help the both of us."

"You're kidding, right?"

"I don't blame you for hating me, but I need you to hear me out tonight."

"Go the hell away."

Adam grabbed my arm to stop me from walking away. It made a nasty red imprint above the elbow.

"If I were about to step out in front of a bus barreling down the street doing ninety miles an hour, I wouldn't want your disgusting hands to pull me out of its path. I'd rather take my chances. You make me sick."

"Okay, damn. I won't touch you again." He held his hands up. "You may not want to accept the fact that you're a part of my story, but you are. I'm not asking you to like me. All you need to do is talk. Just sign the damn papers and stop being a bitch about it."

"I said no."

"I'm dying, Brooklyn. I've taken too many chances with alcohol. I have cirrhosis of the liver."

"Not my problem."

"I'm dying, and this is the only way I can make sure my wife and children will be okay financially after I'm gone."

"How ironic," I rolled my eyes. "Now that you're so-called *dying*, you can finally see beyond your own selfish needs."

"I need to make a difference before I go. Maybe my story will help someone else. Please, I need you."

"You expect me to believe you're doing this out of the kindness of your heart when you've never done anything to help anyone except yourself. I don't want my name attached to yours. Besides, our encounter is not worth rehashing. We met, we dated, and you almost killed me. I hate you. End of story."

"I lost my opportunity to play in the NFL when I did that to you.

No team would touch me. You play a major role in my life, and your story matters."

"You never showed up at the hospital or called to check on me. You didn't care if I lived or died, so I don't care about you either."

"You've never owned up to the part you played. You pushed me to that point."

"Me? I can see as clear as day now. You're the devil in human form. Don't ever call me again. I'm not doing your stupid straight-to-DVD biography."

I stomped to my car and sped away, leaving Adam standing alone in the dark parking lot. The night he left me alone to fight for my life was the nail in the coffin for us.

It'd be a cold day in hell before I do a favor for Adam freaking Williamson.

Chapter 15

Kai and I had a perfect night at the Ourir Touit, but his confession of love was ruined by Adam's shenanigans. Because of it, I didn't get a wink of sleep. So the coffee pot and I would be the best of friends as I dragged through Friday at the office.

I made a beeline to the kitchen. "Thank the lord. It's a fresh pot."

"You look like hell. What did you do last night?" Lorraine asked.

"Forget about my night. What the heck is wrong with Tammy?"

"She took two laxatives the night before her date, but they didn't work until her date," Lorraine replied.

Tammy slid down in her chair with her face covered. "You couldn't keep a secret to save your life, Lorraine."

"You've been going to the bathroom every twenty minutes. Keeping this a secret would be impossible. Be realistic."

I walked over to Tammy's desk. "Why in the world would you take two laxatives the night before a date?"

"I've always done it to get rid of bloating. It usually wears off by the morning, but this time I got them from Lorraine who didn't tell me she got them from NiCole."

"Lorraine," I shrieked. "We agreed not to take anything else from NiCole. Did you forget about the time you ended up in the emergency room on the verge of heart failure after taking one of her miracle weight loss pills? For all we know, Tammy could've taken a dog laxative."

"Now you see why you shouldn't be laughing? I could be dying, and it's all Lorraine's fault."

"I didn't realize they were from NiCole until it was too late. I'm sure she'll be fine."

"How do you know? I could die." Tammy clutched her stomach and bolted down the hallway.

Lorraine and I fell on the floor in a fit of laughter. The three of us had formed a unique bond over the years. We enjoyed a fun atmosphere, but we knew how to buckle down when it was time to be serious.

I took a deep breath. "Maybe you should encourage her to see a doctor now."

"You know Tammy. The harder you push, the more she'll resist."

"If it doesn't slow down, she'll be on a medical drip by this evening."

"I've got my eyes on her." Lorraine wrapped her shawl around her.

"This tops Tammy's list of crazy."

"Neither of you are in a position to judge me." Tammy stood in the hall, fanning her face. "We're all guilty of doing off the wall things around here."

"What are you talking about, Chocolate Nightmare?" I teased.

"Here we go with the name calling. Bring it on. I can take it."

"Chocolate Pudding," Lorraine yelled.

"Are you done?" Tammy asked. "I could seriously be dying and you two are making jokes."

"We're laughing because you walk around like you're a part of the royal family. So when you almost paint the inside of your date's car brown, it's pretty freaking funny." I chugged the last of my coffee.

"Almost doesn't count." Tammy wagged her finger. "It didn't happen. So please, drop it."

"Okay, fine." I waved a piece of paper. "I'll let it go."

"Why are you in such a good mood?" Tammy picked at her nails.

"Yeah, you're usually unapproachable until after ten."

"You should thank Chocolate Syrup for that."

"Ah, another name. You're so clever." Tammy scowled.

"Seriously, you're glowing." Lorraine tilted her head. "What's the deal, Brooklyn?"

I took a seat on the edge of my desk and twirled a pen between my fingers. "It's the guy I told you about when we were at the bar. We've decided to date exclusively."

"I'm so excited for you."

"Thank you." I raked my fingers through my hair.

Tammy bumped her hip into Lorraine's hip to move her away. "I want to see a picture of him."

"What makes you think I have a picture of him?"

"You point that damn camera at everything. You should've been a photographer. Now show us."

"You're right." I scrolled through my pictures.

"Are you in love?"

"Yes, I do love him." I set my phone down and touched my heart.

"Stop stalling," Lorraine said. "I want to see if you and your man are a match or a mix-match."

"What are you talking about?"

"You know how some couples look like they were made for each other, then some look like they don't belong in the same room. Mix-match."

Orange juice shot from Tammy's nose.

"Oh, we're a match."

"Does he have a friend, brother, or uncle? They say birds of a feather flock together."

"Don't listen to Tammy. She doesn't have any room on her roster for another man. Her black book is bursting at the seams."

"Why do you always give me shit about my dating life? Are you jealous?"

Lorraine fiddled with her shawl. "What is there for me to be jealous about?"

"I don't know," Tammy shrugged. "You tell me."

"I'm not jealous of you. I love you, but this playgirl persona isn't working. It's leading you down the wrong path. You're getting old, Tammy. You need to settle down."

"I've been there, done that, and bought the T-shirt. Now I wash my damn car with it. Marriage is your goal, not mine."

I cleared my throat to show the girls a picture of Kai.

"Ooh, he's yummy." Tammy wiggled her fingers.

"Hello, hello." A tall man waltzed inside the office dressed in a dapper suit and tie. He carried a basket of fruit cut into different shapes of flowers.

Tammy raced to his side. "Welcome to Three Angels Event Planning. How may I help you?"

"I have a delivery for Brooklyn Monti."

"That's me." I waved him over.

"Hello. If you sign here, I'll be on my way."

"Do you always wear designer suits to make deliveries?" Tammy circled the man like a buzzard stalking its prey.

"You do when you own the company and have a meeting in the area within an hour." He glanced at his diamond watch. "I figured I'd help my crew make a few of their deliveries on the way. You ladies have a good day."

"Allow me to walk you out." Tammy shoved her arm in his.

After reading the card, I held it to my chest. "It's from Kai. Isn't he the sweetest?"

"Yes, he is." Lorraine snuck a strawberry. "What do you like most about Kai aside from his great gestures?"

"Kai is very forthcoming about his life, flaws and everything. It's actually a trait I wish I possessed. I have a tendency to hold back on a lot of things until I feel the time is right."

"What are you holding back?"

Lorraine had no idea how close she was to discovering the secret I'd been keeping from Kai as well as them. Thankfully, Tammy's timing was better than mine. She danced back into the office, waving her hands.

"Brooklyn, what are you and your boyfriend doing tonight?"

I put my finger up and ran outside to answer my ringing phone. The leaves rustled, and the trees swayed from the cool breeze. "Hello, boyfriend. I got your delivery. Thank you so much."

"Let's do something tonight."

"I can't. I'm sorry. I have plans."

"Cool, how about I tag along?"

"Not this time, sweetheart."

"Am I already suffocating you?"

"No way," I said. "How about we get together tomorrow?"

"Sounds like a plan. I'll give the boys a call to meet me for a drink. They've been giving me a hard time for spending all my time with you."

"Who knew men were so territorial?" I checked a message. It made my blood run cold. I said my goodbyes to Kai and gathered my things. "I'm sorry girls. Something has come up, but I should return tomorrow."

"You can't go. We have end-of-the-month budget tallies to do, and you know Tammy's no help with it."

"Is there anything we can do to help?"

"I'll be back tomorrow." I dashed out of the office mumbling to myself. "Something's got to give."

Chapter 16

It'd been a week since I left work in a rush and now Huntington's had stepped in to keep me away from the office even longer. Luckily, Tammy helped out Lorraine with the end-of-the-month details at the office. Through sleepy eyes, I tripped over my pillow fort in search of my ringing phone. I discovered the comfort of a pillow fort and a good book during the first few months of being diagnosed with Huntington's disease. Whenever there was cool weather, I'd make a pillow fort outside on the balcony to listen to the ocean. Today was one of those days.

I smiled at my phone. "Hello Kai."

"Hi, Lyn, it's been a couple of days since I've heard from you. How are you?"

"I'm sorry. I haven't been feeling well. As a matter of fact, I've been meaning to talk to you about it."

"Wow, I'm getting it from both ends. You aren't feeling well, and my son broke his arm horse-playing today."

"Oh no, are you flying to Winford?"

"That's another reason why I called. I wanted you to go with me, but you don't sound like a woman in any condition to travel. Is there anything I could do to help you feel better?"

I wandered to my vanity. I'd covered the mirror with hand-written notes of affirmations.

This is your life. There'll always be obstacles. You've got to keep pushing. You're worthy of being loved.

"Hello, are you still there?"

"I'm here."

"Why are you sick? What's going on with you?"

"Oh, no. You have enough on your plate with your son." I leaned my elbows on the vanity.

"My flight doesn't leave until later this evening. I could come over and take care of you."

"No. I'll be fine, but I appreciate the offer."

"I love you, beautiful Brooklyn."

"I love you too, and I hope you'll stick around once you learn I'm not as perfect as you think."

"Where would I go?"

"Men are fickle creatures. One day you're here, the next day you change your identity and disappear."

"I know better than to argue with a woman," Kai chuckled. "I want to bring you soup and hold you until you fall asleep. I'll push my flight out for tomorrow."

"No way. Your son needs you. I'll be fine."

"I don't like the idea of leaving town knowing you're sick. I would be devastated if something happened to you."

I fanned my tears away. His attempt to make time for me sent shock waves through my body. The fact that he'd make me a priority in his life gave me confidence in our relationship.

"I appreciate you."

"I need you to know how much I care about you."

"Uh oh," I sat down and propped my legs up on a stack of pillows. "What?"

"Ah, how sweet. You're falling head over heels in love with me."

"I sure am, and I'm not afraid to admit it."

Loud bangs on my front door interrupted our conversation.

"Brooklyn, open the door."

"Is everything okay," Kai asked.

"Brooklyn!" Adam's voice punctuated each heavy bang.

"I'm coming over," Kai demanded.

"Open the damn door, Brooklyn. You can't ignore me. I know your secret."

"What is he talking about?" Kai asked. "What secret?"

"I need to go." I ended the call and cracked the door with the gold chain in the hook. Adam stood in the hallway practically foaming at the mouth.

"Sign the damn papers."

"The fact that you keep intruding in my life tells me you haven't changed at all. I've told you, I don't have anything to say to you. I don't want to talk to you. Yet and still, here you are again. It's beyond pathetic and creepy."

"You don't want to push me too far. I have too much on you that could ruin this perfect little life you think you've got. You owe me."

"That's it. I'm calling security." I fumbled with the phone.

He threw his hands up and walked toward the elevators. "This isn't the end. You have no idea how far I'm willing to go for my wife and children."

"Make all the threats you want." I slammed the door and stomped to bed. But twenty minutes later, the loud bangs on the door started again.

"Oh, that's it." I shrieked. "I'm calling the police."

"It's Kai. Open the door."

My chest rose and fell with rapid breaths. I paced in a circle and pounded my hands together. A thin layer of sweat formed over my forehead in a matter of seconds.

"Open the door Lyn."

I took a deep breath and welcomed Kai inside. His face was almost unrecognizable with anger and fear.

He let out a harsh breath. "What the hell is going on?"

"I told you I was okay. It was just a misunderstanding."

"Do you think I'm a fool? There was no misunderstanding. Who was that guy? What secret is he talking about?"

"There is no secret. It's some idiot guy who can't take no for an answer."

"What the hell?" Kai said with his hands on his hips. "So many bad thoughts went through my mind. I almost flipped my car over to get here. Why aren't you calling the police? This makes no sense."

"Please, sit down and gather yourself. I told you I didn't want you to come over because I can handle this. I need you to trust me."

"I trust you. It's him I don't trust."

"No." I knelt in front of him. "I need you to trust me just like I trusted you with Jees."

He nodded. "Why'd you have to go there?"

"I only want you to give me the chance to take care of my mess the same way you did. Okay?"

"Okay. I'll give you the same opportunity, but who was that guy?"

"Remember the ex I told you about?"

"That was him?" Kai's eyes doubled their size.

"Yes." I finally admitted.

"Oh, hell no. I can't leave you here alone. What if he comes back? I'll kill him myself."

"No. Go see your son. I'm fine. I promise you. No one is in danger. If he ever comes back, I'll call the police."

Kai wrapped me up in his arms and stroked my hair. I could feel his heart pounding. Huntington's gray cloud was slowly fading. My secret was making its way to the light.

"Kai…"

"Lyn," he said simultaneously.

"You go," I urged.

"Thank you for telling me the truth. I can't take the secrets and lies."

I hesitated. Wouldn't telling him about my Huntington's now be tantamount to exposing a withheld secret? Should I do that now while he's already hurting? I bit my lip.

"Thank you for being here for me, Kai. Now go be with your son. I'll be fine. I love you."

"I love you too." He kissed me before leaving me to my own insanity.

My heart refused to slow down. I walked out onto the balcony to inhale the fresh air. I pressed my fingers to my lips and let the tears fall. Things were happening too close for comfort and it left me to wonder who I was becoming.

Chapter 17

Dad ran across the room, almost as fast as an Olympic champion, with his arms stretched. I needed his love after the drama that happened with Adam and Kai three weeks ago. I closed my eyes and slowly exhaled. I've learned to cherish the time with my parents since they decided to become world travelers.

A year after launching my business, Mom and Dad sat me down to tell me about their plans to travel the world after Dad retired. I never realized I'd developed a codependent relationship with my parents until they were gone. They were no longer a drive across town when I was in dire need of companionship. It forced me to work on myself.

After I finally released Dad from my bear hug, he kissed my forehead. He took a few steps back to look at me before returning the bear hug. "Look who finally decided to show up. We've been waiting for you since we made it to town last night."

"Oh, Dad, it's eight o'clock on a Saturday morning. I'd say I'm doing great on time. Where's Mom?"

"The house is quiet. Where do you think?"

"She's in her workspace." I pointed toward the white French glass doors where a sidewalk led to another small structure in the backyard.

Most women wanted a she-shed for a special place to eat cookies and relax in peace, not my mom. She wanted her own workspace to build and restore furniture. She enjoyed breathing new life into unique pieces—much like she did with people.

"Bingo." He touched the tip of my nose.

"I love you more than yesterday."

When I was a little girl, Dad would come home late from a hard day's work and tiptoe inside my bedroom while I slept. He'd kiss the tip of my nose. I'd open one eye and whisper, "*I love you more than yesterday.*"

"What is she working on now?"

"She found a mirrored credenza a couple months ago. She says, 'It's the piece of a lifetime.'" He mimicked her high-pitched voice.

"Mom truly has a gift." I fiddled with a small pillow I'd smashed into my lap. "I wasn't expecting you guys until the end of the month. Not that I'm complaining, but what brought you home so soon?"

"Are you kidding me? We're long overdue to spend some time with our favorite daughter."

"I'm your only daughter." I studied the lines around his eyes. They'd become more distinct since I had seen him last. It triggered my obsession with time. "How long will you be home?"

"We should be homebound for a few weeks, and we better see you every day."

"Oh, you won't be able to get rid of me. I may as well move back in until you're off on your next adventure."

"I know you have a business to run. God knows I could hardly tear myself away from work at your age, but you have to take time off to enjoy the little things in life. Smell the roses. Don't forget our offer for you to travel with us has no expiration date."

"I know, Dad, but I'm too busy trying to have a great career. Hopefully, I'll also get married one day, and start a family of my own," I sighed. "Do you think it's too far-fetched for me to want those things?"

"Of course, it's not." He held my hand. "Since we're on the subject,

I heard from a little birdie you were dating someone. Tell me about him."

"Who's the little birdie?"

"Never mind that." He wagged his wrinkled finger. "Tell me about him."

"I'm not dating anyone."

"I guess you don't think he's good enough for us to know about him."

"I'm not a kid anymore, Dad. Reverse psychology won't work on me now."

He pulled the pillow away from me before I unraveled the gold tassels. "Tell me about him."

"Okay, let's say I am seeing someone. Would that be so bad?"

"Tell me about him."

"Okay, fine." I couldn't keep a lie from him. He's a retired private investigator for goodness sake. He'd wear me down for sure. "His name is Kai. He's a divorced stockbroker with a young son. I didn't tell you because I don't want you to try to talk me out of seeing him. You and Mom have always had reservations about me dating after what Adam did. Kai makes me feel good about myself. He cares about me. He respects me, and he protects me."

"All those things are fine and dandy, but tell me how he feels about you having Huntington's?"

I sat in silence for a moment. "I haven't told him. I can't go back to my life of solitude before him."

"That's selfish thinking."

"Let me explain." I propped my elbow on the back of the sofa to face him. "You know how you love a big, juicy steak cooked to perfection?"

"Yes." He rubbed his stomach with a bright smile.

"Imagine someone serving you a steak, and as soon as you dive in for a bite, they take it away. That's how I feel. Whenever my life is going too good, Huntington's has a way of taking it from me. I can't risk it with Kai."

"If this man cares about you the way you say he does, he won't run away."

"No one has ever stayed. Kai's the one, Dad. I want him to get to know me without Huntington's hanging around. I deserve love too."

He moved to the edge of the sofa. "I don't have Huntington's, so it wouldn't be fair for me to say I know how you feel. I'll get even older one day, and you'll have to take care of me. It's an unavoidable part of life. I could let those thoughts drive me to make selfish decisions, but it wouldn't be right as a man, husband, or father. How serious are you about Kai?"

"I'm in love with him."

"Oh, boy. You threw a curveball. I wasn't expecting you to say the L-word." He ran his fingers through his thick beard. "In that case, you owe him the truth."

"I won't survive if he walks away."

"Cut it out." His stern voice bellowed. "You were living before him, and you'll keep living if he walks away."

"My judgment is cloudy."

He reached over to stroke my hair. "It's my job to lead you down the right path. So far, you haven't let me down. Don't lose sight of who you are because you're experiencing something new."

"I want to get married. I can't leave this world without ever experiencing it."

"Honey, you could be married and still be unhappy. He deserves the truth."

"I need a little more time."

"It's your decision. But remember, the longer you wait, the more likely it'll bite you in the butt later."

Thankfully, Mom ran inside the living room with open arms. Her hugs could put a sunny day on the beach to shame. "How long have you been here?"

"Not a word," I whispered to Dad. "Not long. I heard you found a credenza."

"You have to see it. It's simply magnificent. It'll look perfect in the foyer. Come, come," she said.

I followed Mom outside to her rustic workspace. Even though they lived near the ocean, Mom stuck to her country home style.

"Here we are. Isn't she beautiful?" She extended her arms to reveal her big masterpiece.

"I love it. You should give it to me."

"All of this will be yours in due time. Until then, this beauty will be right here with me."

"Yeah, right. I'd be lucky to outlive you and Dad." My phone buzzed like an annoyed rattlesnake. "I'll be right back. Hello?" I answered with the phone stuck to my ear.

"Good morning, beautiful Brooklyn. What are you up to?" Kai asked.

"My parents surprised me last night. They're home for a few weeks, so I'm spending a little time with them today. How are you? Has Dylan gotten used to his cast?"

"It's been three weeks and the kid is still fighting it," he chuckled. "I'm at my mom's house. I should come over to meet your folks."

"I'm not ready for you to meet them yet."

"Why are you afraid for us to meet each other's parents? You still haven't come over to meet my mom."

"I always say hello to your mom when I'm with you and she calls."

"I want you to formally meet her. This is a perfect day. Come over for a while."

"No way. I look horrible. We should plan something. Make it special."

"I know my baggage isn't ideal. I'm a divorcé with a kid. Now I'm afraid you may not give me a fair shot."

"That's not the case. I just think we should plan a special evening to do those things."

"You can plan something special for your parents. I don't need to plan anything special for you to meet my mom. Come over today."

"I'm wearing a baggy sweat suit, no makeup, and my hair has seen better days."

"My mom doesn't care if you look like a supermodel or the girl next door. All she cares about are your values and your intentions with her baby boy."

"I don't care what you say. Mothers don't want to see their sons with a slouchy ragamuffin."

"When I wake up before you, I brush my fingers over your smooth skin and inhale your sweet scent. I watch you sleep in awe of your beauty. I say a prayer to have you in my life forever. You're perfect in my book. Please, come over."

Kai's and my relationship had a beauty to it, and we had yet to reach our full potential. The thought alone excited me.

"Do you remember the bouquet of roses you gave me on our first date at Ourir Touit?"

"Yes."

"I froze the petals from the flowers you gave me. I look at them often to remind myself how blessed I am to have you in my life."

"This is how I know my mother will love you. Come over when you have time. I'll be waiting."

"Okay. I'll be there soon." I ended the call and held the phone to my chest. I couldn't stop smiling no matter how hard I tried, so I simply stood in the plush green grass.

"You look like a woman in love." Mom leaned against the door frame with her arms folded over her chest. "Who is he?"

"Were you eavesdropping?"

"I wasn't listening. I know that look. I had the same goofy smile the moment I fell in love with your father."

"I'm two for two today. I can't hide anything from you guys."

"What's his name?"

"Kai," I replied. "He wanted to meet you and Dad today, but I was thinking we could meet for dinner this week. I'll make the reservations."

She tucked a lock of her hair behind her ear. "Ah, you two are in the phase of meeting the parents. How long have you two been dating?"

"Nine months."

"Nine months?" Her face twisted in anger. "Why haven't I heard about him before?"

"You throw my past with Adam in my face every time I meet someone."

"That isn't fair sweetheart. You can't use us as an excuse for hiding a nine-month relationship."

"You're right, I apologize. Honestly, things moved fast before I realized how much time had passed."

"I'm your mother, but I'm a woman first. I know a thing or two about love." She kissed my cheek. "Make the reservations. We'll be there," she sighed. "There's something I need to tell you."

"Sure."

"Your father is sick."

"He didn't say anything while we were talking a moment ago."

Mom led me to a bench near the door of her workspace. "He's been having stomach pain, and now there's blood in his urine."

"I talked to him for over thirty minutes. Why didn't he say anything to me?"

"He doesn't want you to know." She squinted at her diamond watch. "I better clean myself up. The doctor ordered a few tests for him today. I can't wear these things." She tugged at the straps of her paint-splattered overalls. Her long mousy brown hair was pulled up into a ponytail and a layer of sawdust covered her honey skin.

"You can't tell me Dad's sick and then run off. What's wrong with him?"

"We won't know until he gets the results from the tests he has to take today."

"I'm going with you guys."

"Take it up with your father. I'll be upstairs." She kissed my cheek before going inside.

I marched to Dad with my hands on my hips. "Why didn't you tell me you were sick?"

"I knew your mother couldn't keep her big trap shut."

"You lied to me. You told me you guys only came home to be with me."

"I didn't lie. I didn't say anything because I don't want you to worry before I know what's going on."

I couldn't keep up with the tears pouring from my eyes. "You chastised me about honesty while you were being dishonest."

"Sweetheart, you'll know when I know."

"Do you think it's bad?"

"I don't know."

"I'm going with you today."

"No," he said.

"So you don't care if I go crazy with worry?"

"My mind is made up. I don't want you to go."

"This is so messed up." I stormed out of the house. My feet pounded against the sidewalk while troubling thoughts clouded my mind. Life keeps throwing me curve balls, and I was becoming too tired to catch them.

Four blocks later, I reached Kai's mother's house. I strolled up the sidewalk to the house and leaned against one of the many white

131

columns. The swell of trees offered a nice break from the sun.

Kai walked outside. "Are you crying?"

"My dad's sick." I tried to blink my tears away.

"Is it serious?"

"We don't know. He has to take some tests today, but he didn't want me to go."

"It sounds like he needs space to deal with this. Give him that. He's got a lot on his mind." Kai stuck his hand out. "Come with me. I'll make you some tea."

I followed him into the kitchen where his mother, Vera, sat at a small bistro table nestled in the corner. She clipped coupons from a newspaper stained with coffee rings.

"You finally made it. Now, I can put a face with your beautiful voice." She shuffled over to me with an enduring smile and open arms. She stood about five-two with long gray hair. She was so tiny, I was afraid I'd break her when we hugged.

"I'm sorry it took me so long. Kai and I have been living in a bubble."

"You look like you've been crying." She turned to Kai. "What did you do to her?"

"It wasn't him." I came to his defense. "I got some bad news before I came over."

"Is there anything I can do to help?"

"Your prayers would be great."

Kai set a hot cup of tea in front of me.

"That tea set has been in my family for many years. When we moved here, we came with that tea set and our clothes."

"It's lovely."

"You're sweet, unlike his ex-wife. I knew she was trouble from hello. Her clothes were too much. She wore too much makeup. She talked too much. She was simply too much."

"Please don't get started," Kai sighed.

"Someone has to warn the poor girl about what she's getting into."

"Oh, I got a taste of her crazy not too long ago," I said.

Vera slapped the side of her leg in a fit of laughter. "I heard about the show she put on for you. I've always said she could start a fight in an empty room."

I let out a much-needed laugh. "I could see that happening."

"Brooklyn," Vera cleared her throat, "how do you feel about my son?"

"Oh we're diving right in there, huh?"

"Look at me. I want to see your eyes when you tell me."

"I love him." I shared an enduring smile with Kai. Always in protective mode, he put his arm around me.

"You'll need to be *in* love with Kai in order to deal with Jeesamyn." Vera reached across the table to touch my hand. "We'll talk again. I feel I should give you some time since you've got so much on your mind. I hope this won't be the last time I see you." She dragged her fuzzy slippers along the wood floor.

"Follow me." Kai took me by the hand. "You can wait here for your parents to return."

"Didn't you tell me you had a younger brother?"

"I do."

"Why are there only pictures of you, your mom, and dad?"

We walked inside Kai's bedroom. Framed poems hung against the pale blue walls. His full-sized bed sat underneath an arched window. A white desk sat next to a matching bookcase by a large walk-in closet. "We moved to this house when I was in my junior year of high school and as you can see, my parents never changed it after I moved away to college."

"Did you ever sneak out?" I pointed to the glass doors.

"I snuck out once. I wanted to go to a party, and I knew my dad would never allow it. But I got scared and came home in an hour because my parents would roam the house at odd hours of the night. They were like zombies."

"I tried to sneak out one time," I laughed. "I got one foot out the door, and my mom jumped out from the dark and asked me where in the hell I was going. She had the craziest eyes I'd ever seen." I sat on a beige leather chair next to a punching bag hanging from the ceiling.

"Your mom's hardcore." He fiddled with a magazine on the desk.

"Are you intentionally avoiding telling me why there aren't any pictures of your brother?"

"It's been that way for a while now."

"Why?"

"When Dad got sick, I called my brother every day. He would never answer. Even when Dad died, he wouldn't answer. I had to leave a voicemail about his funeral arrangements, and do you know what?"

"What?"

"He didn't come to the funeral. After everything Dad has done for us, he couldn't pay his respects."

"That's terrible."

"He came here late at night with a half-naked woman. Mom and I didn't say anything because we were happy to have him home. Then he flew off the handle with the woman, and we had to call the police just to calm him down. After that, Mom would cry whenever she'd see his pictures. I knew she'd eventually make herself sick, so I got rid of them. I couldn't lose her too."

"But he's your brother. You swept the issues under the rug instead of facing them."

"That's something my dad would've said." Kai knelt on the floor and rested his head in my lap.

"Friends come and go, but family's forever."

"My brother knows his way home if he wants to be a part of the family."

I wrung my hand around my wrist to calm my jumping muscles. "Now I'm even more worried about my dad. My parents mean the world to me."

"I've been where you are. It's impossible to tell your heart not to do its job. I'm here for you in any way you need me." He led me to the bed. His hands roamed around my body like a tourist in unknown lands.

I squeezed my eyes shut to surrender to him. My body swayed like fresh linen hanging on a laundry line on a windy day. Kai climbed on top of me, sweeping his tongue around my hot skin. I kicked off my heels and reached inside his jeans to cup his butt. He unhooked my bra, and my nipples hardened as he kissed my breasts and made his way down my stomach.

"No. Stop. I can't do this with my dad on my mind. It just makes it weird."

Kai crawled to the other side of the bed with his knees pulled to his chest. "You're right. We're in my mother's house for God's sake. I shouldn't have gone there."

"You don't need to apologize." I stared at my reflection in the mirror hanging on the wall across from the bed. "I'm scared."

"I'm sure he'll be fine." Kai kissed my cheek and walked over to the closet. "I want to show you how I clear my mind. Maybe it'll help you too." He stood on a chair to bring down a small black case.

"What is that?"

"Try not to freak out. It's a gun."

We walked to the far end of the backyard where three tree stumps met the forest.

"Every woman should know how to use a gun."

"I hate guns."

"You won't after today. Hold this." He set a can on top of each tree stump.

"We're really doing this, huh?"

"Yes." He kissed the back of my neck.

"If you keep doing that, I'll be more than calm."

"I like that." He put my hands on the lock to open the case. "Hold it steady."

"Isn't it illegal to shoot a gun in the city? The police will be here before we know it."

"This long piece is a silencer, which muffles the sound." He kissed my neck. "Here. Hold the gun tight, close one eye, and aim at the can in the middle. Don't be afraid. I'm right here."

I held the gun and shot the first can down.

"You're a natural. Now, try to shoot the next can."

I aimed the gun and squeezed the trigger. The second can went tumbling to the ground.

"You're doing great. Now shoot the last one."

By now, the gun became an extension of me. I squeezed the trigger and the last can went down. "You were right. This is a stress reliever."

"Anytime you need to clear your mind, we'll come out here to shoot some stuff."

"Thank you, but I have a confession."

"What?"

"My dad taught me how to shoot, but I never realized it could help me to relax."

We sat under a willow tree. I fidgeted with my hair and hands, occasionally picking at my beige nails. The chirping birds became a needed distraction from my own nervousness. After nine months, my heart skipped like a school girl whenever I was alone with Kai.

"There's no way I could've gotten through this day without you."

"Thank you for allowing me to be here for you." He kissed my hand.

I succumbed to my happiness. We simply looked at each other and laughed, but my smile quickly faded when the nerves in my cheek twitched. I covered it and turned away.

Kai kicked his feet over the sharply cut grass.

"There are some things I need to…"

"No." He put his finger to my lips. "Don't add to your stress today."

"It—it's not that." I struggled to find the words even with the advice from my dad ringing in my head like a fire alarm.

"I said, no. Not today. I'm putting my foot down."

I dropped my head to rest on him. He reached around to stroke my hair and held my hand with the other one. Love made me feel lighter despite the secrets that weighed on my heart.

Chapter 18

Some people say a day makes a difference. Well in my case, a month makes a difference. Thanks to Kai, Three Angels received a proposal for an event with a budget of a whopping two hundred thousand dollars. The event was to be held in Whitehaven, a flourishing city with a myriad of venues to satisfy their red carpet theme. The month of March was looking up.

Tammy got busy compiling a list of venues. Lorraine made a note of all their requirements to start building a visual presentation, and I created the budget to make sure it would be a lucrative opportunity for the business while still meeting the client's needs.

"You guys, as long as we can stay within budget, based on everything we've compiled today, we could make $129,250.00 from this event." I danced in my seat.

"I knew I liked Kai." Lorraine waved her hands.

"Like isn't the word. I love Kai," Tammy reiterated.

I rolled an ink pen between my fingers. "I say we accept their offer. What do you guys think?"

Lorraine and Tammy looked at each other and flashed the okay sign. I accepted the job and advised our attorney to draft a contract. Tammy ran to the breakroom to grab one of the bottles of champagne we kept on hand to celebrate big jobs.

I held a hand to my chest while Tammy filled our glasses. "I knew we would be successful, but I never expected it to happen as soon as it did."

"That just says you don't dream big enough. I knew we'd be wildly successful. Why do you think I fought to become a third partner in the company?" Lorraine held up her glass of champagne. "Let's toast to our baby, Three Angels Events. You're easy on the eyes, soothing to the heart, and you make me proud. I love you, girls."

We touched our glasses and screamed out loud with our heads thrown back.

"Watch out Forbes. We're well on the way. Here's to Three Angels Events," Tammy said.

"We should keep the celebration going. What should we do tonight?" Lorraine sat on the edge of my desk and chewed a string of licorice candy.

"I can't," I replied. "Kai's meeting my parents and Iris tonight. I'm terrified. My parents have never liked anyone I've dated."

I never asked for much. I liked to keep a low profile and tried to experience life as much as I could without people questioning me. Now, the possibility of my family telling Kai I have Huntington's before I have the chance to tell him has sent my anxiety through the roof.

"What are you worried about? Kai seems like a wonderful man who loves you and supports your business. Why wouldn't they like him?" Lorraine asked.

"They have their reasons to feel that way, but Kai is different. I want them to give him a chance."

Lorraine walked over to the mirror to brush her hair. She'd brush it for hours if she could. She considered it her best trait. "What happened to make your parents feel that way?"

"It doesn't matter what happened."

"I'd like to know why we weren't invited to dinner. I don't have any plans. Do you have any plans, Lorraine?"

"I don't have anything planned." The more she brushed her hair the bigger it grew.

"I'm already stressed, Tammy. Don't give me grief about it."

"I wouldn't bring my man around Tammy if I were you." Lorraine stopped brushing her hair long enough to put on a coat of coral lipstick. She smacked her lips together and dotted the edges with her finger.

"And why is that?" Tammy asked.

"You consider man stealing a hobby. That makes you a threat."

"So what? I enjoy the company of men." Tammy shrugged. "I've never dated a man in a committed relationship with someone else. I have morals."

"What about Ray?" Lorraine asked.

"He was legally separated when we met."

"That's a lie. You bragged for weeks about how you took him from his wife. The man never stood a chance."

"That isn't true."

"Yes, it is. I told you I didn't agree with what you were doing."

"Why would I take advice from you? Michael disrespects you every chance he gets, and you never stand up for yourself." Tammy wagged her finger. "You should leave that guy alone and for goodness sake. Take a break from watching those YouTube conspiracy theories."

"Now you're going too far. Those black-eyed children are freaky, and they're real. Everyone should know about it in case they encounter them."

"No, I'm freaky, and I'm real." Tammy burst into a fit of laughter.

"Okay, that's enough." I stood to gather my things. "I'm calling it a day."

"Hold on. I have something to say before you go. Please try to enjoy your evening. Merging a family into one should be exciting. Sometimes you have to let the cards fall where they may. I'll see you guys Monday." Tammy bolted from the office without looking back.

"You're right," I asked Lorraine. "How late are you staying?"

"I'm leaving after I follow up on the Kennedy account since Tammy left without doing it. Get out of here and do what she said. Relax and take it all in. Everything will be fine."

"I hope you guys are right." I left the office with my phone stuck to my ear. "Hello?"

"Are you on your way home?" Kai asked.

"I just walked out. I'm going to be on time come hell or high water."

"Are you still nervous?"

"My stomach's in knots." I eased into the steady flow of traffic. The seasons had changed, and the stars peeked through the soft blue dusk of the early evening sky.

"Why are you so nervous?"

"I told you about my college fiasco. My family doesn't trust anyone."

"I'm a father too. I understand your parent's plight of trusting a man to treat you with care and respect after what Adam did to you. They may never get over it, but if they need me to spend the rest of my life proving my love to you, I will do that."

"Oh my goodness, I love you, Kai Rahimi."

"Look on the bright side. My mother adores you, so we have one down."

"I get the feeling your mom would welcome any woman into your family as long as it's not Jeesamyn."

His ear-piercing laugh boomed through the phone and poured out through speakers of my racing car.

"What did Jees do to make your mom dislike her so much?"

"She's always thought of Jees as a gold digger with a bad attitude."

"What do you think?"

"I think she never would've divorced me if that were the case. Jees had access to all the money. We only had one account. Honestly, I wasn't the husband I should've been. I focused on my career and put her and my son on the back burner. I failed them. My mom's entitled to her opinion, but she's not so spot-on when it comes to Jees. Hate clouds her judgment."

"Are you sure you're over Jees?"

"I'll always love her. She's the mother of my child, but I'm no longer in love with her because I'm in love with you."

His words turned me into a smiling maniac. "I'm in love with you too."

"You're my perfect girl."

"Perfect doesn't exist."

"I know you're not a perfect human being. None of us are," he explained. "You're perfect for me."

I rolled through the parking garage and there he was, leaning on his car with a bouquet of flowers. "Hey, you're here." I hopped out to greet him with a kiss, and we quickly headed upstairs. "Make yourself at home." I tossed my phone onto an oversized ottoman and stripped out of my clothes, leaving a trail from the living room to the master bath.

Before I left for work, I picked out an ivory embroidered lace dress I bought while Iris and I vacationed in La Cabo. We took a stroll on the boardwalk and came upon a one-of-a-kind boutique. We saw the dress and went for it at the same time. It turned into a cat fight and tested our friendship. I eventually offered it to Iris, but she wouldn't take it. After her second refusal, I bought it. She would've had to have the dress taken in anyways. She's my best friend. Why not save her a few dollars?

I stepped in the shower, hanging my head while the water rained down my body. I clenched the towel rack, waiting for the muscles in my legs to stop twitching.

I need more time.

I dried off and wiggled into my dress. Then I braided my hair down the side and twisted it into a bun. I completed my look with a pearl necklace and matching earrings.

"Well," I stood with my arms stretched out. "How do I look?"

"You're gorgeous, beautiful Brooklyn."

"I can't believe this thing is dead again." I tapped my watch.

Kai rested a hand on my lower back and dipped me with a kiss that melted away my anxiety. "I see you finally hung the painting. It looks good there."

Kai was the best gift giver. He bought the painting last month from an unknown artist. I immediately connected to the woman. She sat on the floor with her knees pulled to her chest, hugging her legs while her right cheek rested on her knee. It was uncanny how her eyes stared right into my soul.

He picked up a box from the counter and placed it in my hand. "This is for you, my love."

"Not another gift? You're spoiling me." I bounced on my heels. "Oh yeah, before I forget, I have great news."

"Lay it on me." He sat on the sofa with his legs crossed.

"So it turns out, when my dad posed for a picture on a formation of rocks by a waterfall, he slipped and bruised his kidneys. The doctor said blunt trauma caused the stomach pain and the blood in his urine. He'll be fine in no time."

"He went through all that for a picture? It better be a damn good one." Kai fell over on the sofa in a fit of laughter.

"Cut it out." I slapped his arm. "You don't know how much of a weight has been lifted off me knowing he's okay."

"I've been thinking about tonight." Kai touched the seat next to him for me to sit down. "I think I could get your parents to come around if I can get Iris on my side."

"So you're strategizing on how to win my parents over?"

"Hell, yeah. I made a plan. You've been so nervous about tonight I'd be a fool not to."

"I'm sorry if I worried you. I really want them to accept you."

Kai extended his arm to escort me to the car. One of the many things I loved about him. My knight in shining armor. At the worst moment, my arm began to twitch.

"What was that?" he asked.

"Nerves," I lied. "Don't pay it any mind."

Kai kissed my shoulder and caressed my arm. "Iris will be putty in my hands after I flash my million dollar smile."

"I love it when you're cocky."

He drove with his hand resting on my thigh. "Open your gift."

"I feel guilty. You've already given me so much."

"There's nothing wrong with a man taking care of the woman he loves. I want you to have nice things, so I do that for you. Please, open it. I want you to wear it tonight."

"You really love me, huh?"

"Yes, I love you with all my heart." He drew a cross over his chest.

I tore into the blue box to find three other individual boxes. The first box contained a rose gold atlas bracelet inside. The next, a rose gold wire bracelet, and the last box made me do a dance. It contained a rose gold and silver dome watch. "I've been eyeing this watch. How did you know?" I leaned over to kiss his cheek. "I love them all. You make me feel like a princess. Thank you."

"You needed a new watch. You've been beating the hell out of yours for weeks now. You know they make batteries for those things."

I playfully shoved his shoulder. "I've got to step my game up. You deserve nice things too. It's only fair."

"Wait." Kai parked in the first open spot outside the restaurant. He looked into my eyes. "I don't buy you nice things in hopes you will reciprocate. I do it because I want to show you I care and to put a smile on your face."

"Ah, Shanice, 'I Love Your Smile.'" I popped my fingers and swayed side to side, singing the timeless tune. "Do you remember that song?"

"Of course, I remember." He sang it with me.

Turning back was no longer an option, even if the guilt suffocated me. I held Kai deep in my heart, and my secret would have to reside on the tip of my tongue for the time being.

I held his hand to my chest. "I need to hear you say you won't walk away from our relationship without at least trying to work through whatever issues we face, no matter what."

"I promise, sweetheart. I love you."

"No. I need to hear you say the words. Say you won't walk away without trying to make it work. I want you to fight for us," I urged.

"I promise I won't walk away. I will fight for us. What is this about?"

"The hardest part of having hope is it could end in disappointment. This relationship has given me a lot of hope. I hope we will continue to love each other. I hope we will continue to respect each other. I hope one day we will get married. I hope to have a family with you. But with all the hope I have, I also have fears of it ending."

"I believe in the law of attraction. What you put out into the universe will come back to you, which means you need to let go of your negative thoughts. They will not serve you. Sure, we'll get on each other's nerves. No relationship is perfect, but I will make all your hopes become a reality. I promise."

"Okay." I let out a sigh of relief after the elephant finally moved away from my chest.

Kai's smile echoed his eternal love. We were a team ready to go to war with anyone who stood in the way of our journey.

My dad was the first person I zeroed in on once we were inside the restaurant. He stood tall with a stern expression. It urged me to come clean and be the good girl he raised me to be.

"Mom, Dad, Iris, this is Kai." I gestured at each person in turn. "Kai, this is my family."

Mom and Iris greeted us with warm embraces.

"It's nice to finally meet the man who's been dating our daughter for nine months."

Dad stuck out his hand to greet Kai.

"Actually, two days ago we made it to ten months," Kai explained. "I really wanted to meet you sooner, but your daughter does things in her own time."

Dad cut his eyes at me. "Yes, she does."

Mom cleared her throat. "Let's cut to the chase." We all took that as a cue to sit down. "Our Brooklyn is a very special girl, and she should be treated as such. What are your intentions for her? That's assuming you have any at all."

"Actually, I do." Kai held my hand. "I love Lyn. I know how special she is and what she's gone through in life. I also know she is kind, resilient, intelligent, and downright beautiful. As I've told Lyn, I'm dating her to get to know her to her very soul with the possibility of one day marrying her."

"Marriage," Dad interrupted. "Brooklyn didn't mention that to me."

"Calm down, Dad. Nothing is written in stone. We're not there yet. It's just on the table."

"How well do you think you know Brooklyn?" Iris asked.

"Well, I know she has a successful business with two partners. She's had an extremely traumatic past with someone she thought she loved." He ticked off the points on his fingers. "I know she thinks of you as her sister. You provide her stability and unconditional love. Family means everything to Lyn because she knows how blessed she was to be adopted by two loving people who raised her as their very own."

"Oh, wow. She told you she was adopted?" Dad leaned back in his chair.

"I guess this means you know what happened to her birth mother," Mom chimed in.

Kai looked perplexed. It was the one thing I hadn't mentioned. They were getting too close to my truth.

"Mom, Dad, slow down. I haven't gone down that rabbit hole with him."

"Tonight's a good night to go there, darling." She gave me a wink. "Her bio mother died from Huntington's disease when Brooklyn was a baby. Her bio father thought it would be best for us to raise her."

"What's that?" Kai asked.

"It's a neurological thing," I replied. "Okay. Who's ready to order?" I motioned for the waitress.

Iris kicked my leg and rattled off her order as the waitress approached. I was practically river dancing in my seat. The curtain was slowly closing, and I was about to make my final curtain call.

"Iris, Brooklyn tells me you're a forensic scientist. That's outstanding."

"Thank you. I'm practically living a dream. Much like Brooklyn," she teased.

This time I kicked her leg.

"Well, I for one hope Lyn feels she is living a dream. I especially hope she is happy with me being in her life because she has greatly improved mine. In fact, the most important bond she has made is the one she has forged with my son. That little man loves her to no end." He turned to me, still holding my hand. "She treats everyone who enters her life with care and respect. That is why I know you will make a wonderful wife, but I don't want to rush our relationship because I plan on making it last with you."

Dad stood from his chair and walked over to Kai. I wanted to take Kai out of there for fear of what was about to happen. But to my surprise, he embraced Kai for what seemed like an eternity.

My secret lived another day.

Chapter 19

After a successful dinner with my parents and Iris Friday night, we spent the rest of the weekend celebrating. So much so, I slinked into the office with fatigue written all over my face. I tried to hide the worst of the wear by sporting the darkest pair of shades I owned.

Tammy bounced her foot up and down to the music blasting through her headphones while Lorraine intensely stapled papers.

"It's ten o'clock. You're late." Lorraine never looked up from her stapling.

"And you came empty handed. You were already late, you could've at least grabbed breakfast."

"Food should be the last thing on your mind. Your hips have gotten wider than mine." Lorraine teased Tammy.

"My hips are fine." She stuck her tongue out. "Is that a stamp on your hand Brooklyn? Did you go out on a Sunday?"

"Why are you two talking so loud?" I closed my eyes and massaged my temples. Visions of our weekend of partying like teenagers ran through my mind like a matinee. "It's Monday morning. Give me a break."

Friday night after dinner, we went dancing at a nightclub. The crowd was way too young for us. There we were a couple of thirty-somethings surrounded by the twenty-ish crowd. We stuck out like wild weeds. A few times, I almost passed out from the rainbow strobe lights. I told Kai it was the alcohol.

Saturday night we went to another nightclub. The crowd was a bit more age appropriate, which was great for me because there were no strobe lights. When Kai held me close on the dance floor, our souls sparked like fireworks on the fourth of July.

Last night, we pushed the needle too far. We drove to Highsea and partied until the morning. We'd danced with abandon in hope to capture the feeling of freedom for as long as we could.

"You guys are lucky I came in at all. I feel horrible."

"You're not doing us any favors if you're not going to be productive." Tammy followed me down the hall, yapping all the while.

I fumbled through the cabinet in search of the tallest coffee mug I could find.

"Where'd you go last night?"

"Kai and I danced until the morning and ended up at a little rundown diner in Highsea. Six o'clock came before I knew it."

"I can't believe you went out on a Sunday." She said with wide eyes.

"Don't look so surprised."

"I'm impressed. This guy has you coloring outside the lines. I like it."

"I like it too." I laughed through squinted eyes, careful not to agitate the monster in my head.

Talk about March madness.

Chapter 20

I woke up and immediately regretted leaving the blinds open last night to enjoy the April showers. The rising sun almost left me blinded. I squinted through one eye to see Kai resting on his side, watching me. We'd been basking in our love for a month since our families got on board with our relationship.

"What time is it?"

"Seven." He raked his fingers through my bed hair.

"How long have you been watching me? You're such a creep."

"Well, this creep woke up early to cook you breakfast. I was about to wake you."

"Thank you. That's so sweet." I kissed the tips of his fingers. "What time did you wake up?"

"About five o'clock."

"Why so early?"

"Your snoring woke me."

"Oh, no. I'm so embarrassed." I pulled the bedsheets over my face. The first night we spent together, I woke up in the middle of the night to find Kai working in his office. His excuse: It was the perfect time to trade stocks.

I knew better now.

I peeked from under the pile of beddings. Kai flashed a goofy grin.

"Maybe I should see a doctor about it. I don't want to run you away."

"It's not that bad. More like a sweet lullaby. Come out from there." He pulled the bedsheets away. "I love to see you first thing in the morning when your curly hair does what it wants. You have the most beautiful smooth skin." He stroked the side of my face. "I'm sorry for making fun of your cute snoring."

"I forgive you." I popped out from under the covers.

"Come downstairs before the food gets cold. You know how much I hate cold eggs. They turn into a rubbery disgusting mess."

Kai escorted me down the wooden stairs to the dining room. He'd gone all out, cooking a feast of eggs, bacon, bagels with cream cheese, strawberries, freshly squeezed orange juice, and waffles.

"This looks amazing. You always take care of me."

"It's my job to take care of you."

"You may not know it, but you're teaching me how to give and accept love. I cherish your presence in my life."

"I need to talk to you about something."

"Okay." I sipped my orange juice and took a few bites of bacon.

"You told me what happened with your ex-boyfriend in college, but I know there's more to it."

"Oh, come on. I don't want to talk about this right now." I held my hands out to remind him of the lovely breakfast he'd made for us.

"This is the only way we'll get to know each other. We have to talk."

"I agree, and I'll tell you everything…eventually."

He leaned into me until our foreheads touched and quickly stole a kiss.

"Sweetheart, please." He tugged on the collar of the silk pajama shirt I'd snagged from his dresser. "Are you afraid to be vulnerable?"

"No, it's not that."

"Do you feel like you can't trust me with the vulnerable parts of your life?"

"None of this seems real."

"What doesn't seem real?"

"You, this, us. It doesn't seem real."

He pulled my chair between his legs. "Sweetheart, this is so real, I want to wake up with you like this every morning. Do you feel the same?"

"Not if you plan to leave your clothes all over the floor." I pointed to the clothes scattered in the hallway. "Your home is much too beautiful."

"Says the messy one in the relationship. Besides, I was trying to tempt you with my birthday suit last night." He fed me a strawberry. "One day, I'm going to marry you, beautiful Brooklyn."

He kissed away a trail of strawberry juice from my chin.

"Oh, sweetheart. Wait. Hold on a second." I pushed my chair back. "You brought up marriage when you met my parents last month and you keep mentioning it. Are you really moving in that direction?"

"I know it's early. I'm trying my best to take things slow. But the more I'm with you, the more I feel the urge. It's been eleven months now. If you haven't given it any thought, maybe you should so we can figure out if we're on the same page." He kissed my hand. "But don't take too long, sweetheart."

I gazed out the window and watched the rising sun be overtaken by rain. Kai's words echoed in my head—*don't take too long*. I wanted to break down right there and tell him everything. Tell him the secret that was holding me back. All I had to do was say the words, *I have Huntington's disease and could die before I'm forty.*

"Hello, Earth to Brooklyn." He snapped his fingers.

"I have a confession."

"I'm all ears."

"I almost lost control last night."

He stood from the table and pranced around with his chest stuck out. "I'm not sure if I told you, but back in college I ran the 800-meter in track. All the girls would come early to watch me strip down to my shorts."

"I probably would've been right there with them."

"Oh, yeah?" he said. "I heard Pinemoor girls were wild."

"Most of them were wild, but I wasn't. I regret it every single day."

"Allow me to help you explore that wild side. I'm a good man begging for you to let me love you. Will you let me?"

"Letting go isn't as easy as you think. It almost feels impossible."

"Nothing is impossible."

"I don't know." I pointed at the silver clock. "Heavy conversation should be against the law before eight thirty in the morning."

"Cool. I have something for you anyways."

"Not another gift."

"This is different." He set a gold key in my hand. "This is the key to my house. I want you to feel free to come and go as you please."

"Is this your way of asking me to move in?"

"If I *were* asking, what would you say?"

"I'd say we're not ready to go there."

"Take it easy." He touched my trembling shoulder with a cunning smile. "This key is my way of showing you I'm committed to our relationship. Please, take it."

"I can't…I shouldn't."

"Why not?" He tilted his head to the side.

"Where would we stand if I don't take the key?"

"I'd be disappointed, but nothing would change between us."

"Okay. Good. I can't take it."

He leaned back in his chair as if the air left him. "What am I doing wrong here? You've got to give me something. I feel like I'm alone in this."

"I thought you said nothing would change?"

"Do you love me?"

"Yes, I love you. I've never felt this way about anyone."

"Then stop fighting it. Give me a chance to show you how a man loves a woman."

I thought about all the nights I'd spent alone and how it nearly suffocated me. My days were empty with the same routine. I'd wake up alone, go to work, and come home to an empty house with nothing to make all the success I'd gained worthwhile. I curled my hand around the gold key with a nod.

"That's my girl." Kai kissed me on the forehead. "You're probably the only woman on earth who doesn't get excited to get a key to her boyfriend's house."

"I'm sure that isn't true." I flipped the key between my fingers. "I can show you how open I am."

"Show me."

"Let's take a shower together."

"Say that again. I don't think I heard you."

"Oh, you heard me." I stepped toward him until our bodies were smashed together. "Come take a shower with me. Today we'll start doing more things we haven't done. You know, get to know each other." I slowly unbuttoned the silk pajama shirt that covered my breast. It fell to the floor on top of his dirty clothes.

Kai sucked his bottom lip as he watched me prance away. "You're serious, aren't you?"

"I'm naked and you still have doubts?" I beckoned him to follow me. "Are you coming or what?"

"I'm scared to move. I may wake up from this dream."

I climbed the stairs, and Kai finally hurried behind me. I started the shower and splashed him with a handful of water. "I want to feel your hands on me. I want to feel your skin against mine." I moaned, hardly able to control myself.

Kai stripped down to his birthday suit. He took a moment to admire me in the shower. A crooked smile appeared over his face. Then he eased into the water and kissed me slowly and deeply, putting all my thoughts to rest even if it was only for a moment.

I smashed my body against his growing manhood and moved from side to side, spreading the soapy water over us. "I love the way you feel."

Kai pinned me against the wall and cupped my face with heavy breaths that turned into moans. He kissed every inch of my body until he was on his knees. The water didn't seem to bother him.

"I love you," he growled.

"I love you too."

His tongue spoke to me in a language only my body could understand. It awakened all the desires I'd buried years ago. Tears began to pour. Somehow Kai distinguished them from the water and kissed them away, but it didn't stop him from exploring my body.

"Open your eyes, Lyn." He kissed my lids. "Look at me. I love you. I'm in love with you." He reached over my shoulders to pull me close.

"I'm in love with you too."

Kai abandoned himself to his pleasures, and I followed his lead.

"You have no idea how much you mean to me."

He carried me to the bed. "I don't want this to end."

"Me either."

"Well, screw it. Move in with me."

"We talked about this."

"Oh, for goodness sakes, Lyn. Stop fighting me. Move in with me." He walked his fingers around my wet thighs. "If you're not here, I'm at your place. Don't you enjoy spending time with me?"

"You're serious this time, aren't you?"

"I hate it when we're apart. Let's do this."

"If I let you see all my flaws before we're married, it'll never happen."

"What else is there for me to learn about you? Come on. Move in with me."

"I said no." I wrapped the gold sheet around my naked body and stood from the bed.

"Okay then, marry me."

"I didn't say that to get you to propose. And FYI, that's not the kind of proposal a girl wants."

"Calm down before you give yourself a heart attack." He took my hand to lead me back to bed. "It's not my intention to pressure you into doing anything you don't want to do. I just want you to know where I stand so there won't be any questions later."

"I don't want to live with you before marriage. That hardly ever works out with couples. I don't want that to happen to us. I love you. Timing is everything, don't you know?"

Chapter 21

We'd spent six months planning the construction of a four-story Candyland-themed castle for a candy factory celebrating a hundred years in business. The clients launched on Halloween, so it came together perfectly. Kai and I stayed in Nova Beach for a week after the event. When I finally walked inside my condo free from all obligations, I locked the door, closed my eyes, and took a deep breath. Not running into my naughty neighbor Nicholas was the cherry on top.

I threw my jacket over the back of the sofa and kicked my heels off into the middle of the floor. Making a beeline for the kitchen, I poured myself a glass of wine and tossed a stack of mail on the counter. A gold envelope peeked from under the mound of mail that caught my attention.

"Britt Thornburg." I mumbled and flipped over the envelope to read the writing on the other side. "Please forgive me?"

My breathing stopped. I'd come to terms with never hearing from him in this lifetime. I set my glass down to find a comfortable spot on the sofa and tore into the mysterious envelope.

October 2, 2022
My Dearest Daughter, I'm not sure how to start this overdue letter, so I'll start by telling you how sorry I am and how much I deeply love you. Please keep reading and allow me to

explain. Your mother, Eva, and I met when we were young. She was nineteen, and I was twenty-one. I fell in love with her the moment she asked me for the time in her thick Italian accent. She was cultured and stylish while I was a meager country boy in the company of someone vastly different from anything I'd ever known. I was so flustered, I forgot I wore a watch and told her I didn't know. She politely said, "Oh, your watch doesn't work." When she touched my arm, and I almost evaporated into a puddle.

I was only supposed to be in Greenview for a couple of days visiting family. But after I met your mother, there was no way I could leave her. Back in those days, we didn't waste time. If you found the one you love, you held onto that person and no one else mattered. We ended up getting married six months later.

We found a little house just outside the city to start our lives together. I was an electrician, and your mother was a painter. I want you to have all her paintings and our family albums. We made a pretty good life for ourselves, and we were overjoyed when Eva found out she was pregnant with you. My fondest memory of your mother being pregnant was coming home from work to find her in your nursery working on a mural for you.

It was one hell of a hot summer, so Eva had her hair pulled up. She wore a cutoff shirt and sweatpants. Her huge stomach would stick out, and by the time she'd stop painting, she'd be covered in it. There's one part of the mural where her stomach smudged it. She didn't dare fix it. She said it was her favorite part because you added your very own personal touch.

When you were born, you filled our hearts and home with

an overwhelming abundance of love. Life was perfect and so were you because you were a spitting image of your mother. You had her eyes, nose, cheeks, lips, fingers, and cute little toes. My perfect girls, my perfect life.

You were almost a year old when your mother took a turn for the worst. The doctor said we should've noticed signs, but I never really paid attention. You two gave me so much joy, I couldn't see anything else. The doctor diagnosed Eva with Huntington's disease, and there was no cure for it.

Eva deteriorated pretty quickly after that. I took care of her the best I could. I bathed her, combed her hair, dressed her, and fed her every single day until the night she passed. But the hardest part of it all was wondering if you had the same illness. I never realized how extremely hard it would be to bury Eva, and I now had this beautiful little girl who was potentially a reincarnation of her.

Your mother was only twenty-six when she passed. I couldn't function anymore. I was so scared I'd have to relieve that pain all over again, and I couldn't fathom it. Then one day while I was in the city, someone told me about a church I should attend. So that Sunday, I dolled you up and we headed to church. That's where I met Sheila and Thomas. They were successful, married, and in love. I would see them every week for almost a year. They fell in love with you. I'd get to church and Sheila would take over. She was a natural.

So one day, I talked to Sheila and Thomas about adopting you. She'd been trying to have a baby for years, but it never happened. I went to their home every night for dinner for a year. I couldn't give you to them without knowing full well they would take care of my baby girl. On the day you were supposed to move in with them, I had a hard time walking away. They let me stay with you for a few weeks. The only thing I asked of them was to send me pictures and updates of you over the years, which they did, without fail. I asked them to tell you about me but not give you my contact information. I wanted you to grow up and flourish. When the time was right, I'd reach out to you. They did such a wonderful job raising you and giving you exactly what you needed and more.

The time has come. I have a heart condition and most days I'm not sure if I can carry on. I don't know how much longer I've got, so I want you to come out to the house. Giving you away is my biggest regret. I let my own fears stop me from being your father. I want to talk to you and spend a little time with you. I want to remind you to enjoy life. Don't let your fears keep you from doing the things you dare or keep you from the ones you love. I've never been the same after losing you and your mother. I never remarried, and I didn't have any more children. That part of my life stopped with you and Eva. I didn't want to give anyone else that part of me.

I'm proud of the woman you've become. I've watched you from a distance, but I should've been there by your side. I understand if you don't want to see me. God knows I don't deserve it. I know your mother wouldn't have ever wanted me to give you away.

If this is our first and last communication, I want you to know I have willed you everything I own—the house, land, all of it. Your mother's insurance was $250,000. I put it in a bank account in your name. The next page contains all the information you need. It's available to you whenever you want to claim it.

Should you decide to sell the house, don't take a dollar less than three hundred thousand. But before you sell it, look at the mural your mother painted. I have pictures, but I want you to see it in person. My insurance policy is another $200,000. The least I could do is make sure you're well off financially.

I love you with all my heart, Brooklyn Denise Thornburg Monti.

Love forever and always,
Your father, Britt Thornburg
P.S. I'd love to reconnect with you. Call me on the
cellphone number included with the bank information. I
love you with all of my heart.

I banged on my chest to jumpstart my heart and called Iris to take a road trip to Greenview with me. I understood the importance of time better than anyone. I needed to know about my roots from the only person who could tell me.

A phone call wouldn't do.

***

Iris and I hit the road after dropping Junior off at his dad's house. For the first time I didn't contest Iris driving like a bat out of hell. We arrived at Britt's house in no time. We sat outside the gate before I could muster up the courage to drive to Britt's house. When I finally walked up to the door, my hands shook so badly I could hardly push the doorbell.

My heart stopped when I heard the lock turn. Britt didn't look anything like I'd imagined over the years. I expected to see a frail old man with a bad heart and a cane. Britt stood tall around six feet with hazel eyes and black hair. If he didn't tell me about his heart, I never would've guessed he suffered from a condition.

161

Good genes.

"You came?" He wrapped me up in a warm embrace. "I can't believe you're here."

"I've been out of town, so I got the letter today. If no one else knows how quickly life can change, it's us. I couldn't put this off. I've waited all my life to meet you." I kissed his cheek. "Where are my manners? This is my best friend, Iris."

"More like her sister," she corrected me. "It's nice to finally meet you."

"It's nice to meet you too. Get in here girls." He waved us inside. "This is your mother." He showed an oversized painting of a woman. I was practically looking in a mirror. A wave of sorrow coursed through my veins.

I walked up to the portrait to touch it. She wore a green dress, and her hair was wrapped up in a scarf with a few curls hanging long. She had a thin frame and a smile that made your soul feel good. Her eyes caught my soul and wouldn't let go.

"It's her. It's really her." I grabbed Iris by her arm.

"She's so beautiful. I'm so happy for you I could burst."

"We have so much to talk about." Britt touched my arm. "But first I want you to tell me about yourself. Are you married? Do you have children? I want to know everything about you."

"I'm not married, and I don't have any children. I've actually had a pretty hard time in the relationship department. I experienced domestic violence in college, and I almost died. It's been extremely hard to move on from that part of my life, but I've been dating an amazing man for eleven months. With him, I'm finally in a healthy relationship."

"I'm sorry you had to experience that. Was the guy in college your first boyfriend?"

"He was my first serious boyfriend."

"Nothing good will happen for that guy. People like him have demons and take it out on everyone else around them. Tell me about your current boyfriend? Does he treat you well?"

"He treats her like a princess," Iris interjected. "He simply adores her."

"Well that's good to hear. You deserve it after all you have endured." He took my hand. "Sweetheart, I want to talk frankly with you. I will be transparent and honest with you. I want you to tell me how you feel about me—the adoption and all."

"Mom and Dad told me the story of how I came into their lives. But part of me always wondered if you truly loved me as your child. Was I a burden that you couldn't stand to endure another day? Did you ever feel connected to me?"

"Oh sweetheart, my love for you is limitless. I was alone in this world before I met your mother. Then you came along. You two were my entire universe. But when your mom died, I did too. I lost my grip on life, and I knew I was no longer in the position to give you what you needed emotionally. But when I met Sheila and Thomas and learned what kind of people they were, I looked into your beautiful eyes and I knew what I needed to do. I had to give you more, and that's what I did. Now look at you, baby girl. You have a successful business with good people in your life." He smiled at Iris. "I'm so very proud of you."

"Why did you leave me and never come back to at least see me or get to know me?"

"I didn't want to confuse you. How would you have felt if I came around only to leave again?"

"You don't get it. I've been living with this God awful disease, and all I know is my dad gave me away as if I was baggage you needed to free yourself from."

His face twisted. "I don't blame you for having those feelings. It's only right." He gripped my hand. "Sweetheart, when you love someone as much as I loved your mother and everything suddenly changes, it's pretty damn hard to deal with. Yes, I may have made a horrible decision, but I know you could've been worse off being raised by a man full of anger and hatred. You deserve to have a life with two loving parents who don't live in fear of a disease every step of the way. They were able to give you a life of happiness and opportunities. They instilled wonderful values and encouraged you. I know all this because I made sure of this over the years. They gave you everything I couldn't. You will understand this when you have children."

I couldn't contain my emotions. They poured from my eyes. They made my entire body tremble. They took over my being. There was a profound love in his eyes. I could see it and feel it. I may not have bio children from my womb, but I could understand his position.

Sadly, it also made me understand Kai's position. "Thank you, I understand and I love you too."

We spent the night touring the house and the property. There was a garden dedicated to my mother's memory in the backyard. I sat alone in the dark, and after a while, I could feel her presence. And for a moment, I could feel her arms around me. I closed my eyes to be there with her in spirit.

The missing pieces of my soul had been found.

Chapter 22

Another month passed, and our days at the office grew easier since we'd finished our last huge event. Of course, you're only as good as your last event. So Tammy and I worked diligently to land another one by following Lorraine's presentation methods while she was out for a few hours for a doctor's appointment. I desperately wanted a fall-themed event because the colors were eye-catching.

Tammy rolled a yellow pencil between her fingers with her head propped on her balled fist. "Just think, in a few hours, you'll be off to vacation in New Bay with Mr. Perfect."

I pushed the pile of folders away. I'd been smiling like a maniac for a month now that Britt was in my life. When Kai surprised me with a romantic getaway to New Bay for the weekend, I turned into the joker with a permanent smile. If this was how we'd start the first weekend of November, I certainly was excited about it.

"Are you all packed and ready to go?"

"I've been packed for days," I giggled. "Kai stayed at my place last night and dropped me off at work this morning. When he picks me up, he'll have our luggage. We'll head straight to the airport."

"Why, oh, why couldn't it be me leaving you peasants behind for a weekend getaway with a sexy man like Kai?"

"Envy is an ugly trait." I pointed at Tammy. "Also, mustard is not your color."

"I'm going to ignore your insults and pay you a compliment instead. Your heels are sexy. I love them." She pointed at my turquoise embellished Indian heels.

New Bay is full of movers and shakers with thriving careers and extravagant lifestyles. It wasn't the type of city where you'd walk off the plane wearing a sweat suit and tennis shoes. I had to step my fashion game up for this one.

"Oh, you like these?" I strutted across the room with one hand on my hip to show them off. "Kai bought them. Actually, he bought me a new wardrobe for the weekend."

Tammy gasped and placed her hand over her chest. "I hate my life. I'm so jealous. Kai is a keeper."

"Jealousy is overrated. You never know what someone else is going through. Appreciate your life and do what makes you happy."

"You went pretty deep there. Do you want to talk about it?"

"Oh, no. Today is a happy day." I waved my hands with jazz fingers. "I'm perfectly fine."

"Okay. But for the record, I love my life. I have two intelligent, beautiful children. I own a third of an amazing business. I have my pick of delicious men to call at any given moment, and let's not forget this body of mine." Tammy ran her hands over her curves with a wiggle and a squeal. "You wouldn't know what to do with all of this." She smacked her butt.

"I'm slim in the waist and pretty in the face. Now sprinkle some salt on it, and eat your heart out." I blew her a kiss.

"You passed thin a month ago." Tammy shuffled a stack of papers.

"What did you say?"

"You've put on weight since you and Kai started dating exclusively. I guess that's how love looks on you."

"You must be blind. Love looks good on me, and Kai loves every inch of my body."

"Guess what I'll be doing next weekend." Tammy batted her eyelashes.

"How do you expect me to guess with a nut case like you? The possibilities are endless." I played with different hairstyles, pinning up one side with a few curls dangling.

"Do you really think I'm crazy?"

"You're a little cuckoo for Cocoa Puffs."

"Oh, how I'll miss your wisecracks while you're on vacation. But since you don't want to guess, I'll tell you. I'm hanging out with Iris Saturday night."

"Someone better alert the authorities." I teased. "What are you girls planning to do?"

"A new bar is having a grand opening on First Ave. She said she's on the prowl."

Lorraine marched inside the office with tears raining down her cheeks like silver lava.

"What happened?" Tammy dropped everything and ran to Lorraine's side.

"Did the doctor give you bad news?" I asked.

"I wished he gave me bad news. That man dropped a bomb on me. I can't even think straight," Lorraine cried.

"Well, what did he say?" I could hardly contain myself.

"I'm pregnant." Her face was etched with despair.

"Repeat yourself," I scowled.

"I hope for your sake it's not Michael's kid," Tammy shrieked.

Lorraine narrowed her eyes at Tammy. "I knew you'd go there."

"Where else would I go?" Tammy shrugged. "The man's got you stuck on stupid."

"It happened two months ago. He came over to talk about our relationship. Before I knew it, one thing led to another, and we were right back where we started." Lorraine clasped her hands in prayer. "I'm having mood swings. I feel run down all the time, and I'm always hungry. It doesn't matter how much I eat, it's never enough. Even still, pregnancy never crossed my mind. I can't believe this. Michael's flighty and self-absorbed. He can't keep his word to save his life. Now he's going to be the father of my child. Why is this happening to me?"

"That's the thing about sex. You could get pregnant." Tammy rolled her eyes.

"What are you going to do?" I asked.

"I don't know. I haven't had time to process it all."

Tammy sat on the edge of Lorraine's desk. "What does dear old Michael think about it?"

"I'll deal with that later. I need to get ready for my last presentation," Lorraine explained. "I hope you have a great getaway with Kai. Have enough fun for me. Looks like my weekend will be full of drama."

"How are sales looking this month?" Tammy asked. "I need to know how to plan my own trip."

"We're up twenty percent. We're on a roll." I danced in my seat.

"That is exactly why I can't let this interfere with me doing my job. This event is ours." Lorraine walked away with an armful of books, swatches, and gadgets to prepare her presentation.

Tammy grabbed the back of Lorraine's arm before she could walk away. "Could I ask you something?"

"What?"

"Does Michael have a huge penis? Does he know how to use his huge penis? Does he do sexual things to you that no man has ever done with his huge penis? Does he make you climax so hard you feel like you are having an out-of-body experience with his huge penis?"

"Why?"

Tammy shrugged. "I just want to know why he has such a hold on you."

"Wow, I've walked in at the worst possible moment." Kai blushed. He was dressed in a designer suit with his hair combed back to show off his chiseled cheekbones—per my request because they're so delicious.

"Hi, honey. Are you ready to go?" I greeted him with a kiss. His cologne soothed my nerves from the office drama. "I want you to meet my partners, Tammy and Lorraine. Ladies, this is Kai."

"Oh, wow. Pictures don't do you justice." Tammy circled him like a buzzard. She would have pulled out every trick in her bag for a date with Kai if he wasn't on my arm.

"It's great to finally meet you ladies." He gave them both a hug.

"Close your mouth, Tammy. You're drooling." Lorraine nudged her. "I hate to run, but I need to set up the conference room. I don't trust these two with my vision. It was great meeting you. Take care of our girl."

"Without a doubt," Kai replied with a nod.

"I'll see you gorgeous girls next week." I held Kai's arm tight. "You look great in that suit."

"You're gorgeous as always. Your hair looks good." He kissed my shoulder. "Tell me all about your day."

"It's just getting started." Kai helped me inside the car.

We rode to the airport hand in hand. Being back in the terminal reminded me of the first time we met. Now a year later, we were taking a trip together. Everything ran smoothly enough for our flight to take off on time. We slept the entire four hour flight so we could be refreshed by the time we arrived in New Bay.

Kai arranged for a black town car to pick us up at the airport and take us to the Starlight Majestic Hotel. We'd rented a presidential suite on the top floor. When the door opened, my nostrils filled with floral aromas. The room had a perfect array of homey hues, which allowed my calm self to relax and breathe.

"I have a lot of things planned for you this weekend. But first we're going to start with a little relaxation at the spa, so get changed into something comfortable. The spa is downstairs and the appointment is in less than an hour."

I took his hands in mine. "I am so thankful to have you in my life. You're thoughtful in everything you do for me—for us. I love you with all my heart. I hope this never ends."

"I was going to wait on our last night to do this, but I believe this is the perfect time." Kai dug inside his luggage and pulled out a small box. He knelt on one knee, and I almost fainted. "I've learned I need to take my time with you, so this is not a proposal but a promise." He opened the box to reveal an extravagant ring. It was silver and its intricate design complemented the delicate bones in my hand. "I promise my undying love to you. I will take care of you and provide for you. I will protect you from everyone and everything. And so you know, the next time I get down on one knee, I will be asking for your hand in marriage."

Chapter 23

Bright and early Monday morning, I waltzed inside the office after an amazing weekend with Kai, shaking the fringe on my brown ankle boots and juggling an armful of shopping bags. I'd bought a ton of gifts for Tammy and Lorraine in New Bay. We'd made a pact long ago that if one of us went on vacation, we'd return bearing gifts. I was eager to show them how much I'd upped the ante.

"I'm back, and I'm sexy," I fluffed my new hair. It smelled like bubble gum and it shined like diamond dust. Then I struck my best 1940s pin-up model pose.

"Look out. You cut your hair. I love it." Lorraine ran over to inspect my new look. "I love the color. The cut is amazing. It has a lot of bounce. I give it tens across the board."

"Looks like you enjoyed your sexy getaway." Tammy stood with pain filled eyes.

I danced across the room to my desk. "We had so much fun. We went to the spa when we arrived Friday and again on Sunday morning before we checked out. We drank margaritas on the rooftop under the stars. We danced on a floating barge and went kayaking downtown." I began to unpack the shopping bags. "Come, come, I have goodies."

I set out a long floral maxi dress and placed a short red mini dress with a plunging neckline beside it. I didn't need to tell the girls which dress belonged to them. They had distinctively different styles.

171

"Thank you, I love it. I'm wearing this on my date tonight." Tammy pranced around the room with the red dress draped over her.

"The black clutch and jewelry are yours, Tammy, and the nude clutch and gold jewelry are yours, Lorraine."

"You know me so well. I love it. Thank you."

"I'm happy you guys like it." I smiled and picked up a text from Kai.

My sweet Lyn with the ruby-red lips. I watch your beauty with intensity like a lunar eclipse. Your kind of love only comes around once in a lifetime. You're worth more than gold, and I would happily give you my soul. I will always be true to you because I was blessed when I found you.

I held the phone to my chest and squealed with a little wiggle.

Tammy pulled me into her arms out of nowhere.

"What's going on? You don't hug."

"I do now," Tammy replied. "We need to talk after you get settled in, but I'm all ears if you want to tell us about the hot love-making you and Kai had this weekend."

"I don't kiss and tell." I zipped my lips with a shrug.

"Oh, come on, Brooklyn. Make an exception for once. I want to know how the handsome Persian man measures up." Tammy leaned against the half wall near my desk and flipped through a gray address book with her glasses sitting on the tip of her nose.

"All I'll say is the sex wasn't dirty." I covered my face with my hands.

"Ooh, you guys made love. Now that's what I'm talking about." Tammy hugged me again and added a kiss on the cheek, which really freaked me out. "Let me know when you're ready to talk."

"This sounds serious."

"It is." Tammy's expression softened.

"Could you at least give me a hint about what it's about?"

"Why didn't you tell us what you've been going through?"

"What have I been going through?"

"We know everything, Brooklyn. Just be straight with us." Tammy pulled Lorraine over.

"I don't know what you're talking about."

"We love you," Lorraine said. "Nothing could ever change that."

"What are you talking about?"

Lorraine cried into a white napkin.

"What's going on with you two?"

"The guy you told us about in college, Adam, came to the office after you left Friday."

My breath evaporated, and I fell back into my chair. My eyes searched for a safe place somewhere far away from Tammy and Lorraine's judgmental stares, but there was no salvation.

"He told us you have Huntington's disease, Brooklyn." Tears rolled out of Tammy's eyes. "Why didn't you tell us?"

It finally happened. My secret sat front and center under a glaring spotlight. I couldn't lie anymore.

"We didn't know him well enough to take his word for it, so we asked Iris to come to the office. She tried to deny it, but she couldn't hide her emotions. Why didn't you tell us? We may be partners, but aren't we your friends too?"

"Of course, you're my friends. It's not what you think."

"Then explain why you never told us you've been living with Huntington's. We've known each other for seven years now." Tammy couldn't control her tears.

Lorraine released a howling cry and disappeared down the hallway.

"You look amazing, and I'm happy it hasn't affected your relationship with Kai." Tammy held my hand where a bold new icy ring sat. The diamonds wrapped around the band to a square stone. "Are you two engaged?"

"No, it's a promise ring." I pulled my hand away and tucked it inside my pocket.

"Do you think he'll pop the question soon?"

"I think so."

Tammy shook her head and grabbed a handful of papers. She pushed her glasses up to read aloud the things she printed about Huntington's. "This explains a lot. I know why you have facial tics, twitching limbs, and why your speech is slurred. I'm ashamed I never asked more questions."

"People don't see me anymore when they find out I have this God-awful disease. They only see a dying patient. I don't need pity. I can be normal around you, Lorraine, and Kai."

"So it's true, Kai doesn't know?" Tammy's eyes widened. "Kai is a good man. I don't want you to lose him over an omission of the truth."

"What do you mean 'it's true'? Who told you that?"

"Iris may have mentioned it."

"Oh, she did?" I sprang from my seat with my phone in hand. "I'll be right back."

"Hey, Brook-Brook, how are you?" Iris answered.

"Don't you 'hey, Brook-Brook' me. Why did you have to open your big mouth?"

"Damn, they didn't waste any time telling you. Let me explain. Tammy and Lorraine called me in a panic. By the time I got to the office, poor Lorraine was in a pool of tears and seconds away from hyperventilating. What was I supposed to do?"

"Keep your big mouth shut and tell them to talk to me."

"Technically, Adam told them."

"Yeah, but you verified it and told them I haven't told to Kai."

"Why is Adam still around? What's going on with that?"

"Don't try to change the subject."

"Explain to me why they didn't know. Tammy and Lorraine have been in your life for seven years. You consider them close friends as well as business partners. You're around them more than any of us."

"I've always respected your privacy. Why can't I get the same in return?"

"I only confirmed what they already knew," Iris explained. "Why are you hiding your true self from everyone? Kai included."

"I'm disappointed in you taking it upon yourself to confirm my reality. Do not rob me of the chance to tell Kai about the depths of this disease in my own time. I don't want to hurt him."

"Now I see why your panties are in a knot. You're afraid one of them will go to Kai. You can't be upset with me because I told the truth."

"It's my truth. Not yours."

"This is the thanks I get for caring."

"No, this is what you get when you overstep your boundaries. You're my best friend. We've been through the fire together. I don't want to throw our friendship away, but you're putting me in an impossible position. Things will change if you keep pushing boundaries." I bit my lip to keep from screaming. "I thought you of all people would protect me from Adam's vendetta." I ended the call and returned to my desk.

"Did you talk to Iris?"

"Tammy, please, back off. I don't need you to tell me how horrible a person I am for keeping this from Kai. I already know. I'll tell him when I figure out a way to say it without scaring the crap out of him."

"I don't think you're a horrible person. I'm worried about you. I want to know how you're doing." She wiped my tears away. "You're stronger than I ever realized. I applaud you for coming in here every day and never complaining. You work harder than the both of us put together."

"No one ever knows their true strength until they're in a situation that tests it. I received the official diagnosis at nineteen. Statistically, that means I have ten years before a major progression then it'll be curtains closed for me. All of you will be left with nothing but memories. I hope you'll cherish the love I have for you. This thing with

Kai came so suddenly, and my fears have controlled every move I make with him. I want to be one of the success stories who'll live over the age of sixty. But even then, I don't think that'll be enough time with Kai, so I'm begging both of you to keep this to yourselves. Don't say anything to Kai. Let me figure this out. I'm going to tell him." I walked over to put my arm around Lorraine.

"You have my word." She said in between sobs.

"Thank you, and please don't treat me any different. Don't ask me if I'm okay every five minutes. I don't want your pity, and I don't want you to worry."

"I have one more thing to say before you close the door on this conversation."

"What is it?"

"Maybe you should take a step back and reconsider how you're handling things with Kai. You should know where he stands once he knows all the details. Then you'll know for sure if he's the one for you."

"You can't see my dilemma."

"Explain what I'm missing," Tammy urged.

"I'm making the best out of a terrible situation. I'm not perfect. A diagnosis of Huntington's doesn't come with a manual. I don't know how or when to tell people. Kai's the first man I've been in a serious relationship with. I am beyond in love with him, but my love comes with fears. One of them is getting pregnant. I don't want to pass this awful disease to an innocent child. I'm doing my best to navigate through life and love with Kai the best I can."

Every part of my body quivered in pain. Still, I pulled myself together long enough to speak my peace.

"You two are my friends. You mean the world to me. I know Iris didn't mean any harm by telling you. The poor thing is so afraid of what can happen, she doesn't even realize she treats me like I'm five years old. She's gotten worse over the years. Loving me comes with worry."

"I haven't slept in days because I needed to look into your eyes." Lorraine touched the side of my face. "I needed to know you were okay. I know you hate it when people change once they know. Like it or not, people change. We can't fathom the thought of ever losing you. To know you is to love you."

"Over the past couple of days, I've prayed more than I have prayed for myself. Gosh, I just love you to pieces." Tammy hugged me again and squeezed me tight.

I touched my face where she kissed my cheek and exhaled, feeling a sense of freedom from my secret.

I needed a shield from Huntington's, which Tammy and Lorraine offered. Though I knew when the time came for Huntington's to take its course, it would break their hearts even more if they didn't know. I never wanted to cause that kind of pain for my loved ones.

"You have the power to make sure people don't worry about your health, and you're failing. You owe one person the truth more than any of us. You have to make it right." Tammy hugged me once more before returning to her desk. "We all love you and want the best for you. But you've got to love yourself as well.

Chapter 24

Kai and I drove to Britt's house to spend the weekend with him. I nervously straightened my shirt while we waited for him to answer the door. I'd left my condo a mess searching for my lucky emerald green mesh patchwork top. I paired it with my favorite denim jeans. Kai complimented my butt whenever I wore them.

Dad's embrace empowered my body, brain, and soul.

"Dad, this is Kai." I moved aside. "Kai, this is my bio dad, Britt Thornberg."

He stuck his hand out to greet Kai, but Kai embraced him instead. Dad gave me a wink over Kai's shoulder and welcomed us inside the cozy house. Kai made a huge production about the portrait of my birth mother that greeted us when we entered. I beamed with pride.

The smell of beef stew and cornbread floated throughout the house.

He asked all the fatherly questions. I sat in silence and munched on cheese and crackers. Kai could handle himself. Like he said, he knew how to win over parents.

When the conversation waned, I invited him to see my nursery, which Dad had left unchanged, and the mural my mother painted. I walked over to the painted wall and rested my hand on it as if I could feel my mother's heartbeat through her meticulous masterpiece. Perhaps that's what love felt like—a heartbeat, a constant reminder.

When I finally took my hand away from the mural, I turned to Kai and Dad. "My mother did this for me."

"Sheila said she died of Huntington's." Kai asked Britt. "What is that?"

"It attacks your brain, and people usually end up not being able to do simple things. In Eva's case, she could no longer walk, talk, or feed herself. I had to do it all. That's what scared me about raising Brooklyn on my own. I was so afraid I'd have to do it all over again. I couldn't have my heart broken twice."

Kai looked at me with worried eyes. "Did Brooklyn have it too?"

"I was too afraid to get her tested before I allowed Sheila and Thomas to adopt her."

"Oh, I understand." Kai held his head down. I could see the wheels turning, but he left the conversation there.

For the rest of the evening, we shared stories, laughter, and love. I sat in between Kai and Dad in perfect peace.

Chapter 25

It had been a week since Kai and I spent time with my bio dad. Work kept us pretty busy. The moment I walked inside Kai's house, he pinned me against the wall and kissed my stress away. I completely melted into him.

"Happy Friday," he whispered in between kisses.

"Amazing Friday," I moaned.

Kai led me through the house. My heels echoed in the foyer against the hardwood floor as we moved further inside.

"Why haven't we talked much since our weekend with your father?" He took my coat and purse.

I shrugged. Nothing I could say would adequately explain my absence.

"I need to show you something."

"What are you up to?"

We walked inside the den. Logs smelling of pine crackled in the fireplace. He'd covered the floor with rose petals and tea candles. A bottle of champagne chilled in an ice bucket next to a silver platter of chocolate covered strawberries.

"What is all this?"

"This is all for you." Kai walked over to a ficus tree. Small tags hung from each branch with a handwritten expression of his love and gratitude.

"What are you doing?" My body wavered like a boat gliding over troubled waters.

Kai knelt on one knee and took hold of my unsteady hands. "I love your smile, your laugh—everything about you from the crown of your head to the tip of your beautiful toes. I've even grown to love the bulging vein in your neck." He nervously laughed. "You love my son as if he's your own, and he loves you the same. No man will ever work harder at making you happier than me. I need you in my life forever. So, on this day, November 18, I want to ask you if you would please make me the happiest man in the world, and be my wife." He opened a small box that showcased a square diamond ring, sitting on top of a diamond band. "I told you the next time I did this, it would be a marriage proposal."

The truth bubbled in the pit of my stomach. My heart and rational thinking were at war. I widened my eyes at the sight of the perfect ring, a symbol of the happy future I'd wanted for so long.

"Please say you will be my wife, beautiful Brooklyn."

"This is unexpected."

"That's the thing about proposals. They're unexpected." Kai squared his shoulders but remained on bended knee.

"My heart is saying yes." I collapsed into his arms and slid on the ring. The fit was perfect.

"Would you look at that?" He kissed me deeply. His hand crept over my body to my shoulder. His fingers gently brushed my back as he unzipped my dress. "You." He kissed my shoulder. "Are." He kissed my back. "The." He kissed my lower back. "Best thing to ever happen to me."

I threw my head back totally immersed in his very essence. Kai's spicy cologne awakened my senses. He swirled his tongue around mine, which made me crumble. I was under his control. Not that I minded one bit. At that point, he could have made any demand, and I would have been all in.

We rolled around the great room amidst the rose petals. They stuck to the crevices of our naked bodies as we wove ourselves together. We were made for each other. He'd become a necessity for me like air and water. I had no worries, no focus, no thoughts, only desire.

After an hour of making our engagement official, I redressed and joined Kai by the lighted ficus tree. He untied a silver ribbon and removed one of the tags. "You make me feel like I'm good enough for you," he read. "You're a successful businesswoman who knows how to turn it off and be delicate with me." He plucked another tag. "I love how we're able to disagree without distress. The circumstances don't matter. We're always respectful to each other."

His heartfelt words were enthralling. I was all ears as he read another.

"I love your honesty and how I've never felt the need to question your motives."

"I don't know how I got so lucky."

"No, I'm the lucky one. You haven't been open to love. But if you let me in, I'll spend the rest of my life showing you how grateful I am to you."

"Could I?" I pointed at the silver platter of poached shrimp and oysters.

"Sure, you can read the rest of these anytime." He dipped a shrimp in the red cocktail sauce and fed it to me. "I love you."

"I love you too. I hope your love for me won't change."

He stroked my cheek with the tip of his nose. Then his lips went on a tour around my bare shoulder, and he slid his arms around my waist to draw me to him.

"When I was a little girl, I dreamed about this moment. I also dreamed about having children. Then, things changed," I sighed, crawling to my purse to check the message chiming on my phone. It was Adam. He had a sick way of knowing whenever I was happy so he could ruin it.

"I feel horrible about this, but I need to go. Something important has come up. Please don't hate me for leaving right now."

"We're celebrating our engagement. I have strawberries and champagne. What could be more important than this moment?"

I kissed him goodbye, gathered my things, and ran into the cold dark night. Though the cold didn't matter much after the message I'd gotten from Adam.

"If you want me to beg, I'll get on my knees. Don't leave."

"I'm sorry. I'll be back in just a few hours, and you'll have me for the rest of the night. I love you."

I hurried to my car and sped down the driveway, forsaking our special night thanks to Adam.

Chapter 26

My blood boiled. The moment I've dreamed about all my life finally happened and Adam threatened to come to Kai's door. I drove away from Kai's house like a bat out of hell to put as much distance as I could before Adam did something stupid, like ringing the doorbell to expose all my flaws.

He flashed his lights in my rearview mirror. I should drive him to the police station, but this harassment would never end. He inched closer and closer to the back of my car until I finally pulled over into a desolate parking lot.

He walked up with a devious grin. "Glad you knew I was serious."

"For the last time, NO." I yelled at the top of my lungs.

"You can either work with me, or I'll make your life a living hell until you hear me out."

"It's always 'I, I, I' with you. News flash, the world doesn't revolve around you."

"Follow me to my hotel."

"Have you lost your mind? I'm not going to a hotel with you."

"I know you miss me, but get your mind out of the gutter. I'm not trying to have sex with you. I want you to see why this is important to me."

"I don't trust you."

"Please. After tonight, I'll leave you alone for good."

I sat in silence for a moment. This could go on for months, but there is no guarantee he'll keep his word. Adam wasn't exactly trustworthy. Still, what else did I have to lose?

"After tonight, I don't ever want to hear from you or see you again."

"Keep your cellphone on, so I can direct you to the hotel."

"I swear I will call the police if you don't keep your word."

"You've changed. You were the first person I could always come to with a problem."

"Your desperation doesn't give you the right to blow up my life or my fiancé's life."

"When did you get engaged? You weren't wearing a ring in Pinemoor." Adam's eyes twinkled as if he'd put two and two together.

"Details aren't necessary."

"Follow me. You'll need to take the exit onto Northwest H Street. We're going to the Sunset Legacy Hotel." He stepped away from my window and retreated to his car. "Your fiancé must be an amazing man to marry a woman in your condition."

"My condition?" I shouted out the window. "You need my help. Insulting me won't get you anywhere."

"I meant to say he's a good man to marry you when death is knocking on your door."

"The only time death knocked on my door is when you tried to kill me. Now, you're begging me for help. Go figure."

Against my better judgment, I followed him to the hotel. I whipped my car into the parking space next to him, and he raced over to open my door.

"Get away from my car," I demanded.

"Okay. You don't have to have a bitch-fit." He backed away. "We're going to the fifth floor."

I stood far away from Adam in the small elevator with my arms crossed over my chest. Every few seconds, I gave him a critical stare.

Each time, more bitter contempt spread through my body.

He opened the door to reveal two little girls playing on the floor and a petite woman lounging on the sofa with her nose buried in a book.

"Brooklyn, this is my wife, Adara. These two beautiful girls are our daughters, Darcy and Regan. You met them in Pinemoor."

"I didn't meet them. You hurried them off before that could happen. This is what's supposed to make me change my mind? I'm out of here."

Adam raced ahead of me to block the door. "They are my family. I know you don't care about them, but I do. I need you to get on board with this documentary." He turned to Adara. "You and the girls need to go to the other room and close the door." The statement was more demand than request, and Adara's only response was to smile with what looked like thinly veiled contempt.

"I've been dealing with cirrhosis of the liver for four years. My health has gotten worse, which means football is in jeopardy. Without it, I have no source of income. My medical bills alone are siphoning my savings. All you need to do is tell your side of the story."

"The one thing I wanted from you that I never got was an apology, but I don't need it now. Besides, people will only see me as the stupid girl who let her boyfriend abuse her for over a year and didn't have the good sense to leave him until he almost killed her. I'm embarrassed for myself. I don't need the world to judge me."

Adara inched next to me and put her hand on my shoulder. "Please, help us. We need you."

I pulled away. "Do you see this ring?" I held my hand so close to her face that if I moved one more inch I could've scratched her cornea.

"It's a beautiful ring."

"My boyfriend proposed to me tonight."

"Congratulations…"

"No, I should be in his arms right now. I've waited a long time for this moment, and I never thought I'd ever experience it." My voice began to shake. "Do you want to know why?"

"Why?"

"I met your jerk husband freshman year at Pinemoor State. He was the 'it' guy on campus. I never thought in a million years he'd give me the time of day, but he did. My inexperience never crossed my mind." I paced the room with my hands on my hips. "I fell madly in love with him. Talk about clueless. We dated for two years. We were perfect in my naïve mind. One night, while I studied for finals, he came to my dorm begging for my attention. When I didn't give it to him, I ended up in the ICU. I was there for six months because of him and he never even bothered to call to check on me. He went on with his life as if nothing ever happened. Adam never took responsibility for what he did. Now I have a great life, and I won't jeopardize it for anyone, especially him. I know you need to take care of your children, but I don't care. I'm not helping him."

Adam's face changed to an evil expression. He marched toward me waving his arms. "I'm sorry for what I did to you. We were stupid kids back then. I treated you like that because I hated myself. I'm sorry for making you feel unworthy. You've always been an exceptional woman."

"I can't believe you. I'm your wife, and you've never apologized for the pain you've caused me." Adara ushered the girls into the other room and slammed the door behind her.

"What are you talking about?"

"When we met, it never took much for you to lose control." Adara unzipped the back of her dress and pointed to her scars, ones that matched mine. "He did this when I forgot to pick up his suit from the cleaners. He went ballistic and gave me a traumatic brain injury. My vision is still fuzzy. My energy plummets at the drop of a dime, and it's difficult for me to take care of the girls most days. Those things are only the tip of the iceberg. I won't even go into the mental anguish. I'm only staying in this marriage for the sake of my girls. For some odd reason, they love you, but I'm probably doing them more harm than good."

Adam wiped a film of sweat from his face. "It doesn't matter what I do. You bitches always bring up my past. I made mistakes. I'm human, damn it. We all make mistakes. I'm sorry," he screamed. "Do you hear me? I'm fucking sorry."

"You should be focusing on your marriage instead of harassing me about some low-budget biography," I said.

"You've always been jealous of me. I was a damn star. You were nothing."

"You're pathetic."

"You're so quick to play the victim, but you never admit the part you played. You pushed me to do those things to you," Adam explained.

"Thank you for showing me what I already knew. You're not sorry for anything."

Adara marched back toward us. She reached out to me. "You deserve to witness this." She held a chrome gun.

"That's my girl," Adam cheered her on. "You're going to sign the papers."

"Wh—what are you doing?" I asked.

"I don't want to hurt you, Brooklyn." Adara pointed the gun at Adam. "I want you to stay for the show. It's vindication time."

"What the hell, Adara? I've been doing all this for you." He looked askance at her.

I grabbed her shoulders and stared into her eyes. "I don't blame you for being upset. Adam's a vile demon, but he's not worth all this."

"He'll hurt me again. He won't change. It's him or me. And for the first time, I chose me. I don't see any other way out of this."

"You have two beautiful daughters who need you. Don't waste your life on him. He's not worth it. I have a business. You could work with us, and I'll make sure you and your daughters are okay. Please put the gun down."

"No, he's going to pay for all the pain he's caused."

"So you two are best friends now. Do you want to braid each other's hair?" Adam teased.

"Tell her the truth," Adara demanded.

"Shut up, Adara."

"Tell her." She put her finger on the trigger.

"Okay, okay, fine," Adam said. "I'm not sick. I just told you that to get you to sign the papers. I'm about to get cut from the team."

"I knew it. You piece of shit," I shrieked.

"Neither of you stupid bitches have a damn clue, especially you." Adam raised his fist in the air and charged toward Adara.

The pair struggled in a tangle of limbs, and the gun clattered to the floor. I grabbed the weapon and fired until Adam fell to the ground. I stood over him with the smoking gun aimed at his chest in case he moved again.

Just like that, Adara and I took our revenge. Adam laid in his own wicked blood. It ran like a red river over the tan carpet. He cradled his stomach with his hands to staunch the bleeding. And for a moment, we locked eyes until his gaze went still and his arms fell to his side.

Adara grabbed me by the lapels of my leather jacket, and I snapped back into reality. "Get out of here now."

"No, I-I can't let you take the blame for what I've done."

"We don't have time to play the blame game. People will be at the door any second. Go right now. I'll take care of this," she ordered. "When you leave, walk, don't run. Don't bring unwanted attention to yourself. Talk on the phone if it helps you look normal."

I reluctantly did as Adara said. There were no sirens. No one ran around the hotel in panic. There were no bells or whistles by the time I made it to my car. I stood in the parking lot and clutched my spinning head. All the emotions bubbling in my stomach came up to my throat and out onto the asphalt parking lot.

All I'd wanted was for him to leave me alone.

Relief and regret remained at the pit of my gut. I shouldn't have crossed the line, but who knows what would have happened if I hadn't.

Chapter 27

Six months ago, I found the Retro Bride Boutique while searching for the perfect wedding dress. It was a cute little place tucked away in the corner of a busy shopping district on the outskirts of town. I was told brides traveled from miles around to shop at the one-of-a-kind bridal shop. The owner, Mrs. Whetzel, prided herself on the unique vintage style wedding dresses.

"When is the wedding again?"

"Next month on June 25," I replied. "I'm such a backward bride. Most women buy their dress first, but it's the last thing on my list." I scribbled my signature on the check and passed it to the perky clerk. I'd frequented the shop for months in search of the perfect dress. When I found my gown, it made my heart do summersaults.

Swarovski crystals covered the off-white gown. The long cathedral train would surely give me the dramatic silhouette I'd dreamed about since I was a little girl. The V-cut draped down to my lower back, and a large satin bow pulled it all together. When I had my final fitting, Mrs. Whetzel clutched her pearls. I couldn't stop staring at myself in the mirror.

I couldn't believe it. I was a bride.

My father, Thomas, had opened a bank account to cover our wedding expenses. He told me to go wild, and I didn't hold back. It was going to be an evening none of the guests would forget.

"Mom, if you keep crying you won't have any tears left for the wedding day."

"I'm happy for you." Mom tweaked my nose. "And don't you worry, I'll be inconsolable on your wedding day. If you want, I'll throw myself on the floor and cry."

We shared a laugh. "You know, Mom, I didn't think I'd ever get married. Kai came out of nowhere. It's really hard for me to wrap my head around all this."

"He's a wonderful man, but you better not forget you're equally amazing." Mom kissed my cheek. She then quickly switched to a poker face. Her tears even dried up in a matter of seconds. "We need to talk."

"Is this going to take long? I need to finish the seating arrangements, and I still haven't listened to the playlist Kai emailed."

"It depends on how you answer my questions." Mom led me to a park across the street from the shop. We sat on a bench near where children played and fitness junkies jogged by every few seconds. I studied the worn piece of paper where I'd drawn seating arrangements for the wedding reception.

"Put that away. How's Britt doing?"

"He's okay. His heart surgery is coming up in the next couple of weeks."

"You did a selfless deed. I'm so proud of you." Mom took a deep breath. "You could've kept all the money for yourself, but you did your research and found the doctor he needed to help him."

"Thanks, Mom. I needed us to have more time together. I really enjoy spending time with him."

"Britt is a good man. It wasn't easy for him to let you go, but he did what he thought was best for you to have a well-rounded life." She drummed her finger against her thighs. "Now let's get down to business."

"Okay."

"I want to know what's going on between you and Iris."

"I don't want to talk about her."

"I've been running around with you for the last six months planning your wedding, and Iris hasn't been with us once. There's no way she'd miss any of this, so what is it?"

"Let it go, Mom."

"I'm not budging until you spit it out."

I glanced at my watch then at my stubborn mother. She wasn't lying. She had no intentions of budging without hearing the truth. So that's what I gave her.

"Iris gossiped about me to my partners. She crossed a line, so I haven't been speaking to her. We need some time apart."

"Iris wouldn't do that. Tell me exactly what was said."

"Mom, please don't blow your top, but I haven't fully explained to Kai the depth of what he's getting into with Huntington's." I looked up to the sky at a plane flying overhead and wished I was on it. "Iris told my partners about the disease and blabbed about me holding the truth from Kai."

Mom clutched her stomach like she was going to be sick. "What are you thinking?"

"I'm thinking about love. I'm thinking about marriage. I'm thinking about becoming a mother. I'm thinking about spending the rest of my life with the man I love. I'm no different from any of you. I deserve it too, and I refuse to allow Huntington's to take it away from me."

A little girl abandoned her shovel in the sandbox and ran into her mother's arms after my outburst.

"Show some respect, and lower your voice," Mom demanded. "Kai still doesn't have a clue what he's getting into?"

I took a deep breath and melted inward. "I don't know what I was thinking. Everything moved so fast."

"So you want the man, but you don't want to do what it takes to build a foundation with him." She shook her head. "The wedding is a month away. You need to make this right, preferably tonight."

"What if he calls the wedding off? We've already sent invitations out."

"Do you remember when you were finding your legs after the doctor diagnosed you with Huntington's? The first thing you said was your life was over." She held my hand. "But you figured it out. You started a successful business, bought a lovely home, and made some great friends. If Kai decides he doesn't want to get married, you will continue to do amazing things. Men are complementary to our lives. They don't define us."

She walked me to my car in silence. The short walk was torture. I could hardly breathe. Kai was the one, but why couldn't I tell him? Because the truth may be the proverbial nail in our coffin.

"I'll tell him the whole story tonight." I climbed into my vehicle.

"Bring him over. You can tell him at the house with us."

"I don't need an audience if I end up with egg on my face."

"How have you been able to keep this secret for so long?"

"You're asking a question whose answer you will never fathom. You should be happy I'm adopted. If I were your biological child, either you or Dad would have this God-awful disease. Respectfully Mom, please don't judge what you don't understand." I started the Mercedes's engine.

"I'll leave you with this," she cleared her throat. "I knew you were my baby girl the moment I held you in my arms. You'll always be my sweet little angel. We may not understand what you're going through, but we will always be in your corner. We will always root for you. I love you, honey."

I drove off into the setting sun. It's colorful hues reminded me of the first picture Kai and I took by the ocean. I'd lived long enough to know we shared the kind of connection that could never be replicated. What should have been a beautiful memory morphed into mild panic. Would we ever be happy again after he knew my secret?

Chapter 28

I lounged on the sofa massaging my temples, attempting to soothe my pounding head while pondering over the choices I'd made. I'd promised my mom I'd tell Kai the whole truth a week ago, but I was a prisoner to my fears. I may as well have shackles on my ankles in a dark abyss of nowhere.

Add to that, I felt like a fugitive buying time after shooting Adam. Sure, he wasn't a good person, but who was I to play God with his life? It didn't make me any better than him. I didn't gain any peace from it. So if the police threw me in a cell, it all would've been for nothing. Thankfully he survived, and hopefully it changed him for the better.

I stayed in contact with Adara and persuaded her to move here permanently with the girls. We set her up with a full-time job with Three Angels Events. It was the least I could do after the mess I made that horrible night.

The ringing phone interrupted my thoughts. "Why do you keep calling me, Iris?"

"Why are you avoiding me?"

"I'm not avoiding you. I wasn't ready to talk to you. What do you want?"

"I don't want anything. I've been worried about you. How are you doing?"

"Do you give your son the amount of attention you give me?"

195

"You're only upset because you know you were wrong."

"No, I'm upset because you stuck a knife in my back."

"I didn't realize you'd take it like that, and I apologize for breaking your trust. I was in a tough position, and I wasn't going to call you with that on your weekend getaway. I'm human, Brook-Brook. You have to know I'd never do anything to intentionally hurt you. I love you," Iris explained. "When are you coming over to spend some time with your godson?"

"I'll come by soon. It's not like I'll have any other plans."

"I talked to your mom. You've been planning your wedding without me. Why? We're sisters."

"I didn't think you'd want to hang out with a heartless liar."

"I should be able to tell you when you're messing up without being punished for it."

"I should be able to respond to the hurt you caused in any way I need."

"I see you still need a little time. Please call me when you're ready to let me back into your life. I will be here." She sighed and hung up.

Honestly, the drama with Iris was small peanuts at this point. I needed to talk to Kai, and I knew the perfect person to call. Britt. He lived it. He felt every emotion that came with the discovery of Huntington's invading his life. Now that my future was hanging in the balance, I needed to know how to face this without bringing my house of cards down.

Chapter 29

Later that night, I wandered inside the small bar where we had our girl's night. People stood shoulder to shoulder in the cramped space, schmoozing and making business connections.

"Hello there, pretty lady. Pick your poison." The bartender set a bowl of mixed nuts in front of me.

"What's the Bridesmaid drink?"

"Ah, that's a good one. It's my specialty for the week. It has raspberry vodka, peach schnapps, a little lime juice, pineapple juice, cranberry juice, and cherry juice. It's juiced out. Want to give it a try?"

"The name's ironically befitting. Lay it on me."

A slender man eased next to me with his hand stuck out. His heavy cologne overpowered the cigarette smoke and booze. He wore a gaudy silver and black shirt. He'd left it unbuttoned to show off his bird chest. "Hello, how are you?"

"Oh, I've seen you here before. I was with my friends having a girl's night and you winked at me after you'd already talked to about five other women."

"That was you," he snapped. "Please, allow me to start over. My name is Tony. What's yours?"

"Brooklyn. Now go away."

"Do you come here often?"

"Wow." I cringed. "That's wildly original."

Tony had the kind of laugh that sounded like nails on a chalkboard—a type of laugh that reeked of arrogance. It made my skin crawl.

"I can tell you have a lot on your mind. Lay it on me." Tony clapped his hands.

I looked him over again. It was even worse the second time. "Yeah, I don't think so."

"Okay, fine. We don't need to talk. Give me an hour, and I can put a smile on your face that'll last for weeks."

"Wow." I touched his shoulder. "You could use a good kick in the butt."

"Are you going to do it?" Tony asked. "Give me your best shot."

"Tell me my last name."

He shrugged.

"Tell me one thing you know about me."

"Your name is Brooklyn."

I downed the last of my drink and set a few dollars on the bar to tip the bartender. "You only know my first name. Yet, you asked me to share the most precious part of myself with you. Something a person should only share with a connected soul. You're barking up the wrong tree." I touched the side of his face. "I've made my decision. It's high time I start living in my truth. I'm going to start with you because you need a wakeup call," I explained. "I have Huntington's. In the blink of an eye, my life could change. I wished my life wasn't so complicated. So, the last thing on my mind is sex with a player wearing cheap shoes and an entire bottle of funky cologne." Everything spilled out of me. I'd finally reached my limit.

"Hey, wait." Tony ran after me, waving his hands.

"What?" I asked. "What do you want?"

"Could we at least have a conversation?"

"What do we need to have a conversation about?"

"I spent years researching Huntington's disease after the only woman I ever loved died from it. Her name was Diane Richards. She was the funniest woman I'd ever known. We were a couple years out of college when she died. Since then, I've done extensive research on Huntington's to try to understand, but the pieces aren't coming together all the way. How do you feel daily? How does it affect your life? I want to know everything."

"I'm sorry you went through that but this isn't a Q&A session." I climbed into my car and started the engine. "I need to go."

Tony tossed his business card through the small opening of my open window. It landed on my lap, and the first thing I noticed was his title as a TV producer.

"Please call me. We should talk."

"I don't think so. Have a good night." Luckily, I was saved from further conversation by the sound of my phone. "Hello?"

"Hi, sweetheart, how are you?" Kai asked.

"Better, now that I hear your voice."

"How was your day?"

"I picked up my wedding dress. It's in the backseat as we speak."

"Oh man, I'll bet it looks sexy on you," Kai gasped. "I can't wait to see you walk down the aisle to become Mrs. Brooklyn Rahimi."

"I hope you won't be disappointed."

"You're a beautiful doll. You could never disappoint me."

Despite my inner turmoil, I managed to create a deep connection with Kai. The thought of soon telling him my horrible secret caused me great pain, but it had to be done. Everyone was right. A marriage built on secrets and lies would never survive.

"Do you tend to hold grudges?" I asked.

"I guess it depends on the situation."

"Elaborate."

"It depends on how much the person means to me. With you, I'd try my best to work through any issue," he paused. "Forget the hypothetical talk. Is there something you need to tell me?"

"You're my prince charming. I'll always love you for giving me everything I've ever wanted in a man."

"Why does it sound like you're breaking up with me?"

"No. There's something I should've told you the first day we met, and I need to tell you before we get married."

"If this is about your past, leave it there. Horrible things happened. Now it's time to move on to better days." He sucked his teeth. "You know, I don't understand why you won't allow yourself to fully commit to our relationship. I can't keep ignoring it anymore. Our marriage won't survive if you keep doing this."

"Please don't give up on me. It'll all make sense when we talk face to face."

"Something in my heart is telling me we should wait."

"Fine, consider it done. The wedding is on pause." I threw my phone in the passenger seat and wiped the tears from my eyes. They were coming so fast. I couldn't keep up. I massaged my chest to ease the burning pain shooting through my aching heart.

A ring echoed from the passenger seat. I answered it in a panic. "Kai?"

"No, it's your Dad, Britt. I wanted to let you know my heart surgery is next week. So, put it in your calendar."

I'd offered to take care of him so I could hear more stories about him and my mother. But now, with the tension between me and Kai, all I wanted to do was curl up in a cocoon and sleep my troubles away.

Both of us needed a new heart because mine was broken.

Chapter 30

I drove home from the bar in a blur. My emotions were running high, and I needed to be alone before I did more damage. I changed into a comfy pair of pajamas, grabbed a box of Kleenex, and stretched out on the sofa to stare out into the starry sky.

"Why can't I just say it? Why can't I just tell him?" I blew my nose then smothered my face with the tan sofa pillow for only a moment when my front door opened. It was locked, so I already knew the uninvited visitor.

"What do you want, Iris?"

"What the hell is going on with you?" She stood over me with her hands on her hip. "You won't answer your phone and people are worried about you." She flipped on the lights.

"I'm fine. The wedding is off. I'm sure that makes you happy. You've been against my relationship with Kai since the beginning."

"You know I love you. It doesn't make me happy to see you in pain. Why is the wedding off?" She sat down, swinging her keys around her finger.

"Adam was right. No man wants to be with a dying woman, and they sure as hell don't want to marry them."

"Oh, you really have lost it if you agree with the asinine things that come out of Adam's mouth." She sat next to me. "Does that mean you told Kai you have Huntington's?"

"There was no point. I knew he'd leave when he found out anyway."

"Please don't tell me you called off the wedding without first discussing it with Kai. You overreact all the time, but this time you've gone too far."

"Technically Kai said we should wait."

"I don't know what to say to you anymore." Iris put her face in her hands. "This shit isn't funny anymore."

"It doesn't matter. It's over now."

"I have to be honest with you," Iris said. "Kai may be on his way over here." She ran her fingers through my bed hair, tugging at knots along the way. "Is this why you haven't gone to work in a week?"

"How do you know I haven't been to work?"

"Tammy and Lorraine called. They were worried about you."

"Why do you keep doing this? You won't stop talking about me when I'm not around."

"Nobody's talking about you. You should be more focused on why you're sabotaging your life. Yes, you have Huntington's disease. No, it's not the end of the world. You have so much to give. I wish you could see that."

The doorbell interrupted our come-to-Jesus moment.

"That's Kai," Iris said. "I wasn't sure you'd let me in."

"Brooklyn, open the door." Kai knocked.

"What am I supposed to say to him? I don't want to see him."

"Listen to me." Iris grabbed my shoulders. "You are an amazing person. You have a huge heart. You're a damn catch. He should feel proud to have you as his better half. Tell him the truth. It's beyond time." She pushed me toward the door and walked away to my bedroom.

I opened the door and welcomed Kai inside. His eyes were red and worried.

"Hi sweetheart, Iris asked me to come over to check on you. What is going on?"

I held Kai's hand and asked him to take a seat. "There is something very important we need to talk about."

"I'm listening."

"You know my mother died from Huntington's disease. You've heard how my father had to take care of her during her last days. Well," I inhaled deeply and clutched my stomach. "I have Huntington's too."

He reached out to pull me close to him and rested the side of his face on my belly. "Why has it taken you so long to tell me?"

"I was afraid. I didn't want to lose you." I bent over to hug him.

"When were you going to tell me? Were you going to wait until after we were married? You know everything about me."

"I wanted you to get to know me first, but things moved so fast. The next thing I knew, we're in love. Then we got engaged and started planning our wedding and life together. I got lost in it all. I was wrong, and I apologize. I never meant to blindside you with this."

"Wait, hold on," he stammered. "This is the same thing your mother had? You said it was neurological, right?" This is serious. You should've at least told me when we began dating."

"I know, I know. I was wrong. I hate myself for keeping it from you. Please forgive me." I buried my face in my trembling hands.

"How could you keep this from me?" His voice broke with every word.

The table had turned. Now Kai couldn't make eye contact with me.

"I apologize for keeping this from you. I was wrong. It's the most selfish thing I've ever done. I never intended to hurt you. I was experiencing and feeling things I never have before." This time I lifted his face the way he usually lifted mine. "We were this thing overnight, and you became a permanent fixture in my life. I fell hopelessly in love with you. I just wanted the chance of having something with you without the fear of my disease looming over us like a gray cloud."

"I understand all that, but you should have told me. I could've had the chance to make sense of it all. This is too much at one time. You're my best friend—the love of my life. How am I supposed to handle seeing you the way your dad did with your mother? That scares the hell out of me." Grief poured out of him in an uncontrollable flood of tears and angry sobs.

"I operated out of fear, but now I know that wasn't fair to you. No matter how afraid I was of losing you, I should have told you the truth. I take full responsibility for not telling you the truth. I will never keep anything from you going forward. I will be completely honest no matter what fears loom in the back of my mind. I desperately want to marry you. Please tell me you still want to marry me."

Iris poked her head around the corner. I narrowed my eyes hoping she'd get the hint to retreat.

"To love someone beyond boundaries comes with fears." Kai squeezed my hand. "I fear losing you. Now, that probability is extremely high, and I'll be honest, it terrifies the hell out of me. I don't know if I'm strong enough to be the man you will need when that time comes. You are a beautiful person inside and out. You deserve to have a mate who could rise to the occasion when you need them most."

"Death is the only certain thing about life. No one is exempt. You promised to love me no matter what. You said we could work through anything. Please don't give up on us."

Kai pulled me into his arms. His tears saturated my messy bed hair. "That's the problem, beautiful Brooklyn. I don't know what to do right now. I need time to think."

He held me tighter as if he were trying to keep me from drifting away. By this time, Iris had made her way back inside the living room and sat in a chair by the doorway. She tried her best to hide her tears with no luck.

"Please understand it wasn't easy keeping this from you. It killed me." I kissed his hand. "You're my carpe diem. I saw a future with you the moment we took that picture by the beach. I thought if you got to know me it would lessen the blow of my disease. Huntington's is frightening on its own. But sweetheart, don't toss me aside as if I never mattered. You've asked me to lower my wall. Well, here I am, totally naked. Am I not good enough for you now?"

"Of course, you're good enough." Kai drew his lower lip between his teeth. "But I can't watch you wither away. It would be selfish of me to enjoy this part of you and not be there for you when you need me the most."

"You promised, Kai. You promised."

"I know I did, and I'm sorry, my love. I just need time to think about everything."

"Don't call me 'my love' if you don't love me."

"Please don't do that. I love you with all my heart." He kissed my hands. "When my father died, I barely survived it. I'm used to your laugh, your smile, your sweet voice, and your touch. I don't want you out of my life, but I need time to take this all in, and I believe I've earned the right to have that time."

I slid the diamond ring off and placed it in Kai's unsteady hand. "Give this back to me when you come back. If you don't, then I don't want it."

"I'm not taking the ring back."

"Please, I can't look at it. My heart will continue to ache until you come back. If you don't, I don't know how I will handle that." I held the side of his face. "You're amazing—everything I've ever wanted. Could you do something for me?"

"Whatever you need?" His eyebrows shot up.

"A love like ours only comes once in a lifetime. Please make sure you really think about what you could be giving up."

"I will." He kissed my forehead and marched out the door, taking his heart with him.

I wandered out onto the balcony and gazed at the dark sky. "I'm not suicidal, Iris. I won't jump."

"Your words, not mine. I'm only here for emotional support." She eased beside me. "I'm proud of you for expressing your feelings. That's something you've never done before."

"Where did it get me? I'm alone again."

"You're not alone. You've got me. We're the Dynamic Duo. Always."

"This is my biggest screw up in life. I should've listened to you and told him when we first met."

"Maybe he's the launching pad to your next great love."

"We only get one great love, and I blew it."

"How do you know we only get one great love?"

I turned my back to the dark sky and leaned against the silver rail. My shoulders hung lower than my spirits. "I've survived twelve years with Huntington's. You'd think I'd have a handle on it by now, but I'm in the same sad state, feeling sorry for myself. What the hell am I going to do without Kai?"

"Your presence brings joy to everyone you encounter. Kai doesn't define you, and your happiness doesn't end with him. Love will find you again when you least expect it. I've seen you grow since college whether you know it or not. You're assertive, successful, and people can count on you. Either you'll deal with this, or you'll allow it to break you."

"I don't want to hear your motivational speeches right now. I may as well gain weight, get a cat, and let the hair grow where it wants."

"You said you wanted to experience love. It's not all rainbows and blue skies. I mean, I know you live in the clouds." She stretched her arms out. "But when the heart is involved, you'll have some pains. You've dated, kissed, made love, and got engaged. You did it all, my friend. You're living. Can't you see that?"

"I did live, didn't I?" I leaned over the side of the rail and let out a loud howl. Not that I'd ever admit it, but Iris often gave great pep talks. Even though excruciating pains shot throughout my body, I couldn't help but celebrate my evolution. "I even had the chance to experience motherhood with Dylan. That little guy opened his heart to me. I've experienced earth-shaking romance. Kai knew how to make me feel like a woman. I was his one and only. Oh baby, I lived."

"There, you see," Iris said. "This is only the beginning. Mark my words."

"I can't believe it's over." Pain coursed through my body.

"It's not over yet. He will be back once he has time to sit with it. Give it time."

"I used Kai as an outlet. He's an extraordinary man who pulled me out of my darkness. I'll never forget the way he muscled himself into my life at the airport," I laughed. "I hate myself for hurting him, but I needed to know how it felt to be loved." I walked Iris to the front door with my arm draped over her shoulder. "It's the best feeling in the world."

"I'm here for you whenever you need me. I'll even come over with a bucket of ice cream and unwanted advice at a moment's notice. I've got you, girl."

"Maybe I'll call Kai in a few days to talk after the shock wears off. And maybe, I could convince him to come over. I know it's a shot in the dark, but I can hope, can't I?"

"There's nothing wrong with hope. You're in love with him."

My arm jerked so hard I inadvertently slammed the door shut. "Oh, crap."

"How long has that been happening?"

"About two weeks."

Iris leaned against the wall with heavy breaths. "Don't do this to me. My heart can't take it anymore."

"I'm okay." I braced my hands on Iris's shoulders. "I owe you an apology. You were right to tell Tammy and Lorraine I have Huntington's. I should've told them when we first went into business. That was totally irresponsible of me. I had no right to push you away."

"You're my sister. Even when you push, I won't go too far for too long. I'll be by your side until it's not physically possible. You have my word."

"You're a constant person in my life, and I love you very much."

"Get some sleep. I'll come by in the morning with breakfast. I love you too."

After we hugged goodbye, I watched Iris walk to the elevator and thought about the first time we met at Pinemoor State.

I was sitting alone on a bench eating an apple underneath two trees. I imagine I looked like I hadn't slept in days. Iris walked up to me with her big personality and asked if I wanted to get away from campus for a few hours to explore the city.

First, she took me to Pizzaandu, and then we went to the beach. We spent the entire day together talking about our hopes and plans for the future. After that, we were never apart from each other for too long.

I locked the door to carry on with my night, wiping away a single tear. It would take time to get over Kai, but I was holding on to the hope of his return.

Chapter 31

After Kai and Iris left, I took a deep breath to start cleaning the mess I made during my week of being out of commission mentally. I thought the task would keep me from thinking about my failed relationship, but my moment of peace was interrupted by the knock of an unexpected guest.

"Who's there?"

"It's Nicholas."

"What do you want?"

"Your boyfriend left the door open earlier. I heard you guys talking. I figured I'd come over to check on you after they left."

"I'm sorry if I caused a disturbance. Everything's fine. Thank you for checking on me. It won't happen again." I stepped aside to close the door.

"Please, wait." Nicholas grabbed the door. "Could we talk? I promise I left the jerk at home."

"You heard about my illness, didn't you?"

Nicholas didn't have to say anything. His face said it all.

"Suddenly, I've become quite interesting to everyone."

"I come in peace. I just want to talk."

I reluctantly welcomed him inside.

"You were interesting before I knew any of that," Nicholas explained. "I'm sorry to hear you're dealing with this terrible disease. I feel like an idiot for putting you through all that unnecessary drama. I have a lot of growing to do."

"Thanks."

"You don't look sick."

"How is a person with Huntington's supposed to look?"

"I don't know. Sick? But I don't see anything other than beauty. You have a beautiful smile, beautiful eyes, and a beautiful personality. Everything about you is beautiful and that's only the surface. You're a nice person and intelligent as all get out. Maybe that's why I've been acting a little crazy. You're a remarkable woman who wants nothing to do with me. My ego was bruised."

"I appreciate the compliments, but one day this disease will take its course, and I won't be able to string two words together. All those things won't matter."

"Is your illness the reason you pushed me away that night?"

"No, I pushed you away because you were a jerk."

"So you are attracted to me?"

"How did you get that from me saying you were a jerk?"

"You didn't say you weren't attracted to me." He relaxed as if we'd become fast friends in a matter of minutes. "How do you cope with it?"

"Tonight I lost someone extremely special to me, so I'm over everything. Life can have its way. I'm not coping anymore."

Nicholas grabbed my hand. "You can't give up."

"As you can see, I have a lot to do around here." I pulled away. "Could we do this another time?"

"Wait, before I go. I want you to know you won't have any more problems out of me. You have my word."

"I appreciate that."

"Still friends?" He stuck his hand out.

"*Friends*, you're using that word a little loosely."

Nicholas made a cross over his heart and stepped out into the hallway. "Hey, my offer still stands. A spot is still open for you in our office."

"You were serious about that?"

"Hell, yeah I was serious. Our company's drowning in new accounts. We need intelligent people who catch on quickly. I know you'd catch on quickly. I can feel it in my bones."

"I wish people who hardly know me would stop saying I'm strong."

"Ah, now, I see your weakness." Nicholas knocked on the wall before walking away.

"Wait. What is it?" I poked my head into the hallway.

"You don't know how resilient you are. You're a fighter, Brooklyn Monti." He blew me a kiss before closing his door.

I stood there drenched in regret, ready to surrender to my pain.

Chapter 32

A week later, I had a hankering for a Bridesmaid drink at the bar. I pushed my way through the crowd and beckoned for the cheerful bartender. He was busy admiring a woman in a tight red dress. For a moment, I envied her. She seemed free and happy without a care in the world with a gorgeous man fawning over her. She flipped her long red hair, batted her icy gray eyes, seduced with her pouty lips, and stuck out perky breasts. She exuded confidence, a trait I'd struggled with for the better part of my life.

"You're back." The bartender slapped a coaster down. "I'll bet you want another Bridesmaid, huh? You liked it."

"Yeah, it was pretty good."

"I knew you'd like it." He mixed the pink drink all while casting flirty glances at the lady in the red dress.

"It's different."

"That goes to show ya. Different is good." He winked. "Here you go young lady."

"Thank you."

"High five." He held his hand in the air for me to slap it. "I'll be over there if you need me."

"Yes, with the woman in the red dress." I nodded before guzzling the tall drink.

"Well, well, well, look who's back." Tony pranced my way with his chest stuck out. He downed the brown tonic in his shot glass and slammed it on the bar with a loud sigh. "You never called me."

"Why would I do a thing like that?"

"Mind if I sit here?" He signaled for the bartender before I could answer. "Give my friend another one of what she's having, and I'll take a crown and coke."

"No thanks. I don't need you to buy me a drink. This one is good enough." I grabbed my purse and moved a seat over to escape the smell of his loud cologne and the cloud of cigarette smoke coming from the couple standing behind me. "Is this what my life has become?" I stared blankly at the last of my pink drink.

"I'd like to talk to you a bit more."

"Why?"

"You know," he pondered. "I went home that night and for the first time in a very long time, I reevaluated my life because of what you said."

I strummed the rim of my glass. It was all I could do to keep from falling apart in a bar full of strangers.

Tony held his glass in the air. "Whatever you're going through, this too shall pass."

I tapped my glass against his. "Not soon enough."

"I want to pick your brain. I have a million questions about how you live with Huntington's disease."

"No way," I put my hands over my ears. "I don't want my brain picked."

"But you could help millions of people." Tony waved his hands. "Allow me to explain. I'm a TV producer for a nationally syndicated talk show called, *Social Talk USA*. We focus on health and public issues. You could help us shine a light on this awful disease."

"What is it with everyone lately? I don't want the world having full access to my life. People aren't compassionate. They don't think before they speak and could care less how their words affect me. I'm not interested."

"Your story could give hope to millions of people. You could save a life." Tony pounded his fist on the bar.

"Yeah, that's easy for you to say when you're not the one who'll be in the spotlight."

"Think about it before you totally write me off." He passed me another business card. "I have a feeling you threw the other one away."

"I don't want to do it. That's final."

I never cared for the limelight after my stint at Pinemoor State. Everyone knew me, which meant I became the talk of the school's rumor mill after Adam's departure and my return as a different person. Their whispers and dirty looks were more than I could bear. I never wanted to go through that again.

"I'm not a motivational speaker. I just want to live a quiet fulfilling life."

"Sleep on it. We could make a difference. We could save the world one viewer at a time." He put his hands on his hips in the Superman pose.

I laughed for the first time in days. "You're living in a fantasyland. No one cares about my story. I can hardly stand it."

"I've been at the top of my career for over twelve years. I know what works. You'd be the perfect person to give this topic legs."

"You think you have me figured out, but you don't."

"I don't care what you say. You're likeable, you speak intelligently, and you're very easy on the eyes. I'm sure we could make our mark with my knowledge in producing."

"I'm a private person. Only a few people know I have Huntington's. I ruined a relationship with a man who only comes around once in a lifetime because I was too afraid to be upfront with him about my disease. I don't want to change the world. I want to build my legacy, you know. Get married, have a family of my own, and grow in my career. For anyone else, those are simple things. For me, it's like asking for the sun and the moon."

"Those things will happen when it's your time."

"Are you the same man who tried to jump my bones five minutes after learning my name? Also, knowing you produce TV shows about health is ironic with you approaching unknown women for sex." I swallowed the last of my drink.

"I apologize for being a foolish selfish man. I told you about my ex who succumbed to the disease. Since then, I've operated from a place that doesn't allow me to get too attached, so I won't get hurt. Call me a fool if you must, but it's worked so far."

"I accept your apology, but that doesn't mean you should go around humping everything with a pulse. Do you think you'll ever get over it and have a real relationship or get married?"

"I think marriage is cool. I hope to meet an exceptional woman one day, but it isn't the end-all for me."

"Well, look at Mr. Playboy," I chuckled. "Sadly, I'll bet you get married before I do."

"People with Huntington's get married and have children all the time. I've done the research. I've talked to many people. We've done a couple shows about it. There are a lot of success stories. I know you don't want to hear it, but I have to throw it out there one more time. Consider doing a show. You have an *it* factor. People will be drawn to you." He straddled his stool. "Which one of your parents had Huntington's?"

"My birth mother." I took a long gulp of my drink.

"Has she passed?"

"Yes, when I was a baby."

"What would you say if I asked you to have dinner with me?"

"Oh, no." I shook my head. "I don't think so."

"Indulge me, please." Tony pressed his hands together in prayer. "I'll beg if you want."

"I don't want you to beg. I suppose I could use a little company and a hot meal. It'll soak up whatever this is." I pointed at my empty glass.

"You lead the way, and I'll follow. There's a line of restaurants in the area."

"Don't make me regret this."

We filed out of the bar. Even though Tony wasn't the man I was hoping for, his company might be just what the doctor ordered. I drove towards a small family-owned Mexican restaurant with Tony following in his own vehicle.

I sat for a moment after parking to consider if this was a good idea, but Tony raced over to open my door before I could talk myself out of it.

"Allow me to help you."

"I never pegged you as a man who opens doors."

"My dad raised me to be a gentleman. I may stray away from time to time, but my values always surface when I'm in the presence of a lady."

"Good to know," I replied with narrowed eyes.

"It's nice to finally spend time with a beautiful woman and have an intelligent conversation. Thank you for agreeing to come."

"Like I said a moment ago, don't make me regret it."

A waitress showed us to a small table with two chairs after I quickly denied a booth. A booth seemed too personal. It makes it feel like a date. This was not a date. She took our drink orders and hurried away to fill them. The small bells hanging from the fringe of her apron kept ringing.

"Care to talk about what's got you so down?" Tony flipped through the menu.

The restaurant showcased its authenticity right down to the line of colorful sombreros hanging along the walls. All the waiters were dressed in ponchos displaying the same colors as the Mexican flag.

"Life is unpredictable. Every time I think I have it together, it all falls apart." I thanked the waitress for the massive margarita and gave her my dinner order.

"It happens to the best of us." Tony fumbled with his phone that he kept glancing at every two seconds.

"Are you expecting a call?"

"Hoping for one in particular." He set his phone down. "You know, maybe you should look at your situation a different way. We all take risks daily just by leaving the house. We don't know what'll happen from the time we leave until we return. Life is unpredictable. You don't have an expiration date. Don't allow Huntington's to control your life."

"You've got to feed your nice guy persona in small doses. It's hard for me to separate it from the man I first met."

"Okay, okay," Tony chuckled. "I know I almost fouled up our newfound friendship."

"Friendship?" I scratched my head.

"Aren't we building a friendship?"

"I'm not doing your talk show. So you don't need to try to be my friend or any of that."

"Oh, we're going to be friends." Tony moved things around on the table to help the waitress with our steaming plates. "Why didn't you call me?"

"Do you think you can handle the truth?"

"Lay it on me. I can handle it."

"You came off as a bar bum with one thing on your mind. You took your life for granted. I'm fighting for something you're throwing away, and I didn't like that."

"Damn, that hurt." Tony paused his assault on the refried beans to clutch his chest. "I've never looked at it that way."

"Life comes and goes so fast."

"I want to know more about you," he urged.

"Hell no, TV producer," I joked.

"You're a hard shell to crack, Brooklyn. Give me something."

"All you need to know is I haven't had an easy life, and I don't share every detail with people so easily."

"I'm sure those things have helped you recognize your value and worth." He wrestled with his ringing phone. "Please excuse me for a second."

I gave him a nod and opened a picture of Kai and me on my phone. It was the picture we took the night Kai met my parents. We were both dressed in black. I wore an A-line black dress, and he wore a tailored black suit. We were standing outside the Kizomba dance club. We both had goofy grins that wouldn't go away because of a successful night with my family. We danced, kissed, laughed, and drank all night. It was one for the books.

"Sorry about that." Tony returned with more pep in his step. "I got the call I've been waiting on for weeks." He shook his phone in my direction.

"Good for you. Was it a special lady? Do you think she'll restore your faith in love?"

"No, it was my brother. We aren't exactly on speaking terms. But the last time I went to our parent's house, I took a package of his that had been delivered and told him he would have to see me to get it. He's on his way over, and I'm a nervous wreck."

"Why did you need to go that far to get him to speak to you?"

"I did a lot of stupid shit in the past that tore my family apart. They tried to get the truth through my thick skull but eventually gave up on me when I shut them out. I've seen the error of my ways, and I miss them. Now, I'm doing everything I can to repair our relationship."

"That's brutal. But look on the bright side, it can't be as bad as Huntington's."

"My problems may not compare to Huntington's, but they're still my problems."

I covered my face with the tan linen napkin and apologized for my toxic comment. I was becoming much too comfortable in toxicity and negativity.

"I recognize I don't know you very well, but I think you're strong. Would you like to know why?"

"Sure, why not."

"I know the statistics for Huntington's. One in four people commit suicide when they're diagnosed. You've already beat the odds. This is the kind of encouragement people need to hear. What do you do for a living?"

"Hear me out." My chest rose and fell with rapid breathing. "A person diagnosed with Huntington's has more than likely watched a parent die from it. They know the outcome, and there's absolutely nothing they can do. It's quite terrifying. Those people who choose an alternate path aren't weak."

"You're right. I never thought of it that way. I guess I was just thinking about some of the symptoms—fatigue, tremors, muscle contractures, impaired balance, incoherent speech, irritability, and social withdrawal—and noticed how well you're coping. If you're worried about what people see on the outside, you shouldn't."

"I get all that, but my life isn't for the entertainment of others. Please respect that."

"Now I'm afraid to ask my next question."

"Take it easy on me, or I'll leave you sitting here alone." I took a bite of taco salad.

"How soon do you tell a man you have Huntington's when you start dating? Are you as upfront with them as you were with me?"

"Well that came out of nowhere." I clutched my chest. "What do people expect of me when I meet someone? Should I say, 'Hello, my name is Brooklyn. I have Huntington's disease. Still want to talk, or should we call it a day?'"

Tony laughed so hard he almost choked on a mouthful of his fajita. "You're finally showing a sense of humor."

"It's my only selling point these days."

"Hey," he snapped. "You never told me your last name."

"Yeah, right. Like I'm going to tell a talk show producer, who's interested in my story, my last name. Better luck next time."

"What does my profession have to do with knowing your last name?"

"I can see it now. I'll be channel surfing, and boom, a complete stranger will be telling my story. Not in this lifetime."

"Why are you so guarded?"

"People stop treating me like a normal human being after they find out about my illness. Even if you have an agenda, and we just met."

"It's not about your disease. People become invested in you because you're a fascinating woman. I guess it's a blessing and a curse."

"I'm not fascinating. My disease is fascinating."

"My gut has never steered me wrong. We should work together."

"Nope, nope, nope." I crossed my arms and leaned back in the chair.

"Brooklyn, what are you doing with my brother?" Kai stood with wide eyes.

Tony leaped out of his seat to draw Kai into a bear hug so tight he almost lifted him off the floor. "It's great to see you. How do you know my friend?"

"Your *friend* is my fiancé."

I sat frozen with wide eyes.

"I thought your fiancé's name was Lyn."

"Lyn is short for Brooklyn." He turned his attention back on me with an angry glare. "How did you find my brother?"

I took a deep breath, beating my chest a few times. "You never told me your brother's name, remember? How are you doing? Where have you been?" I touched his hand. "I miss you."

"I've been around. I miss you too."

"Could we talk?" I asked.

"It doesn't appear you have time to talk to me." Kai pointed at Tony and walked away.

I put all my fears aside to chase after him. "This isn't a date. Tell him, Tony."

He grabbed Kai's shoulder. "She's right. This isn't a date. She's too good for me."

Kai reached out to open his car door, but I couldn't let him go—not while he was angry and thought the worst of me for having dinner with his brother.

The waiter raced outside, waving a piece of paper. "Hey, someone needs to pay the bill."

"Sorry, this should cover it." Tony passed him a crisp hundred dollar bill. "Do you really have Huntington's, or did you make it all up?"

"Yes, I have Huntington's." I stomped my foot in frustration sick of Tony's questions and the interruption. "Kai, do you still love me?"

"Why are you here with my brother? I've been at home crying and fighting with myself, trying to find the strength to move forward with you. I don't want to lose you. I want to marry you."

"Then marry me."

"My brother doesn't hang out with women unless he wants to have sex with them. He's a pig, so explain to me why you two are here together."

"You don't have anything to worry about, I promise."

Tony tried to put his arm around Kai. "Forget about me. I was trying to convince her to do a show with me about her having Huntington's disease. She's a good person. I wouldn't let her get away if I were you."

Kai stared down at me with red, watery eyes. "How could you confide in a complete stranger about something so personal so soon, but leave me in the dark? You should've opened up to me as we were getting to know each other. It would've given me the chance to process it."

"I could apologize a million times in a million different ways, but I don't believe it will help the situation. I never meant for you to find out the way you did. I blame myself for my omission of the truth. I wanted you to get to know me. I wanted a chance with you. I never would've experienced your love had you known from the beginning. It would've scared you away. I love you, and I'm extremely sorry for the pain and confusion I've caused you."

"You wouldn't have scared me away, but you would've given me the chance to understand it."

"Do you think you will ever forgive me?"

"I forgave you the day you told me. I was hurt and scared." He turned to Tony with a blank stare. "Were you trying to sleep with her?"

"I won't lie. I tried when I first met her, but she shot me down in two seconds. The only thing we've talked about is Huntington's. I offered to produce a special around her story to help raise awareness. That's it." He held his hands up in a surrendering motion.

Kai kissed my forehead. "That's my girl. You came into my life at a time when I wanted to give up on love. You're funny, intelligent, gorgeous, and so damn amazing. You have my whole heart. You're my perfect match." He rested his hand on the side of my face as he often did to reassure me of his words. "I love you more than you'll ever know, beautiful Brooklyn."

"Losing you hasn't been easy. I couldn't get over you even if I wanted to."

"You've been the highlight of my life for three years. Wait right here." Kai reached inside his car to retrieve a small box and got down on one knee. "Brooklyn Denise Monti, I love you, and I know I'm strong enough to be the man you need. Would you please say you'll be my wife again?"

"Are you sure you can handle the baggage that comes with me?"

"I don't know what the future holds, but I'm willing to find out as long as we do it together. You mean that much to me. I'd marry you right here if I could."

"This may get heavy, Kai. It won't be easy. One day you may have to watch Huntington's take its course, and you won't be able to save me. Are you sure?"

"I need you in my life, and I've had more than enough time to think about it. Please, marry me." He asked with tears in his eyes. "Well?"

"Yes, I'll marry you." I fell into Kai's arms. He rocked me side to side.

Impossible dreams are challenges, and we were impossibly in love even though we knew time would challenge us every step of the way.

Tony pounded on his chest and released a hard cough.

"Are you crying?"

"Brooklyn, you need to tell your damn story. You've beat the odds." Tony wiped his eyes.

"When her mind is made up, there's no changing it. Let it go."

"Now I'm sure you know me. God, I love you." I kissed Kai again. I looked into his eyes and said, "I don't know what I've done to deserve your love or your forgiveness, but I'm thankful. I love you with all my heart."

Chapter 33

The day had finally come, June 25th. Kai and I would become husband and wife at the Scarlet Temple Hotel right in the heart of downtown in Highsea.

I'd practically stolen the venue from another bride-to-be who had to call her fiancé to verify the date before making her deposit. A quick wave of a check under the nose of the hotel manager sealed the deal to secure our date.

Thank goodness I never officially called off the wedding. Something in my heart held onto hope Kai would forgive me and move forward. For the first time, Huntington's couldn't take my happiness away from me.

I stood in front of the gold antique mirror and ran my hands down the side of my beautiful wedding dress. Iris stood on the other side of the room putting the finishing touches on my veil. Earlier, Mom pulled me away from everyone to give me her diamond teardrop earrings. She wore them on her wedding day forty-five years ago, and her mother wore them over fifty years ago on her wedding day as did her great-grandmother.

Iris smoothed a flyaway hair on my fishtail braid. She set the diamond crown on my head and covered my face with the lace veil. I was transformed. I was a bride. Kai's bride.

Tammy and Lorraine spent the week decorating my bridal suite to Iris's demands. You'd think she was the bride the way she carried on. Lorraine found a pair of tailored off-white curtains with gold thread. Tammy created an accent wall with large white three-dimensional paper flowers from ceiling to floor. I couldn't wait to see what the photographer came up with.

I leaned over a round glass table to read the gold and silver wedding program one last time. Iris laughed when I read my name as Mrs. Kai Rahimi. I used my sexy voice and did a little dance afterward. I then closed my eyes and kissed the program, leaving a faint print of my ruby-red lips.

"I need someone to tie my bow."

Tammy raced over, wiggling her fingers.

"You're the last person I expected to be so excited about a wedding."

"Weddings don't excite me when I'm the bride, but I'm happy for my friends. Kai is a catch. I know you two will make a beautiful life together."

Tammy cupped my face. We didn't speak. We didn't need words. Seconds turned into minutes before she finally let go with a long sigh and pulled me into a tight embrace.

"Thank you, ladies, for decorating Brooklyn's bridal room. It's fit for a princess. You two have blown me away." Mom held my bouquet of calla lilies. They were bound together by a white satin ribbon with champagne pearl pins. "This is it."

I turned my back to everyone to deeply inhale the sweet scent of the fresh flowers. I needed a moment alone to think about the day Kai and I first met.

"We made it." I wiped away a single tear.

"Look at my baby girl." Dad held me in his arms. "You're not my little girl anymore. You're about to be a wife."

"I'll always be your little girl."

"Are you ready for me to take you to your groom?" He stuck his arm out. "He almost looks as good as I did when I married your mother."

"I'm more than ready. And for the record, no one could ever look as good as you, Dad."

Before he led me away, Iris took my hands. "You deserve all the happiness in the world. I'm so happy for you. Kai is an amazing man. I know he'll take care of you and protect you. He's your one."

When Dad opened the door, there was Britt. They would both walk me down the aisle.

I watched the guest file inside the hotel earlier. They were all dressed in silver and light gray just as we asked on our invitations. The padded chairs were also silver, arranged in a circle with a three tier arch in the center where Kai and I would say our vows. A path of white lily petals created a runway to the arch. A magazine sat in each chair outlining our love story, complete with pictures of Kai and me, starting with the first one we ever took together on the beach after our impromptu coffee date.

When the horns blasted, a series of soft white lights spilled through the canopy of sheer curtains to let our wedding guests know the ceremony would begin. A hush came over the crowd. The flower girl marched out first. She wore a silver dress of tulle and lace and carried a white satin basket of blush lily petals. She sprinkled them along the floor as she marched down the aisle. Dylan followed her, carrying a white satin pillow with my diamond wedding band.

To keep the ceremony intimate, I only had two bridesmaids, Tammy and Lorraine, and Iris as my maid of honor. After Tammy and Lorraine joined Kai and his two groomsmen, Iris and Tony walked arm in arm down the aisle.

I reminded myself to breathe.

The minister made an announcement for everyone to stand. They gasped as I marched down the aisle, but I couldn't see anyone except Kai. He stood tall and handsome in his tux with tears in his eyes. Tony patted him on his shoulders every two seconds.

Iris hired a harpist to play while I walked down the aisle. Every time she plucked at the harp, it made my stomach swoosh like the ocean waters during hurricane season.

A spotlight followed me down the aisle. Without Dad squeezing my arm, I would've shivered right out of their hands onto the floor. They kissed me on the cheek before giving me away.

Kai leaned in to steal a kiss.

"Slow down, young man." The minister laughed. "We haven't gotten to that part yet."

Kai blew his mother a kiss. She sat in the front row, wearing a champagne dress with a big smile.

"Who gives this woman away?" the minister asked.

"I do." Dad and Britt answered simultaneously.

"Very well," he said. "You may all be seated."

I stared into Kai's eyes, fading in and out during the ceremony in a dreamlike state. His lips moved, but I couldn't hear the words. It was actually happening. I was becoming a wife, and Kai knew everything about me. He loved me in spite of it all.

"Brooklyn," the minister extended a hand. "It's your turn to recite your vows."

"Love is flawed. But when it's between two people who were made for one another, it's perfect in every way. Your love flows through my veins. It keeps me going. You have been a defining person in my life. I've forgotten all the bad things in my past. Because of our love, I'll always find my way. For the rest of my life, I'll be your friend, your partner, and your lover. I'm forever yours, Kai Adar Rahimi."

"And with that, I now pronounce you Mr. and Mrs. Kai Adar Rahimi."

Everyone rose with a thundering round of applause, whooping and hollering while we shared our first kiss as husband and wife.

We danced through a cloud of bubbles down the aisle hand in hand, dipped in happiness as we headed up to our suite to change into our reception attire.

"We're married," I screamed.

Kai couldn't keep his hands off me on the short elevator ride upstairs. They wandered from my face to my neck then back over the rest of my body.

"We're married. It was you all along."

He brushed my tears away with the tip of his thumbs. "After you, my lady," Kai opened the door to our suite. "When I saw you walk down the aisle, I couldn't stop crying. I never imagined you could look more beautiful than you already do."

"Yeah, you were crying so hard you could hardly talk."

"What's so funny? This is why men hide their emotions."

"I apologize, husband. I love your vulnerability more than anything. Please don't change." I kissed his cheek and wiped away my lipstick stains from his handsome face.

"You've got twenty minutes to get changed for the reception. We'll dance and visit with our family for a few hours, and then we're off to our honeymoon."

"Yes, sir, drill sergeant." I wiggled out of my wedding dress and slipped into a white lace off-the-shoulder princess gown. The dress hung low in the back but was cut short in the front to show off my toned legs.

I paid special attention to the smallest details in hopes of taking Kai's breath away—my clothes, the decorations, and most of all, our honeymoon. I even took a crash course from my girlfriends on how to drive him wild when we consummate our marriage. Tammy's tips alone would leave Kai begging for more.

"You're gorgeous." He glanced at his watch with a mischievous grin. "We have a little time, you know."

"Not yet."

"Oh, come on, Mrs. Rahimi."

"Don't Mrs. Rahimi me. You have no idea what I have in store for you. I'm going to blow your mind." I'd tapped into a new level of confidence. For the first time, I knew the meaning of endless happiness.

Kai took my hand to escort me back downstairs. "Are you ready?"

"Let's do it."

The elevator ride was a steamy one. We kissed my lipstick away. It was becoming hard for us to maintain ourselves while we were alone. Unfortunately, our time alone had come to an end. I wiggled as Kai opened the double doors to a crowd of screaming guests.

"Attention. Attention, everyone." The DJ screamed into the microphone. "Say heeey, Mr. and Mrs. Rahimi!"

"Heeey, Mr. and Mrs. Rahimi."

"What took you two so long to get down here? What were you doing?" One of the guests screamed.

I embraced everyone as we passed through the crowd. Even my college crew made it.

"Okay, everyone." The DJ lowered the music. "It's time for the bride and groom's first dance."

"You look good in that dress, girl," someone yelled from the back of the room.

I interlaced my fingers with Kai's. The melody from the music overpowered gravity and lifted us into the air. My tears soaked his white shirt, but Kai didn't seem to mind.

"Say your vows to me again," I whispered.

"I knew you zoned out during the ceremony."

"Please say them again, honey."

Kai leaned into my ear. "Brooklyn Denise Monti, from the day I laid eyes on you, I knew you would be the last woman I'd ever love. I got to know you. I got to experience your infectious personality, and I fell for you hard. I promise to love and respect you all the days of my

life. I will always be honest with you. I will encourage you. I give my
heart to you as a sanctuary. You are my equal in all things." He kissed
my earlobe.

Our souls floated back to Earth as he dipped me and the song faded.

"Thank you for loving me beyond my flaws. You kept your word.
You're an incredibly special man. I'm proud to say you're all mine."

"I love you with all my heart."

For Kai to keep his word meant the world to me. Many people had
come and gone in my life, but he showed me loyalty through all the
hurt and disappointment.

Chapter 34

Kai and I ran through the lake house in a frenzy to make sure everything was in order for our weekend with friends. It'd been a month since our wedding, and we wanted to show our appreciation to our wedding party for standing up with us on our special day. So we invited them to spend July 4th on the boat to watch the firework show.

The first to arrive were Iris, Lorraine, and Tammy. "How was the drive?"

"We almost got lost thanks to Lorraine."

"It's not my fault this place is in the middle of nowhere."

"Don't knock it. It gives us much-needed peace from the hustle and bustle of the city out here," Kai explained.

"They're a bunch of city rats. They can't appreciate this level of solitude," I teased.

"You don't know everything," Iris pushed me aside to enter the house. "Tammy threw a hissy fit because she drank like a fish and had to pee on the side of the road. Lorraine drove away while she was pulling her pants down."

"It wasn't funny. People are killed in the middle of nowhere every day. I could've gotten my head knocked off. Then you'd all feel bad." She pointed at each of them with evil eyes.

"Go sit in the corner," Lorraine ordered.

"I don't know why you're worried about being in the woods.

Whatever's out there is more than likely afraid of you with your big mouth." I gave Lorraine a high-five.

Tammy shot us the finger with her tongue stuck out.

A red Porsche raced up the private road kicking up a trail of dirt clouds.

"That would be Tony," Kai said. "The other guys couldn't make it."

Tony stepped out of his sports car dressed in a black and white shirt with jeans and black pointed toe shoes. He held a bottle of wine in each hand. "You can't start a party without me."

Tammy's eyebrows rose. "You get more interesting every time I see you."

"Oh, you have no idea." Tony winked at me and Kai. "I brought something special for this weekend. I don't know if you can handle it."

"Oh, I'm intrigued." Tammy high stepped next to him.

"Will we have to keep our eyes on you two?" I asked.

"Too late," Lorraine chimed in. "They kissed at the wedding."

"You really don't know how to keep your mouth shut," Tammy chastised her.

Kai put his arm around Tammy to keep her calm. "We all saw it."

Her cheeks turned two shades red. "Blame it on the alcohol."

Tony waved the bottles. "Drink up," he chuckled. "But seriously, I thought you liked me. That hurts my feelings."

"I'll help you get the glasses." Kai showed Tony to the kitchen.

"I want to put it on the record that this thing between you and Tony will never work," I said.

"Why is that?" Tammy shrugged.

"You're both players. Neither of you want to settle down."

"I guess you're right." Tammy sunk into the sofa with her legs crossed. "I thought you were inviting your college friends? I wanted to meet them."

"Yeah, you guys were a hoot at the wedding," Lorraine added. "That story Roxie told about your other friend was hilarious. Did the guy really bark like a dog when you had sex?"

"A loud vicious dog." I chuckled and nestled into the couch beside Tammy.

Kai and Tony returned with a large cooler and the basket of food we made to enjoy the fireworks. "Okay ladies, we're all set. Let's get on the boat already."

"Thank you guys for coming. I usually spend the fourth of July by myself. I'm so excited," Lorraine said.

We slowly drifted away from the colorful graveled shoreline into the bonny waters. The other neighbors waved hello from their boats and some picnicked in their massive backyards waiting for the festivities to begin. A few people flew by on jet skis.

The aroma of food grilling and freshly cut grass lingered in the air. I snuggled under Kai's arm convinced I had the most comfortable spot on the lake.

"I'm so happy for you guys. When are you going to tell us about your honeymoon?" Lorraine said.

"It was amazing. Thank you guys for holding—what did you call it?" Kai asked.

"Honeymoon Sex Positions 101." Iris and Tammy slapped hands. "Did she do the spin?"

"Oh, yeah. She did the spin." Kai grinned and rubbed his chest. "She also did the leg thing."

Tammy jumped up with her hands in the air. "That was mine. That was mine."

"Tell me more about that move later, bro." Tony roared the motor as he passed a swell of colorful boats. "Are you guys ready? It's about to start." He killed the engine as we'd reached the perfect spot to watch the fireworks.

Tammy helped herself to a few macaroons and a glass of wine. "We couldn't let our girl go on her honeymoon without a little excitement. Tony, you know about excitement, don't you?"

"Oh, I know all about excitement." He pulled her close to him, his eyes steady and full of enough heat to cause us all to break into flames.

"Enough of that." Lorraine turned on some jazz music.

The fireworks exploded, creating brilliant pieces of artwork in the sky. We sailed around the lake until there was only the smell of rotten eggs from the potassium compounds of the fireworks remaining. Tony got us safely back to the house, and I showed everyone to their rooms.

As I climbed into bed with Kai, a stomach full of terrible pains came out of nowhere.

"Is this Huntington's?" Kai asked.

"No, maybe I ate something bad."

"Well, just to be on the safe side, I'm taking you to the doctor in the morning."

"No way, we can't leave everyone here. Couldn't we wait until next week?"

"Your health is more important. I'm putting my foot down," Kai said. "They'll be here when we get back."

"Great." I submerged my face into a sink of warm water. I had no idea what the doctor would say, but I knew I didn't want to deal with that part of my life this weekend. Kai undressed me and showered me and held me in his arms for the rest of the night.

Chapter 35

Kai woke me up first thing in the morning to take me to the doctor. I melted into the leather passenger seat, but no matter how far I slid down, I could still see the angel statue perched on top of the clinic. The image was embedded in my memory after my first appointment at nineteen years old. That statue was the first thing I'd see when my parents would take me to the doctor every week. Depending on my mood, it could be the angel of life or the angel of death. Seeing it perched above, tall and proud while my friends were at the lake house, signaled the angel of death.

"Stop making that face, honey. We can't take any chances when it comes to your health. I want us to have as much time together as possible." Kai reached over to calm my trembling leg. "I'm sure you're fine. This is just a formality. It comes with the territory."

"How can you be so sure?"

"I have faith, that's why."

"I hope you're right."

A nurse who looked like she'd been working a month with no days off greeted us at the front desk. She had a gold pen sticking from her messy bun. The bags under her eyes were so big, she could pack the entire office and work out of them.

A much younger, perkier nurse came around the corner holding a stack of folders. "Hello Brooklyn, I hear congratulations are in order. You ran off and got married."

"I sure did." My smile was big and proud. "Where have you been? My husband has become a regular around here."

"Don't even get me started. For some reason, they chose me to train the staff at the new office and held me hostage there for a few months. But I'm back now." She bounced on the balls of her feet. "Follow me. We'll get you ready for the doctor. Gosh, you're married. I'm so happy for you." She barely took a breath in between sentences. "Your husband says you've been feeling faint and nauseous. The first thing we need to do is get some blood from you. How long has this been going on?"

"A few weeks," I replied. "Today's the first time I've actually vomited. Now, my husband is all worked up."

"It's good to have a husband who cares. You have no idea how many married women I treat on a daily basis, and they're always alone. I feel sad for them. Don't be too hard on him. When did you eat last?"

"Around noon yesterday. Nothing today. We snuck out early in hopes of not disturbing our weekend guests."

"Ooh, weekend guests." She pressed a needle in my arm to draw blood. "That sounds fun, but it also sounds like your sugar levels may have plummeted, which would explain why you feel faint. Of course, the doctor will put a rush on your results. Let's keep our fingers crossed that it has nothing to do with Huntington's." She held the tubes of blood in the air. "I'll run these babies to the lab, and we'll see what's going on with you."

I swung my feet from the edge of the exam table and twirled my hair around my finger. Life always throws me a curve ball.

"You're going to drive yourself insane." Kai stepped into the exam room. "I told you everything is fine."

"This is a bad idea. You won't be able to handle bad news. I shouldn't have married you. I'm beyond broken."

"I don't want to ever hear you say that again. Our marriage isn't a mistake. I can handle whatever comes our way. I knew the deal when I married you. I'll walk to the end of the earth for you. Now cut it out."

Thirty minutes later, Dr. Dunbar swung the door open with a broad smile. "What do bees do if they need a ride? Wait at the buzz stop!"

"Ha! Clever."

Dunbar's joke must've touched Kai's soul, or maybe he was nervous, but the cheesy dad joke did nothing for me.

"I've got your results." He sat on a black stool and rolled in front of me. "Take a guess."

"Please just tell me. I can handle it."

"You're expecting. A week and two days to be exact."

"No, no, no, no," I cried out. "Kai, why are you smiling? This isn't good."

"It's not necessarily a bad thing, but this is important," the doctor explained. "Women with Huntington's have healthy babies every day. Don't automatically assume the worst."

"The baby could be born with Huntington's. Babies don't live long with this God-awful disease."

"Not necessarily, Brooklyn. Look at you. You were born with it." He gave my hands a gentle pat. "We could do prenatal genetic testing to decide whether the baby is carrying the gene."

Kai paced the room with his arms folded over his chest. "What are the chances that the baby could be born with it?"

"The odds are very low," Dr. Dunbar replied with bright eyes. "If you decide to get tested, you'll need to do it within ten to fifteen weeks of the pregnancy. Unfortunately, you're already at that stage. So, you have the rest of this weekend. If you should decide otherwise, give us a call Monday, and we will go from there."

I hopped off the bed. "I need to get out of here."

"Be careful. Don't hurt yourself." Kai grabbed me by my waist to steady me.

I raced outside and drew in a series of breaths to regain control of my nerves.

"Sweetheart, stop. Please calm down."

"How could I bring a child into this world?" I asked. "If I pass this disease to my child, I could never live with myself."

"Come here. Have a seat." Kai led me to a bench under a sweetgum tree. "I've been studying Huntington's since I found out you had it, and I came across an article about a woman who tested positive with Huntington's at twenty-two. She talked about how she gave up on her dreams after her diagnosis. She gave up on love, becoming a mother, and even pursuing her career goals. Remember, she was diagnosed at twenty-two. She was fifty-five when she did the article and still had no symptoms of the disease. She never had children. She never got married. She gave up any idea of a career. She wanted to be a painter. She was studying at the time of her diagnosis. I refuse to let that be your story. You will have a family. You will be a mother. You will pursue your dreams. You will have all your heart's desires. I will make sure of it. We're just getting started. Do you understand me?"

"I'm still amazed at how much you're here." I pointed to my chest where my heart beat double time for him. "I need this baby, Kai."

"And you will have it." He rubbed my belly. "We're going to be parents."

"You know this means we got pregnant on our honeymoon. It's so cliché, but I love it."

Kai poked his chest out with his hands on his hips. "I'm the man."

"Look how proud you are of yourself." I typed a group message to Mom, Dad, and Britt.

Love is a powerful emotion. It takes my breath away. My heart is finally full. You're about to be grandparents!

"We don't need to wait. Let's get back in there and check on the fate of our baby," Kai stuck out his palm.

I took his hand and left my fears on that bench. I was a mama bear on a mission.

Chapter 36

The smell of burnt bacon greeted me at the door upon our return from the doctor's office. Kai distracted them enough for me to sneak away to our bedroom before anyone spotted me to ask questions. I sat on the bed coddling my stomach.

I could see my sweet baby being born, saying her first words, taking her first steps, going to her first day of school—all of it. I could even see her becoming president and getting this crazy world in order.

"I cooked your favorite." Tammy walked inside the room and sat on the foot of the bed.

"Thank you for trying, but the bacon smells burnt," I teased.

"It is burnt," Lorraine confirmed from the doorway.

"I tried to stop her." Iris waltzed in and stretched out next to me.

"I did my best. All of you can suck it." Tammy had enough.

"I told you to cut the fruit and stay away from anything that required heat," Iris fussed. "Go sit in the corner."

"You're always telling someone to sit in the corner. You must have us mixed up with Junior." Tammy rolled her eyes. "I also made the scrambled eggs. All of you ate them."

"You ruined an entire package of bacon and a dozen eggs," Lorraine said.

"I would've stayed in bed if I'd known my help wasn't appreciated. I need all the beauty sleep I can get. That Tony is a looker. We could have some fun."

"I think you should let that go," I said. "I don't see anything good coming from it."

"What makes you think he wants you," Iris interjected. "He gave me a look a few times that said he wanted to get to know me too."

"Whatever," Tammy turned to me. "You've been hiding all morning. Kai is a vault. What's going on?"

"You trained him well." Lorraine popped a raspberry in her mouth. "I need some pointers. Maybe it'll work on Michael if we ever get it together."

"You are the most naïve person I know," Tammy said. "Just because you're pregnant doesn't mean you have to ruin the rest of your life marrying a man like Michael. Don't be stupid."

"Okay ladies. This is about Brook-Brook." Iris moved closer to me, walking her fingers around my arm. "I can tell she's hiding something."

A soft knock on the bedroom door offered me an escape from my prying friends.

"This is your room, Kai. Why are you knocking?" Tammy teased.

"I'm no fool. When a group of women are gathered behind a closed door, you better knock." He touched my shoulder.

"Damn, I like him. Your husband's a smart man." Lorraine winked and followed the girls out the room.

"How are you feeling?" Kai and I sat on the small bench by the window overlooking the lake. The morning dew on the grass glistened and a fog hung over the earth. The water in the pond resembled smooth glass and reflected bits of blinding silver from the sunrise.

"Waiting for the results to know if the baby has Huntington's has my anxiety through the roof, but I won't allow it to take full control of me."

"What did we say?" Kai asked.

"Kai, please don't."

"No. What did we say?"

"We said we'd make the best decision that suits our family—yadda, yadda, yadda."

"We're having this baby no matter what the results say. You're a mother. Smile." He gently tweaked my nose then pointed at the closet. "What do you think about that dress?"

"It's my favorite. Why?"

"Put it on and go downstairs. Your friends will keep your mind off the results. Besides, I'm not sure how much longer I can keep quiet about this."

"I don't want to go downstairs. The girls already know something is going on. I can't hide anything from them. I'll fold."

"Then fold," he declared. "They are your friends. You're in good company to be vulnerable. Besides, you need to eat and relax. You're carrying a baby."

"Okay, Mr. Bossy."

"I'm only bossy when it calls for it." He kissed my forehead.

I walked downstairs with Kai in tow to join our loud friends.

Iris walked out of the kitchen screaming. "I made mimosas. Here Brooklyn, drink up. It's the perfect way to get the day started." She pushed the glass in my face.

"She can't have that," Kai blurted. "She's pregnant."

"You're pregnant?" Iris repeated. "Why didn't you tell me?"

"Yeah, more secrets," Tammy said.

"Kai, we agreed to wait on telling people. Why did you do that?"

"I didn't know a smoother way to stop you from drinking in case you forgot."

"How would I forget I'm pregnant? I was going to turn it down."

"What about Huntington's?" Tammy stood in the middle of the room. "Are you even thinking about the baby?"

"What kind of question is that?" I asked.

"Watch yourself." Iris stood in front of me to be my defender at all costs.

"What kind of life will your child have if it's born with Huntington's?" Tammy crossed to the chair next to me.

"Brooklyn doesn't owe any of you an explanation. She has every right to have children the same as us. She's no different." Iris stood over Tammy with her fists clenched.

"Listen, I've known about this disease for many years," Tony explained. "I lost the love of my life to it. I can assure you, Brooklyn is as healthy as you and me. I know what a progression of Huntington's look like, and this is not it."

"I shouldn't have said anything." Tammy held her hands up. "I was only worried about her."

"You have no idea what I'm going through." I moved Iris out of the way to share space with Tammy. "I never thought I'd have a family of my own until I met Kai. Now my life is finally moving in that direction. I'm pregnant with my first child, and I'm married to my best friend. You may look at it as catastrophic, but it's perfect in my eyes. We made a plan with the doctor. I've taken the test to see if the baby has the trait. We should get the results this week. I don't need your opinions, and I can assure you we're thinking of our child's well-being more than anything. So you can take your judgement and shove it."

"I-I'm sorry." Tammy rubbed her watery eyes.

"If you're against us, be clear about it. I don't want to have to share my space with you," Iris added with shrewd eyes.

"I'm your friend," Tammy replied. "I can't help that I'm comfortable talking about the hard stuff. I'm a mother and no mother wants to see their child die young. You may be strong, but that kind of strength is almost unbearable. It could change you forever."

"Brooklyn knows what she's doing. She needs your support, *friend*." Iris marched back in front of Tammy.

"I just think we should all think realistically."

"*We*," I said. "You don't have a say in the matter." I was on the verge of hysteria. My voice commanded every eye in the room. "Shut the hell up or get the hell out, *friend*."

Tammy held up her hands and backed away. "I apologize for causing you to feel anything other than my love and support. I love you."

"I accept your apology. Now, can we move on with the day outside of my uterus?"

That joke lightened the mood and cooler heads prevailed. We were all once again on one accord.

Chapter 37

Kai and I played cards by the fireplace in our new home. My belly stuck out from under my crop top. It'd grown massively in five months. I slammed my cards down and screamed. "Off with your pants."

Kai stood in front of the crackling fireplace and dropped his pants. He shook his hips side to side to show off the see-through boxers I'd bought for our strip poker nights.

"That's what I'm talking about. Strip." I held the bottom of my heavy stomach.

"Your pregnancy hormones have turned you into a bad girl." He grabbed the bowl of fruit salad and peanut butter pickles he made before we started. He always kept my favorite cravings close by just in case.

"Have I changed that much?" I asked.

"I love you with all my heart, but your mood is up and down. Monday you were happy. Tuesday you were a fire-breathing dragon. Wednesday you were horny from sun up to sun down. Thursday you nagged me the entire day, and now you're happy and horny. I take it as it comes."

"You try sharing your body with another human being who's constantly hungry. And even when you give it what it wants, it still kicks the shit out of you." I rolled my eyes. "You can't expect me to be Mary Freaking Poppins. Give me a break."

Kai stretched out on his back with his arms behind his head. "This has been an interesting five months."

"This has been an interesting game, loser." I slammed down another hand of cards. "It doesn't feel good, does it?"

"If kicking my butt makes you happy, I'll gladly lose every time." He stripped out of his boxer to bare it all. "Get a good look at me because once the baby is here privacy will slowly become a thing of the past."

"When you say things like that, it makes me have second thoughts about giving up my ocean view condo for good. Don't tell me we'll have to give up strip poker too. What the hell?"

"Your due date is getting closer and now you're talking about having second thoughts as if you can stop it from happening. It's a little too late for that," Kai laughed. "But yes, you'll have to give all this up." He popped his hips back and forth hypnotizing me like a Newton's Cradle.

"Damn it, Kai. Stop talking. You're freaking me out. This is my first child. It's scary as hell."

"Okay. I'll stop since you can't seem to take a joke today. I wouldn't want to piss you off. I've had more than I can stand this week."

"We've given up so much. I'm selling my condo, and you've already sold your house. Do you think we'll lose the essence of us?"

"You don't need to sell the condo. We could hang out there when we go to the beach. As long as we've got each other, we won't lose the essence of us." Kai walked his finger from my earlobe to the corner of my curled lip. Goosebumps rose over my body. "Nothing else matters anymore. It's all about our family now." He touched my chest where my heart fluttered. "How was your visit with your dad today?"

"Great. He's up and going. He came over to cook for me and rubbed my feet. Oh my goodness, he pampered me like a queen."

"I'm really proud of you for giving him a second chance. I'm sure it wasn't easy for you."

"Thank you, baby. It's been an emotional rollercoaster. But I've learned so much about myself. For the first time, I'm not walking through life clueless and it feels amazing."

"I love the woman you've become. You were so timid and shy when we first met. Now you're confident, fearless, and carefree. I'm proud of you." He crawled over to kiss and hold my baby belly.

I looked down at Kai resting his head on my stomach with his arms wrapped around me. We were everything I'd ever wanted. All the things I'd been afraid I'd never experience were in the here and now. Our life was pure joy.

"I used to hate when you'd call me perfect, but now I understand because of this moment—our life—it is truly perfect. I love you, Kai Rahimi. Now dance sucker." I slammed another hand of cards down.

Chapter 38

The girls came over for one last get together before the baby's big arrival since I was due any day. They babbled about their hectic lives and not one of them stopped talking long enough to give the other one the floor. Yet somehow they never lost the thread of the conversation. I just sat there watching them go on and on.

"Before we call it a night, I have something for Brooklyn." Iris pulled a white box from under her chair. The top was tied with a blue bow. My name was written in bold letters on the tag.

"I've been eyeing that box all night. Give it." I wiggled my fingers before tearing into the gift.

"Do you remember that blanket?" Iris asked. "We brought Junior home from the hospital. I thought you'd like to bring Cas home in it as well."

I ran my hand over the soft blue blanket as I thought about the first time I held Junior in my arms. He was so tiny I was afraid I'd break him. Then my happiness turned into fears that I'd never have a baby. Before I knew it, I baptized Junior's forehead with my salty tears.

"I want you to take this all in. Drop all your fears and think of the future," Iris explained.

"I have a question that I'm a little afraid to ask," Tammy said. "We all know how that turned out the last time."

Iris stood in a huff. "I hate it when people play the victim instead of admitting they were wrong. You know you ruined a special moment when we found out Brooklyn was pregnant. If you think you're going to try that shit again, you're mistaken."

"Both of you stop it," I said. "What's on your mind, Tammy?"

"What does Cas' name mean?"

"It's Persian, it means king of treasure. Since he's my treasure, it suits him. I never thought I'd be a mother. Now, my baby boy is on the way with no traits of Huntington's." I massaged my lower back. "I need to talk to you all about something important. So, please, put your phones away, and don't say anything until I'm finished talking."

"Oh, this sounds serious." Lorraine sat up straight.

I took three folders from my briefcase. "My lawyer and I have come up with a plan for Cas. I don't know if my health will take a turn for the worse before he's of age. My father gave me away when my mother died. I'm not saying Kai would do the same, but I'm not taking any chances with my son." I leaned forward and clutched my stomach.

"Are you okay?"

"I've had a few sharp pains today, but I'm okay." I swallowed back the pain. "I need to make sure my son is in a stable environment if Kai doesn't step up to the plate."

"Oh, please. Kai's a good father. He'll do what's right."

"The decision has been made, so please listen. This is important to me."

"Why?" Iris shrugged.

"Time isn't a luxury for me. If you have a problem with my decision, don't sign the papers. This isn't up for debate."

"I thought you stopped thinking that way. But if you must, go ahead."

"What about you two?" I looked at both Tammy and Lorraine.

"I'm in," Tammy said.

I turned to Lorraine. "And you?"

She nodded with an uncomfortable smile.

"Good. Now, let's get down to business. Iris, you're first in line to take custody of Cas if Kai decides he can't do it. Lorraine's your back up person."

"Hold on," Tammy yelled. "I should come after Iris. Lorraine is a new mother. She's clueless."

"You were the only one who didn't think she should even have a baby. Why in the hell would she trust you to raise him?" Iris shrieked.

"I expressed my concern out of love. You can't always be the good guy when you care."

"There's no point in arguing about it. I'm not making any changes." I clutched my stomach again and leaned forward. "Tammy, I didn't think you'd want to raise another child since your kids are grown with a family of their own. You'd have to start all over again."

"That's exactly why I should come after Iris," Tammy explained. "My children are successful, intelligent, thoughtful people. They are the perfect example of how capable I am of raising your son."

"Don't make me say it, Tammy," I said.

"You're a grandma." Lorraine exploded in laughter.

"Shut up, shut up." Tammy covered her hands over her ears.

"No, seriously, that was my biggest concern. You've always talked about how you hated changing diapers. You hated their teenage years. You hated most of the things that come with motherhood."

"I hated the smell and sight of poop. Show me a mother who loves it, and I'll show you a damn liar," Tammy explained. "Teenage years come with combativeness and know-it-all attitudes, but I got through it. I know more about raising well-rounded children who'll strive for greatness than the two of them combined. My children are exceptional. My daughter is a lawyer, and my son is a doctor. Neither of them had children before marriage. They have great values, work ethic, outstanding attitudes, and I did it on my own. Hell, if you ask me, I should've been your first option."

"Primera opción." Iris yelled in Spanish with angry eyes. "Have you lost your damn mind? Brooklyn is my sister. Her child's practically mine, and it doesn't matter if she's here or not. You could never be her first option."

"I know, Iris. I'm not trying to take your place, but I should come after you. Lorraine's a rookie. She has a one-year-old for goodness sake. I should come second."

"Okay, okay, let's get to the gist of it. I'll be giving birth any day. Your arguing isn't helping the matter and won't change anything." I rubbed my stomach in a circular motion to soothe my karate kicking baby.

"You should rethink this. I should come before Lorraine."

"My decision is final." I touched Tammy's hand. "Could you do me a favor?"

"You insult me, and then you ask me for a favor?"

"It appears that way."

"What do you want?"

"Will you help Lorraine if she needs you?"

"I help her now," Tammy exclaimed.

"It's a yes or no question. Now give me an answer right here and now."

"Yes, I'll help her if she needs me."

"Thank you. Now sign the damn papers. I want to get them back to my attorney tomorrow." I passed each of them a folder with their names on them.

"This is a waste of time. Kai isn't going to abandon his son. Look how great he is with Dylan." Iris scribbled her name on the paperwork.

"I know Kai's a good father, but this is a tricky situation. Nobody knows how Kai will react if I take a turn for the worse. I'm sure my mother didn't expect my father to do what he did." I rested my hand on my stomach. "I need you three to make sure Cas understands a woman's point of view. Make sure he's a gentleman and teach him how to cook, and I don't mean simple stuff. I want him to know how to throw it down in the kitchen. I want him to know how to cook for his family instead of being useless to his wife when he gets married. Wives need breaks too. And make sure he appreciates the simple things in life more than anything. I don't want him to work his life away."

"I've got your back Brooklyn. I will hold him in my heart as if he's my own if need be," Lorraine said with an obsequious grin.

"I'll be there for him," Tammy agreed.

"And you, Iris?" I asked.

"You're not going anywhere. You'll get to teach him yourself."

"Say yes, Iris. It's not hard." I held my hand out for her folder.

"Nothing's going to happen to you."

"Say yes, or I'll smack you with my sandwich. Say it."

"Fine. Yes, I will step up and raise him as my own and teach him all the things I should and love him with all my heart. Are you happy now?"

"Yes, I'm happy now. Thank you all." I stuffed the folders back inside my briefcase. "You've made my night. Now I can relax and wait for my little man to make his big arrival into the world and give me my body back."

"Can I go now that you've got your little papers signed?" Iris stood. "I need to drop my lab coats off at the cleaners before they close."

I grabbed her hand. "I love you."

"I love you too," she replied.

"Wait, you're my ride." Tammy grabbed her purse and raced after Iris.

"Those two kill me. They scratch each other's eyes out, and the next minute they're Shirley and Laverne."

"I'm just glad Tammy has someone else to fight with besides me." Lorraine drummed her fingers against her thighs. "Do you need anything? You look uncomfortable."

"I'm embarrassed to say, but I've been sitting here for so long my legs have gone to sleep, and I need to go to the bathroom."

"Don't be embarrassed. I remember when I was pregnant with Violet and I peed on myself more than a few times. At least it's not running down your legs."

She helped me to my feet and quickly went back to the half glass of wine she'd been babysitting most of the night.

My eyes blurred as I rounded the corner. I used the wall to make my way down the hallway, but I still rammed my stomach into the corner of a mirrored table Kai insisted on squeezing into the narrow hallway. My feet faltered and a blood-curdling scream escaped my throat.

Lorraine ran to my side in a split second.

"Brooklyn," she shrieked, knocking over a gold heart sitting on the edge of the offending table. "I think your water broke. Where's your hospital bag? Do you have a bag packed? Where is it? We need to go."

"Yes." I blew a series of breaths. "It's in my bedroom by the door."

"Stay right there. I'm taking you to the hospital."

"Wait, wait." I sucked in a belly of air. "You have to call Kai, Iris and Tammy."

"I'll call them on the way to the hospital." She ran away. I could hear things breaking all the while. She returned and gasped. "I see blood. This isn't normal. There's too much blood. Something's wrong."

"This can't be happening. Let's go. I can't lose my baby."

Lorraine summoned every bit of her strength to drag me to the car. I drifted in and out of consciousness. My breaths came a few far in between. I rested my head against the cold window and focused on one star that shone brighter than the others.

By the time we reached the highway, everything faded to black. My hands fell from my stomach down to my sides. Still, pain surged through my body reminding me I still had life inside me, and I needed to continue to fight.

And so I did.

"Brooklyn, stay with me." Lorraine tugged on my arm.

I opened my eyes and took a series of deep breaths to push through the pain.

"We're almost there," she squealed.

She drove faster as the directional signs for the emergency room whizzed overhead. Drivers honked, but Lorraine paid them no mind. She sped into the parking lot, peeling the tires to reach the emergency entrance. I focused on the red emergency sign while the attendees pulled me out of the car.

"I'm bleeding. I hit my stomach on the corner of a glass table."

They put me on a stretcher and rolled through the hospital so fast the overhead fluorescent lights went by in a blur.

"Don't you worry." A matronly nurse with kind blue eyes looked down at me and stuck a needle in my arm after we reached a sterile room. "We'll take good care of you."

A doctor entered and examined me as the nurses gave him the rundown.

"Is my baby okay? Someone, please talk to me. Tell me what's going on. Please say something."

"My name is Dr. Harold Clay. You're suffering from a condition called placental abruption. You'll need an emergency cesarean to get the baby out safely. I know I'm not your OB/GYN, but I have twenty years of experience. You and your baby are in safe hands."

I wanted to scream, but my body lacked the energy. I drifted in and out of consciousness. My mind drifted to my baby's perfect nursery. His little clothes were tucked away in a silver dresser. He was already a part of our lives. I had to fight for him even if it was only through will and energy.

The doctor gave me an epidural. After twenty minutes, I couldn't feel anything below my waist, but my heart felt everything when Kai walked into the room.

"I'm here, beautiful Brooklyn. I'm right here." He held my hand.

"I'm sorry it took so long." He kissed all over my face and hand. My eyes darted beyond him to the doctor and nurses. They worked ferociously. I could see the doctor pulling and tugging, but I couldn't feel anything. I glanced at the clock and more than forty minutes had passed when Cas made his grand arrival into the world. It was worth everything I'd gone through. I was a mother.

The nurses huddled on the other side of the room. We heard a smack followed by the glorious sound of Cas wailing at the top of his little lungs. The sound of his cries soothed my soul.

Slow and gentle tears poured out of my eyes as I watched the nurses dart around the room with Cas.

He's here. He's here.

"You have a handsome healthy baby boy." The nurse laid Cas on my chest. "He's six pounds and five ounces with ten fingers and toes."

He curled his tiny hand around my pinky as I cradled him. I ran my fingers through his thick curly black hair. His face made me forget about the doctor on the other side of the curtain taking care of me.

"I've got you all fixed up. You aren't bleeding anymore, and I don't foresee any complications. The nurse will move you to a room shortly. I expect you to recover very soon. You did great, kiddo." He gave my shoulder a gentle pat.

"Hello, baby boy." I kissed his rosy cheeks. "You're more beautiful than I imagined."

"He looks just like you," Kai said. "I'm sorry I was late. I told you I didn't want to go hang out with the guys."

"It's okay. I was okay. I held on until you got here."

"See, you're stronger than you know."

"I never thought anything could override my love for you, but this level of love is unexplainable. All I want to do is protect and love him."

"You deserve it." He held me and Cas close as I drifted off into a deep slumber.

Huntington's finally had to take a backseat to allow me to enjoy a bit of sunshine, and I unapologetically basked in its glory. My obstacles and past may have caused me pain, but the birth of my son made it all worthwhile.

Chapter 39

It was a brilliant September night a year after the birth of Cas when everyone gathered at the house for Sunday dinner. Mom and Dad stopped traveling to assume the role of grandparents and to give us the opportunity to start a tradition of Sunday family dinners.

Vera and Britt arrived together. They adamantly denied dating. Vera says the only things that interest her are good friends, good conversation, and hot tea. Britt filled that void and also gave Kai more freedom since she didn't need him as much anymore.

We were loud, rowdy, and full of love when we cooked together. We'd start early in the day. I looked forward to our conversations more than anything else. Cooking gave us the chance to catch up. We benefited from each other's wisdom.

Adara and her beautiful little girls had also become a part of our fold after I gave her part of my ownership of Three Angels Events. She had a great business mind. All she needed was a chance. I felt it was my duty after all she'd done for me that night at the hotel.

"Where's the salt?" Tammy asked.

"Hopefully it's somewhere where you can't find it."

"What's that supposed to mean?" Tammy turned to Iris with her hand on her hip.

"Your food is way too salty. It's just too salty, and I'm not the only one who thinks so. My blood pressure went through the roof after I ate your Swedish meatballs last week. I've had a headache for days, so you're on a salt restriction."

"I'm offended." She put her hand over her chest.

"Don't act surprised as if this is the first time you've heard of your food being too salty." I shook my head at Tammy. "I tell you about it every week. Dad almost choked to death when he ate a spoonful of mashed potatoes." I shook the spoon I used to stir the batter for my famous three-layered chocolate cake. A dollop of the mixture splattered onto the marble countertop. "I refuse to let you take my dad out."

"It wasn't my food he choked on. He choked on your green bean casserole. I told you to cook them longer. They tasted like little pieces of plastic."

"Now, girls." Mom stood in the middle of the kitchen wearing her retro sweetheart red and white polka dot apron. We bought it for her for our first Sunday dinner.

"Oh, hey, guess what," Adara blurted out.

"What?" We all said at the same time.

"I checked the messages at the office before I left, and we landed the Dowdy Christmas Event in Red Valley."

"That's the big one." Tammy's scream made everyone cover their ears. "We're going to make a lot of money from this account. I'll be able to buy my new car." She shimmied her shoulders and did the limbo dance around the kitchen.

"I'm using the money to send Dylan to basketball camp." I poked at the lumps in my cake mix. "He doesn't want to go to any old camp. He wants to go to the Elite National Ballers camp in New Hampton, and it's not cheap. The kid has high standards."

"Do you think he'll be okay so far away from home by himself at eleven years old?"

"Kai and Cas are going with him. I'll have five whole days to myself. You have no idea how excited I am. Cas's little one-year-old self gives me a run for my money."

"Oh, he's Mr. Big Baller these days," Iris teased.

"You should thank Kai for that. He's always preaching to the boys about dreaming bigger than everyone they know."

"I applaud Dylan's mom for giving Kai full custody. I'm sure it wasn't easy for her to do that, but a boy should be with his father," Tammy said.

"Why?" Iris crossed her arms over her chest.

"I wasn't talking about you. Junior has both his parents," Tammy explained. "Rodney only lives twenty minutes away from you." Tammy turned her attention back to the stove to keep her sauce from burning. "Could someone put a little salt in here since I'm not allowed to do it?"

Lorraine reached under the island deep beyond a stack of pots and pans to get the salt. "I'll do it for you." She ran over to give it a pinch of taste.

"This is unbelievable. I'm the best cook here," Tammy exclaimed.

Mom waved her hands. "Hello, am I invisible or what? You all know I'm the best cook. I have more wisdom and experience in the kitchen than any of you."

"I agree, but I'm the runner-up." Tammy backed down.

"Okay. As long as you all know I'm the queen bee." She pointed her spoon at each of us. "I'll be back. I need to make sure the men have set the table. If not, there will be hell to pay."

"Uh-oh," we said simultaneously.

I poured the big bowl of chocolate batter into three round pans. "You know it wasn't easy for Jees to give Kai full custody, but I respect her for it. The first few months were hell. She was a basket case. She called every day because she wasn't sure if she'd made the right decision. We've shared long talks about motherhood and sacrifices, but she made peace with it without the court's intervention. This was about two parents making the best decision for their child. I'm very proud of them, and now Jees is pregnant with a baby girl. We make sure Dylan is home with her whenever she wants, as long as it doesn't interfere with school, and he spends most holidays with her. She should have that after the sacrifice she made for him."

"I tell you," Iris said. "Being a mother has a way of expediting wisdom. Look at Lorraine. She's been a mother for four years now, and she's got it down pat. I'm proud of you ladies."

"Should we attribute your new and improved attitude to your ex-husband's return?"

"No way," Tammy screeched. "I'm trying to get him out of my house and back on his feet as soon as possible. Iris is the one in love."

"Don't throw me under the damn bus just because you don't want to talk about your husband moving in with you."

"Ex-husband," Tammy corrected her.

"Are you girls about done? The table is set, and I hear stomachs growling. I'm afraid those fellas will pass out from hunger if we don't feed them soon." Mom grabbed a stack of serving plates. We filed out of the kitchen one after another each holding our dishes.

"Choc cake." Cas sang, dancing in his seat.

"Of course, mommy made your favorite dessert, but it has to cool off first, honey."

He raised his little hands in the air with the biggest smile a child could have. He'd been that way since he came into the world a year ago.

Kai hit the rim of his glass with a silver spoon as he stood at the head of the table to give his usual spiel about family togetherness. He'd become much more sentimental than me. He'd cry at the drop of a dime.

"This has been a great ride. The boys are growing so fast. Brooklyn is killing it in marketing and kicking Huntington's butt."

"Huntington's who?" Iris held her glass in the air. "I told you. I knew you'd beat the shit out of it."

"Mind your manners, Iris. Kids are at the table." Mom swatted Iris with a linen napkin.

Kai cleared his throat. "I want to thank each of you for being a part of our lives and our journey. You all play an important role. I know there's no such thing as perfection, but I'd be lying if I didn't say we're pretty damn close." Kai reached out for me to join him. "Brooklyn and I kind of have an announcement to make."

"Is Brooklyn pregnant again?" Iris asked.

"Spit it out."

"Close, we've decided to adopt a baby girl."

"What in the world? That's wonderful news!" Mom leapt from her seat almost hitting the ceiling.

"You and Dad are the reason why we've come to this decision," I explained. "I don't know where I'd be if it wasn't for the two of you."

Britt hung his head and rubbed the back of his neck.

"Please don't make that face. You gave me a new lease on life." I hugged Britt. "Mom and Dad, you've taught me that unconditional love doesn't end with blood. I want to give a child the same thing you have given me."

"You overwhelm me," Mom cried.

I looked around the room at all the people I loved and respected. Tears of gratitude welled in the corner of my eyes. Life wasn't easy by far. I'd given up more times than I could count, but each of those tearful beings sitting at the dinner table made it all worthwhile. My family and friends encouraged me even when I gave up on myself.

I returned to my seat in between my boys and held them in my arms, rocking side to side. "Love, marriage, children, family, and friends are the things of life. I've got it all." I held them tighter. "My life has come full circle."

I glanced at the three vases of tulips in the center of the table—orange for appreciation, pink to celebrate our accomplishments, and yellow for happiness and cheer.

There were more than a few broken petals spread over the surface, but broken and all, they were just like me—viable and beautiful.